Fast forw

Kit Runyon isn't looking for a man to keep—she's happy with the occasional one-night stand and no strings. Making sure her family's electronics repair shop is profitable enough to support three generations is her main focus. But when Brian Hendricks walks into the store, one look, one word, and she knows he's not wired like any man she's ever met before . . .

Brian's attracted to Kit's strength and no-nonsense attitude, but he's tired of the one-and-done dating scene. He's ready to settle down with the right woman, even if that means he'll have to play things slow and stay out of her bed to show her there's more to love than just mind-blowing sex. But at this rate he's liable to short all the circuits . . .

Books by M.Q. Barber

Neighborly Affection Series
Playing the Game
Crossing the Lines
Healing the Wounds
Becoming His Master
Finding Their Balance

Her Shirtless Gentleman
An Accidental Gentleman

Published by Kensington Publishing Corporation

An Accidental Gentleman

M.Q. Barber

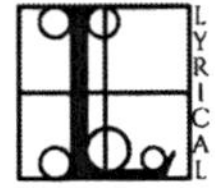

LYRICAL PRESS
Kensington Publishing Corp.
www.kensingtonbooks.com

Lyrical Press books are published by
Kensington Publishing Corp. 119 West 40th Street New York, NY 10018

All Kensington titles, imprints, and distributed lines are available at special quantity discounts for bulk purchases for sales promotion, premiums, fund-raising, and educational or institutional use.

Special book excerpts or customized printings can also be created to fit specific needs. For details, write or phone the office of the Kensington Special Sales Manager:
Kensington Publishing Corp.
119 West 40th Street
New York, NY 10018
Attn. Special Sales Department. Phone: 1-800-221-2647.

First Electronic Edition: August 2016
eISBN-13: 978-1-60183-549-9
eISBN-10: 1-60183-549-3

First Print Edition: August 2016
ISBN-13: 978-1-60183-550-5
ISBN-10: 1-60183-550-7

Printed in the United States of America

For Cat, who opened the door

Chapter 1

Brian drummed the steering wheel, half in time with the radio pumping out classic rock, half in annoyance at the truck ahead.

Racks of shiny diamond-tread toolboxes rode the bed rails above a pristine white body. Early June sun meant good things for the fields of patchy green blobs slipping past in neat rows. Near-sunset glare off the truck meant less-good conditions for his eyes. Shouldn't have stayed late to finish the terrain analysis and forgotten his sunglasses at his desk. He flipped the visor down.

They cruised along at the speed limit, courtesy of the work truck's driver. Dead-on, not even the nickel above everyone did. Good thing the delivery menus plastered on his fridge wouldn't complain when he walked in late on a Thursday night.

Eight-inch-high black letters taunted him from the tailgate. *You break it, we'll take it.*

Towing company, maybe, but the back lacked a winch or a hoist or—

The tail-end bounced. The back tire uncoiled. Pop-thud-*smack*.

As thick rubber flapped and flew, he jerked the car hard right. "Motherf—"

Streaking past the driver's side in chunks, the tire missed the windshield by inches. The burnt rubber stench invaded his coupe via the open window. Close enough to singe a cat's whiskers, Christ.

The truck wobbled but recovered, coasting in a straight line without the knee-jerk flash of brake lights. Good man behind the wheel to keep a steady hand in a blowout.

Matching the driver's gradual slowdown, he tamed his roaring pulse and coasted his coupe onto the gravel shoulder. No traffic in the rearview, but he snapped on the flashers for good measure. Light bounced off the truck's tailgate deco.

Might as well help the guy get back on the road.

The pickup driver shoved open his door. Hefty dude with a beer gut descending in three, two—

A tanned beauty hopped out of the cab, raised her hand across her brows, and stared toward him.

Boner in the lunchroom. Christ Jesus, his jeans hadn't shrunk so damn fast since seventh grade.

The sinking sun cast her in gold, a shining statue gorgeous and false as a heat mirage. No way had that woman emerged from a pickup that'd probably rolled off the assembly line the year she'd been born. He'd gotten hit by tire shrapnel, swerved into a roadside ditch, and lay hallucinating in a busted metal shell. Percentage-wise, the winning explanation.

Arm outstretched, she planted her hand above the wheel well. "Fucking great."

If she meant her damn fine ass, he silently agreed. Or her long legs, stretching as she covered the twenty feet between them in a no-nonsense stride that nonetheless gave her hips an agreeable sway.

Slamming his eyes shut, he clenched the steering wheel and mumbled a string of names. Amundsen, Scott, Shackleton. Thank Christ, the icy tombs of polar explorers cooled his blood.

Voice low but feminine, the woman called out, "You all right? Tire didn't clip you, did it?"

Opening his eyes, he faced the ribbed texture of a royal purple tank top disappearing into the worn edge of faded jean shorts clinging to her hips. Denim and cotton pulsed in the slow beats of her breath. The tire hadn't stunned him, but she sure as hell had.

"Low blood sugar?" She bent sideways and touched his shoulder. Freckles sprinkled her cheeks and spotted her arms. A cheetah, fast and deadly, frowned at him. "Sit tight. I've got a granola bar in the cab." Trotting away, she flashed her rounded ass and muscled calves as her tennis shoes spat gravel.

A phantom straight out of junior high shoved him in the shoulder blade. *Get the fuck over there before someone else asks her, fraidy-cat.*

He fumbled for the door handle and launched himself into the traffic lane. "Hey, don't worry about it. I'm fine." He feinted left and shot right, smooth moves as irresistible to women as the A-okay sign he flashed. "See? All in working condition, except the frog in my throat. Those buggers'll jump into the damnedest places."

She eyed him askance and leaned into her truck. "So you're a frogman?"

"Combat diver? No." Might've gone that route, if he'd taken the spec ops weather tech track, but those choices lay twenty years in the dust. "Air Force data intelligence and analysis for a while. I'm in the private sector now."

"Huh? I meant because of the frog. In your throat?" She flipped him a granola bar and tore one open herself. "He must've hopped outta the way of the tire." Lips clamped, she threatened a grin. "Sorry for the fright."

Her smile begged to be kissed free. The breeze caught the sharp points of her hair, an earthy-rich shade of red clay skittering along her forehead and ears. Lizard-brain urged him to slip his fingers through those flyaways, press her back against the truck, and hold her still while he tasted—

Plastic crackled in his grip. Coughing, he ripped the granola wrapper open. The last time he'd fallen so hard and fast, he'd landed in that god-awful mess senior year. "You have some serious road skills. Pick the wrong move, and that shredder would've knocked you sideways into a roll."

"Not my first blowout." Bar jammed between her teeth, she rolled up the lid on the aluminum toolbox running the length of the bed. Her quick rummage produced a folded tarp, a roped pair of chocks, a cross-socket lug wrench, a small plank, and a red jack shaped like a fire extinguisher. Between peeks down the deserted stretch of road, she piled the gear alongside the shredded back tire. Standing straight, she leveled her gaze at him and retrieved her granola. "Thanks for the overlap parking job and the flashers. Traffic-side changes are a bitch with no lookout."

"No problem." He stepped back as she went to circle him. They played backsy-forsy twice more before he snapped to attention and held his ground. "Howsabout I stay still and let you make all the moves?" Preferably before his dick saluted again.

"Fine by me." She flashed a broad, beautiful smile with a thin gap between her front teeth. "Watch and learn." Her arm brushed his chest as she squeezed by beside the truck. Crouched at the back, she reached under the bed.

Her boxy truck, its mirrors and dash free of fancy electronics, wore its age well. The side panel bore the same lettering style as the tailgate, bigger on top: *Runyon's Repairs: Rapid, reliable and right the first time*. Be a surprise if she rode on shoddy tires. A sharp bit of nothing in the road must've jumped up and said hello.

The remains of the tread hung like so much rubber and metal confetti from the rim. Explosive failure. Scrapes decorated the wheel well. No gouges, twisted steel, or axle bits sticking out. With a spare on, the truck would be drivable.

"I'm no expert"—wouldn't Rob kill to hear him admit that one—"but intel from my preliminary scouting report suggests something large and round ought to be here but isn't."

"That's the best you got, huh? The Air Force pay you for that top-notch analysis?"

A metallic smack and a hollow thump sounded from under the truck. Her shorts hugged her ass as she wiggled back, dragging a full-size spare. A lime green strap escaped the edge of her tank top.

"You giving me a hand or standing around to gawk?" Her gaze dropped, a split-second blink at the lug wrench lying near his feet.

Creeper. Self-defense.

He rushed in, steadied the tire's bouncy landing, and rolled it around the side. He pegged her for late twenties, wiry and strong but wary. Appreciating a stranded woman's assets on a deserted roadside fell dead last on the list of brilliant dating strategies for a guy on the wrong side of thirty-five.

"Your truck here is a little before my time." So old the dash might house a tape deck. "You need to analyze satellite data, I'm your guy. But I've got a friend who's great with machinery." Married, too, and not about to steal this self-assured woman away before he took his shot. "I could give him a call."

"Relax, I'm hot shit with machines myself." Shooing him off the tarp, she held out the chocks. "Think you can put the squeeze on a tire for me, Brainy?"

"Brainy?" He'd earned his merit badges in class clownery. She numbered first-and-only among those defining him by his intelligence. Tempting. The class clown label chafed when the twenty-year high school reunion loomed next summer with at least one likely attendee he'd rather not see again. He snagged the chocks dangling from her palm. "Yeah, I guess I am."

Tarp spread, she waggled grease-smudged and muddy fingers. "I'm a hands girl."

Show me. Mouth firmly snapped shut, he scooted around the truck. He didn't score on every at-bat, but his comedic charm meant he rarely suffered droughts. With this woman, the easy way cramped his chest. His nervous system second-guessed his movements and paralysis overtook his command center.

Her laughter followed him. “Don’t crack your teeth holding back that filthy remark, Brainy.”

“So you run a psychic business at your repair shop, too?” He nestled the sloping wood beneath the curves of the undamaged front passenger tire.

“Men all think alike.” Her casual cynicism floated above the grind of metal on metal. “No special powers needed.”

“Ouch. If I’d known I’d be answering for my entire gender this evening, I’d have called my mom to tell her I love her.” He sauntered around the front and jerked his thumb at the field beyond. “Got a shovel in your toolbox? I’ll get started digging my own grave.”

She spun the lug wrench in two hands, push-pull, her confident execution fucking hotter than a sauna in July. Damn yeah, she deserved her hands-on pride.

“Nah, you can skip the grave-digging. Just fling your body between me and any cars that come along.”

Shit, he’d have done that anyway. Odd, because he’d never been the overprotective-of-women alpha—and sure as hell not for one who so obviously didn’t require protection. A chunk of rubber hurtling past his window had reset his signals. Concussion and hallucination remained the likeliest answer. “Your wish is my command, Ms. Fix-it.”

He stood guard. Cranked the jack once she’d fussed the cylinder into place on a plank. Team-lowered the blown tire, minding his fingers around the exposed metal threads. They worked steadily, her issuing orders and him following. Been a while since he’d maintained strict discipline, and she sure as fuck didn’t resemble any of his commanders, but the rhythm crept over him slick as a second skin.

He planted one knee on the tarp and gripped the tread on the replacement. They lurched upward in sync, heaving the full-size spare onto the bolts. Leaning in, he inhaled sweet pineapple and salty feminine sweat, a pairing as perfect as the prime posting in Hawaii he’d chased and never landed.

She finger-tightened the nuts, spinning in a star pattern, and gave him the okay to release the jack. The final twists she claimed for herself. Little proprietary about her four-way wrench—or determined to bust his jeans with her hand-over-hand work and swaying tits as she locked the sucker down tight.

The wrench slipped off the last nut. She grunted and patted the sidewall. “That’ll do it.” With the metal tucked under her arm, she scooped up a rag that’d been the victim of too many washings.

"Solid job." He grabbed the road tarp, shook off the dust, and started folding. Work wasn't done until the tools had been inspected and stowed. "Nothing cements a bond faster than shared terror and a successful mission."

Stuffing the gear back in the toolbox, she shot him a side-eye. "Yeah, that special connection between nameless strangers changing a tire on a dusty roadside'll get you every time."

"Brian Hendricks." Kneeling side by side for twenty minutes and he hadn't fucking introduced himself. Every smooth move he owned lay a hundred yards back with the rest of her shredded tire. "Sorry, I should've said that first."

Blame the dark brown rims of her eyes holding in orange fire and her sexy, confident strut.

He handed off the tarp, heaved the mangled tire into the truck bed, and tossed her the chocks. "Let me take you out to make up for my bad manners."

She dropped the lid on the storage bay. "No can do, Brian. I'm late to dinner."

"Tomorrow, then." He dogged her steps toward the cab. Not near enough women had the height to match him on equal footing. This one did. He dug for his phone. "What's your number?"

Flinging open the driver door, she flat-palmed his chest. Her bicep flexed. "You were sweet to keep me company and play lookout while I changed the tire. I appreciate the help."

She swung in with the handgrip and scooted her ass in the seat. With a reach through the open window, she dragged the door shut. "You're a nice guy."

Solid and warm, she patted his cheek. "But I don't date." The engine turned over as she withdrew. "I fuck."

The big pickup lumbered forward, guided off the shoulder and onto the blacktop by those same sure hands. Her arm rested on the window frame, her freckles fading in the flash of sunlight off the silver toolboxes.

He stood in the road with a grime-streaked button-down and aching knees. She'd knocked him so far off his game he might as well have spun out in the ditch. Trudging back to his car, he spat a curse for his own stupidity.

He hadn't even gotten her name.

* * * *

Babying the white whale's substitute tire, Kit held the needle under forty. She dropped to twenty-five when she hit the concrete curves of their neighborhood. Rancher after rancher, copycat products of the seventies, distinguished themselves from one another by siding color and lawn décor.

The streetlights waited to do their duty, but no kids raced across lawns to sneak in extra fun before dusky judgment prompted moms to shout them home. The neighborhood had aged with her parents. With her.

Parked in front of the garage, she silenced the engine. Twenty-eight and yet to move out. She lived in the house with the uneven sidewalk where she'd tripped and chipped a baby tooth loose at four. Puttered in the garage where she'd first learned to rebuild a radio, kneeling on the workbench with Grandpa Jake looking over her shoulder. When the station had emerged from the plastic shell, she'd shrieked her seven-year-old heart out and Grandpa had hoisted her in a victory dance.

She hopped out beside the six-seater minivan they'd gotten used a dozen years back. The old sedan wouldn't have fit four adults and two car seats. The minivan marked the dull gold legacy of one deadbeat coward. She slammed her door as the garage rattled up.

"Sounded like my girl was home." Perched on a stool, Dad hunched over their latest garage sale find, a busted espresso machine. Fixed, the basic home brewing setup might bring a decent profit at the shop. Parts lay scattered across the table. "Late night. Trouble?"

"Tire blew." She jerked her thumb toward the offender.

Dad laid aside a gasket and wiped his hands on his pants. "You all right?"

"Uh-huh. Good Samaritan stopped and gave me a hand." More he'd stayed out of her way, but he'd lent her muscle and acted the charming gentleman.

Pleasant, sweet, and so not her type. Didn't explain her goose-bump shivers at the thought of him. Brian. Hugging herself, she rubbed her upper arms.

"Tire's shredded. Rim's good. I've got the spare on." They'd have to take the truck in to get checked anyway, replace the—

"We'll have to take her to Tom." He ambled past her and squatted by the back tire. "Get him to give her a look-see and pick up a replacement."

As alike as peas in a pod, Mom always said. Tinkerers and problem-solvers. "I know, Dad."

He patted the fender with the gentle care most reserved for children and beloved pets. "The old girl brought you home safe, though." Standing, he cracked his back. Grandpa's death last year had aged him more than hitting the big six-oh. "Go on inside with you." He shooed her through the garage. "Your mother's keeping a plate warm."

She slipped into the house as he settled back at the workbench. The wall hook accepted her keys. The laundry closet welcomed her purple tank, so grubby that stripping the grime would demand a miracle. The lime one underneath would do for now. She scrubbed her hands at the sink in the half bath, her fingers sore and pinched and her palms red beneath the dirt. Burdened by more than a year's worth of road salt and mud and nameless gunk, the tire had thoughtfully transferred its collection to her skin and under her nails.

Brian wouldn't be so rough and dirty. Him in his office-guy dress shirt with his I'm-a-regular-Joe jeans, driving his older but still fancy Audi, asking for a date as if people whose hormones clicked needed to pretend to like each other for a few hours before the clothes came off. He'd be one of those tender nice guys sucking on her fingers and gazing at her with eyes green as new shoots in a flower bed.

As she shut off the water, giggles filtered through from the living room. Better than her nieces fighting. The Squabble Sisters' screeches demanded high-quality ear protection or escape. So-called nice guys seduced women with their bullshit, and when they walked out they left behind babies who grew into bickering teens. The house had enough of those.

She dried her hands on a shaggy rose-petal towel Dad had picked up for Mom at a garage sale a dozen years ago. Sorry, Brian, but her fingers would stay unsucked. Shoes toed off on the rug, she sock-footed into the kitchen.

Wiping down the cheery Formica floral counters, Mom half-turned. The way the spots darkened her vision, a full-on stare would've meant less attention than a sidelong glance. "Hiya, sweetie. Did you lose track of time on one of your projects again?"

"Hey, Mom. Something like that." She squeezed tight in a come-from-behind hug. Her height hadn't come from Mom's side of the family—her mother fit under her chin. Had since she'd hit eighth grade. "Thanks for holding dinner for me."

Mom patted her hands and swiped at a stray smudge on an upper cabinet. The stenciled yellow flowers on the white cupboards matched the counters, scaled bigger. Hand-cut by Mom, hand-painted by Kit and Erin when they were small. "Mm-hmm. Your plate's in the oven."

"Erin working tonight?" Keeping up with her sister's picker schedule at the warehouse took a color-coded calendar.

"She went in at four." Mom hung the washrag over the faucet, neat and tidy. Dirty dishes wouldn't dare linger in her sink. "Second shift this week."

With an unevenly stitched potholder birthed in a middle-school home ec class, she pulled out her dinner and shut off the warmer. Meatloaf and mashed taters. "Are there any—"

A jar of dilly beans landed in her hand. "Last one until this year's are ripe. You girls best make them stretch until August."

"Sure, if Dad doesn't find them." She carried her loot to the table and dug in. A glass of iced tea appeared at her elbow, and she mumble-chewed her thanks. The granola bar had helped, but lunch lay eight hours past, and her stomach had started in with reminders three hours ago. She fingered the seam of the table leaf. Thirteen years ago, the extra board's appearances had been limited to holidays and potlucks. Once Erin moved home and brought the girls with her, the leaf had taken up permanent residence.

If she'd accepted Brian's invitation, she'd be dining somewhere else instead of her usual chair tonight.

Mom slipped into her seat in front of the sliding door to the backyard, keeping her company at the table because she'd never let one of her girls dine alone. She'd like Brian's politeness. "Bring that nice boy over," she'd say. "A hot supper will thank him for stopping to help my baby."

His blond hair and trim body made judging his age tough. His smooth cheeks and peach-fuzzy arms lent him youth. The crow's feet embracing his eyes marked him as more than a boy, though. His manners sure as fuck didn't scream twenties. Older than her, but how much?

Half listening to her mother's rundown of the day, she nodded and hmmed between bites. Brian intruded with silent persistence, more distracting than a macho jackass throwing attitude. If he'd called her "little lady" or taken the wrench from her and tried to change the tire himself with less skill, she'd have shut him down and sent him on his way. Instead, he'd complimented her mechanical skills and joked to entertain her. And paraded around with his tight ass, trotting to and fro on her orders.

Arms bared by his rolled-up shirtsleeves hinted at a balance of brawn and brains, the peak before sexy fell toward overbearing posturing. His spiky hair ruffled on top as the wind directed, but the front tendrils flowed down his forehead and the tips promised curls if he delayed a haircut. Brian was a real guy, not a badass punk.

Exactly why dating him would be a train wreck. He'd make her life messy. Entangled, connected, and longer than one night. Ditching assholes came easy. They didn't give a shit why she refused to bring them home or insisted on fucking in the parking lot. They cared about two priorities—when and where they could stick their dicks.

She'd be an unfair bitch to lead on nice-guy Brian when he should be looking for a settle-down girl. He didn't behave like a fuck-and-run, and she didn't do long-term investments. And if he was faking like all so-called nice guys, he'd get bored and walk away once she'd gotten hooked.

Mr. Frog-in-His-Throat. A real Prince Charming. The minute she kissed him, the world would drive her toward fairy-tale princess dreams she'd shunned since childhood. Her happily ever after came with a mess of metal and wires under a work light, not a white gown and a gold ring under the eyes of God.

* * * *

Gravel crunching under his tires, Brian pulled up to the farmhouse and parked alongside Rob's pickup and the SUV they'd gotten to replace Nora's beater. Fuck takeout. He'd run his ass off cramming best-man duties in the narrow window between Christmas and New Year's. A bachelor deserved to dine off that apology at least through summer grilling season. After Labor Day would be soon enough to call them square.

He took the porch steps in one leap. Rob understood women. He'd landed Nora despite the awful introduction Lucas would never live down. And Nora, she'd know why his nameless Amazon had rejected him. She'd decipher woman-code, he'd track down said woman, and the date would be on.

The unlatched screen door invited him on inside. He poked his head 'round the corner toward the kitchen as the screen snapped shut. After eight. They might've eaten or be out back finishing up.

"Hey, Sherwood, Maid Marian, what're you serving tonight?" he yelled toward the stairs as he patrolled the empty first floor. The dining room sported actual furniture instead of Rob's piles of someday projects. Living with a woman changed a man. "I come bearing no gifts."

"Brian, I swear to—" Rob's deep bark cut off, and the peal of Nora's laughter followed. "If you're staying for dinner, grab a beer and go the fuck outside for at least fifteen minutes."

He slumped over the banister and howled his laughter. Heading into month six and they still went at it like newlywed rabbits. "You're only giving her—"

"Make it thirty." Nora shouted louder than her husband. Bedsprings creaked.

He sucked back the laughs to get words out. "You two trying for a baby up there?"

"Go grill the damn steaks." Nora wasted no time hollering orders. Helluva shift from the shy blusher he'd met last summer. "Beer, fridge. Steaks, grill. You, outside!"

Shit, these days she scared him more than Sherwood did. "On my way. You folks take your time, now."

The fridge held the promised beer and a platter of beefy red beauties. He hauled both outside and fired up the grill. Fifteen minutes to kick back before that puppy heated. Bypassing the picnic table smack in the setting sun's path across the yard, he dragged one of the sloping loungers into a shady spot on the porch and slapped his feet on the rail. Not bad. The balcony on his apartment measured three by six in a generous accounting. Rob's place, now—room to sprawl, no neighbors setting off smoke alarms—this was the life. Except the huge fucking yard to mow.

He'd put a good sear on the steaks and lowered the temp on the grill by the time Rob trotted out, barefoot and in jeans, wrestling a T-shirt down his back. "Sorry, Surfer Boy. You drop by unannounced, you gotta expect to wait."

He saluted with his longneck. Condensation splashed his cheek. "Husbandly duties. Far be it from me to stand in the way of a man getting some regular."

"Regular." Rob snorted, snatched the tongs, and prodded the meat. "With Nora, every time's a fresh adventure. You ought to give long-term a try. Find a woman, settle down."

"Thanks, Mom. I'll get right on that." The woman tonight, though. Casual competence and a brilliant smile. "I did, actually. Find one."

"Are you bullshitting me?" Rob dropped the lid on the grill. "What's her name?"

He scrubbed his head. Maybe a genie would pop out and deliver the answer. "I don't know her name. Yet." Thank God her truck offered a clue. "But I know where she works."

"Didn't get her name. Uh-huh." Standing in the yard, Rob knocked Brian's feet off the rail and planted crossed arms in their place. "Sounds like the Brian I know. Let me guess—you got distracted by her bouncy bits, deployed your tongue, and forgot to ask after."

"Shows what you know, married man." He swigged his beer, the last of the bottle coating his throat. Taking her at her word, mystery woman loved to fuck. Just not him. "She thinks I'm a nice guy. A smart, non-sexy nice guy. Says she doesn't date—she fucks. I gotta find a way to get her to date me."

Easy, except she turned him into the flustered seventh-grader clutching his math book over his intractable hard-on and rehearsing his invitation to the dance for Jenny Shlovski. He'd whiffed with his knee-slide and Bon Jovi serenade. The first girl to pick someone else over him, but not the last. At least she'd had the courtesy to tell him to his face.

Nora swished by in a blue sundress. "You sure it's really this woman you're interested in?" She deposited a lumpy foil packet beside the grill and plates and silverware on the picnic table. "Not the challenge of chasing her?"

"Hey, I don't chase women." His class clown routine roped them in and gave him his pick. Always had. Almost always. "They chase me. I'm good-time Brian, the life of the party. One and done."

True for twenty years. If she wanted one night and he wanted the same, they could have an explosive experience. But the words tasted sour this time around. Anticipating a single all-night fuckfest ought to make him energized, not weary. At the least, the sex ought to be more enticing than a vision of her guarding his flank next summer when he walked into a gym full of balloons, streamers, and people he hadn't talked to in those two decades.

Rob hung back and drummed his thumbs on the rail. "You do have a hard time letting a victory flag go, though." Shading his face, the porch brought his narrowed gaze into focus. The ex-sarge's inspection attitude signaled a demanding interrogation in the offing. "You mad she's one-upped your usual move?"

"Whoa, unfair." He set his empty beside the chair and rolled to his feet. He didn't leave a string of broken hearts behind or lie to women to get them in his bed. "I've always made it clear up front when I wasn't looking for more."

"And so is she." Nora, plates distributed, had claimed a corner of the picnic bench. Frowning, she rubbed her stomach. "What, a woman can't be looking to skip the date and go straight to the after-party?"

"Not this woman." The answer punched out without a speck of thought, faster than a Navy fighter catapulting off the boat and twice as cocky.

Mouth clamped tight, Nora stalked past him and into the house. Hawk-alert, Rob stared after her. The screen snapped and bounced twice in the frame before settling.

His unaccustomed defensiveness retreated into a touch of panic. Rob had been closer than his brothers for twenty years, and in the last year Nora had become the closest he'd ever had to a woman friend. "Shit, did I piss off your wife?"

Rob quirked his lips and shook the tension off his shoulders. "She'd let you have it if you did." Meandering to the grill, he waved him over. "Tell me about this woman."

Where to start, Christ. He hopped the porch rail and landed in a crouch on the grass. This woman out-toughed the obstacle course at Lackland, and he quailed before the flutter in his chest. "She's got this no-nonsense tone, but then she'll throw a deep curve on it and fire a sly laugh in the pocket." As Rob lifted the silver lid and the last rays of sunlight flashed, he circled the smoke. "She talks like she's got places to be, and I want to be the place she's going."

"Conversation, laughter…" Grill sizzling as fat burst into flame, Rob snatched the steaks clear. He tossed the foil packet in. "What's she smell like?"

"Sweet and thick." Mmm, yeah, she did. Her short-cropped hair made her neck a tempting target. "Pineapple, salt, and motor oil."

Tongs frozen in hand, Rob stared.

"What?" Brian yanked his shirt from his jeans and stretched out the tails. The spare's tread pattern across his chest would give his dry cleaner fits. "She was fixing a car when I met her."

Rob took his time tenting the steaks under foil and slotting the tongs over the tool rod. "You know this is the first time you've described a woman you wanted to bang and didn't lead off with the size of her tits?"

They'd landed in the same training squadron as eighteen-year-olds. Longer ago now than the years they'd counted behind them then. The charge couldn't be true—but Sherwood didn't lie, and no name came to mind to refute him. "Maybe."

Feet planted at-ease, Rob crossed his arms. The screen door claimed his full attention. "Conversation. Laughter. Scent. My daddy told me that's how you know you've found the right woman."

Right meaning Nora. Marriage. A house together. The total commitment to one woman for the rest of his life. Fuck no, not for him. Maturing beyond banging a nameless woman along the side of the road didn't transform him into a slack-jawed, yes-dear spouter. He tamped down a patch of uneven grass. "My dad advised me to 'clean up your act, you smart-assed punk, and stay out of jail.'"

The screen crept open, Nora leading with her back and making a slow turn. An oversized salad bowl occupied both hands.

"Flip the veggies in a minute." Rob shoved his shoulder and hustled to the porch steps. "You all right?" He jammed the bowl in the crook of his elbow. "Let me take that. You need anything?"

Smile growing, Nora gripped his free arm and descended. "I just got a little queasy. We're fine."

"Sure?" Rob rubbed her stomach, his broad hand flattening her dress to her body. Her not-quite-flat body.

"Holy shit. You two are growing a baby?" They didn't waste time. Engaged at Christmas, married at New Year's, a squaller any flipping minute. Guess the newlywed honeymoon phase— "Goddamn, Rob, you were fucking your wife when I got here. What if you hurt the kid? Shit, should she sit down? Nora, get off your feet."

"Oh God, now I have two of you to contend with." Burying her face in Rob's chest, Nora slapped her husband's shoulder and laughed. "Rob, you tell him the ground rules, because I'm not putting up with male nonsense for the next six months."

"I will. Promise." Salad in one arm, wife in the other, Rob kissed the top of her head. "Are you sure you don't want to sit down?"

As Nora delivered a proper kiss, Brian turned his back and flipped the foil pack. A baby, hell, that'd be over the top. But the easy trust and friendship with a woman? A dinner companion and bed partner who got beyond, "So, what do you do?" and "Where's the condom?"

Envy flickered quick as the lightning bugs buzzing around the lawn in a mating dance. The first star winked into existence past the roofline. Pretty as a fucking postcard. *Wish you were here.*

* * * *

Kit closed the door behind herself and leaned against the wood in the house's last refuge. The girls' clutter covered the sink surround, and the extra towel bars created dual-level drapery for the peach walls, but the bathroom came the closest to privacy in a home crowding six.

Washing up for dinner hadn't cleared the road grime and stray grease streaks from her knees and elbows. A hot shower would soothe tight shoulders, too. Knocking the lug nuts loose had demanded brute strength.

She dropped her clothes in a heap and cranked the shower. Too tall, more giraffe than gazelle in school, her lanky height a deterrent for teen boys whose insecurities ran as deep as the girls'. She owned her skin now, all five-foot-nine of her from pixie cut and freckles to rounded biceps and nick-scarred fingers to padded thighs and arched soles.

Prince Charming had noticed. His roaming gaze had crisscrossed the border between blatant and subtle often enough to unlace a thousand inhibitions, but his move had been a polite request for a date. She intimidated him. Too much for his nice-guy sensibilities.

On a Saturday night at the dirt track, she'd have grabbed him by the front of his white-collar button-down and dragged him out to his car for a hard-and-fast fuck. Sat on the trunk, worked his jeans open, and played with the cock bulging beneath denim.

He'd tried hiding those flashes of interest. As if she hadn't stolen glances of her own. Crouched beside her, one knee down as he hefted the spare, he'd managed a simultaneous stiff declaration and hair-sniff.

Hot water blasted her tight back. No—a sun-warmed car trunk. She propped her feet on the bumper as he muscled between her legs. Thick and solid, he claimed the space in a wrangle of teasing pressure. Rough and dragging, he popped her fly and unzipped her shorts.

"This what you want, Kit?" Her gruff gentleman asked and assumed in the same motion.

She climbed his sturdy frame, hooking her legs around his waist. Her ass lifted off the car. "What do you think?"

With a sharp yank, he shoved her shorts and panties to her knees. Locking them together, he drove her legs to her chest with his weight. "I think I'm gonna take what you're offering."

Dragged to the edge, hot and wet, she flexed into his first plunge.

He sucked the salt from her neck, his hips snapping an unstoppable rhythm. Their sweat steamed the air.

"One time only." She huffed half-truths through short breaths. One night, but she'd take him as often as he managed to stand up for her before dawn. "Better make this count."

"You counting?" Perfect and relentless, he pumped. The tendons in his neck strained. "Count for me, Kit. Every thrust."

"One." She rose and met him in the squeeze between his body and the hot metal.

"Two." Rocket fuel raced along her blood vessels.

He clamped his teeth in the curve of shoulder and neck. His breath soaked into her bones. Their bodies rattled the car, challenging the suspension to keep up.

"Three." His fine hair defied her. She scrabbled for purchase. "Four."

"You can count faster than that, Katherine." He drove her hands down and pinned her wrists. Their arms lined up, his blond fuzz atop her freckled tan, same length, same muscled strength. Her world ignited.

"Aunt Kit!"

Her back thudded against the plastic tub-shower combo. Frantic fingers froze. As the door banged the wall, a blast of cool hallway air rustled the shower curtain.

"Have you seen my aqua scoop neck? I need it for tomorrow." Abby talked a mile a minute while cabinet doors opened and slammed. "Jess swore she didn't take it, but she's a liar, and I know…"

Flinging the handle to cool, Kit pounded her fist on her thigh. So damn close.

The teenage diatribe dragged on. "…that time she stole my red top, you know, the one with the white flowers."

Good God, an opening. "Did you check the hamper? If your mom or grandma found a shirt on the floor, that's where it'd go."

"Thanks, Aunt Kit." The shout faded in retreat as feet scampered down the creaky hall.

The shower curtain still rustled. She launched a desperate plea. "And close the door!"

The creaks returned. Sans apology, but the bathroom door clicked shut.

Too late. Her Brian-gasm had disappeared. Furtive strokes under the bedcovers or a Saturday night hookup might restore the passion, but shower satisfaction soared out of reach.

Didn't matter. Condomless car sex with her hot-as-fuck bad boy belonged to fantasies. Brian was a nice guy. And he didn't even know her name.

Chapter 2

Cruising slow, Brian circled past the faded yellow-brick drugstore and came around the block again. At the consignment store with bright summer clothes on display, he slipped the car into the parking lane and inched forward.

Runyon's Repairs occupied the first floor of a red brick tri-story so old the side wall boasted faded advertisements for refreshing Coca-Cola and whites-whiter, colors-brighter Borax. Fancy pavers, swept free of street litter, lined the sidewalk out front. A "closed" sign hung on the door.

Thank Christ. The shop lacked a website or any online presence, and he had no reason to show up on a Monday after work—or any time, truly, given Ms. Fix-it's rejection. Better to survey the landscape in the clear before confronting his hostile quarry.

Ducking and staring through the lowered passenger window limited his view to a narrow strip of storefront. An old typewriter occupied one display. Model trains and slot cars seemed poised to race in the other.

He killed the engine. Three full days he'd wrestled the urge to track her down. Staying away, starving the thoughts of her, would've been the smartest play. Shake off her fierce grip on him, the one drawing him to see her and pushing him back to cautious recon. Saturday softball had nailed the lid on his coffin. Not the rug rats running wild, but the partnerships. Most of the guys had a wife or girlfriend who watched their backs. An elite squad of two assigned to each other's support and defense.

He hadn't believed, not really. For years he'd preferred one-nighters and sweet freedom from drama while Rob had dated one special lady for months on end and showed up with a case of beer when the relationship inevitably went south. One woman with a blown tire, and he stood on the verge of the same painful leap. Turning bachelorhood into breakups and loneliness. The fuck had gone haywire in his head?

Heavy as a thunderclap, his car door slamming cut through the traffic noise. He stood outside, unsure when he'd opted for a closer look or why his feet dragged him over the curb and the brick pavers to the storefront. Sun-bleached stencils promised warranty repairs, in-home service for large items, and a three-day turnaround time for appliances with parts in stock. His would-be partner spent her days behind the green door with its white lettering.

"Partner. Christ." They hadn't fucked. They hadn't so much as kissed. His brain answered the age-old question of how long it took to go 'round the bend: thirty minutes of conversation with a woman. But grease stains and road grime had painted the target, and whatever demanding fucker had taken charge of calling the shots for him refused to lock on anywhere else.

Hands cupped across his forehead, he peered through the window. Electrics and motors. Household appliances, radios, and hobby toys lined shelves back to a wide counter. Crock-Pots and big kitchen mixers flanked the typewriter in the window.

Not a damn thing he owned. He'd made his whole life disposable. Well, if he had nothing busted to bring her, he'd have to borrow an appropriate whosie-whatsit. Scanning the list, he unsnapped his phone and placed a call.

Rob picked up on the second ring. "You miss me in the twenty minutes since you left work?"

"My heart's pining for you something awful." He dropped his ass on the passenger window frame and bent back over the top of the car. Clear blue sky absorbed his sigh. "Can I borrow your mower? Or your vacuum?"

"You don't have a lawn." Dead silence transformed to suspicion just so. "And the last time you cleaned your carpet, the rivers ran red with blood and the sun went out."

"I know." The building's maintenance guy managed the lawn, and his maid service dropped by once a month to keep a lid on his mess. Valid objections, but neither helped his case. "It's for a friend."

"I know all your friends." Rob tried to cover, but fuck if he wasn't laughing.

"Dammit, man. Can I borrow one or not?"

"Easy, airman. First time I've heard of impressing a woman with a lawn mower."

"He's doing what?" Nora chimed in from the background.

A spreadsheeted breakdown and overhaul loomed for his whole dating strategy. "Oh, for the love of—"

"Yeah, yeah. C'mon over, man. Bring a six-pack." Muffled chatter alternated high and low, Rob's phone likely smothered against his shirt. "And fishsticks." The garbled speech continued. "With brown sugar barbecue sauce."

"I see who's queen of your castle."

"You want our mower? Beer. Fish. Barbecue sauce."

Call ended, Brian hustled around to the driver's side. The Vanderhoffs lived clear across town and beyond, a good fifteen or twenty minutes. He swung by the grocery store for the essentials.

* * * *

The customer bell over the front door tinkled a warning an hour before closing Tuesday evening. Pickup, more than likely. The extra hour gave office jobbers unable to fix a loose screw with two hands and a flathead time to drop their problems in Kit's lap and take pieces good as new home for dinner.

From her workbench in the back, she hollered a greeting. "Be right with you."

The stand mixer cracked open on the operating table would have to wait for its fresh worm gear. As she walked to the front, she wiped food-grade machine grease from her fingers. "Can I"—holy fuck, Prince Charming had tracked her down—"help you?"

His dress shirt sported navy pinstripes today. No grease stains, but she could change that.

He rubbed the back of his neck, driving his short hair up, and flashed her a toothy grin. "I was going to bring you a lawn mower."

Snail-slow, she tilted from the waist and scanned the shop floor behind him. She loved a good laugh, but fucking with Brian delivered a charge her body hadn't learned to measure. "You showed up empty-handed."

"Yeah." He kept his distance, ten feet back from the counter, between the refurbished kitchen appliances and the working antique radios. "It wasn't mine. Or broken." Two steps forward, he dropped his hand and lifted his head. In his unblinking stare, his eyes glowed green as a solid grounded connection. "I wanted an excuse to see you."

The corner of the intake ledger hung off her side of the counter. She aligned the edges. The leather cover had collected stray scuffs in the sixty-five years since Grandpa Jake had opened the shop. The softness stretched over the unyielding boards beneath, protecting the pages between. "What's your replacement excuse?"

"No excuse." One shoe rapping in place on the vinyl, he created sharp tick-tock beats over the air conditioner's low hum. "Games are for boys."

"And you're not a boy." Sometime between Thursday and Tuesday, he'd gained confidence. All kidding aside, he'd be a hot fuck if he didn't insist on the dating part. Her skin prickled with the charge of an approaching storm.

"I acted like one for a long time." Shrugging, he gained another stride. Two feet back from the counter, he spread his hands, palms up. "I'm tired of that life. Something's changed for me."

Her heart demanded more amperage to keep up the pace. "What changed?"

"You." He dropped the word like a stone in an old well, all else quiet as they waited for the splash.

"You don't even know my name." Her own fault.

"You want me to?"

No. Maybe.

The no-strings fuck she'd turned down Saturday at the track despite being revved and ready to race she blamed on Brian. His damn soft-looking hands and the challenge in his tone, and the way in her fantasies he hadn't been afraid to use her real name—

"Katherine." Sonova-fucking-bitch. "Kit. Everyone calls me Kit."

The wattage on his smile for sure blew out a fuse box somewhere. He closed the gap to the counter. "So which is it for me?"

"Kit. It's Kit." Much safer. He owed her two orgasms—the one interrupted in the shower and the one she'd given up Saturday. Wouldn't telling him shock his good-guy sensibilities.

"Okay. Kit. For now." He unsnapped a smartphone from his geeky-as-hell belt holster and held it up. "But I'm putting 'Katherine' in my phone."

"Did you just take my picture?" Jesus, fucking him would be dangerous if he meant to make more out of it, but the danger added to the attraction. The thrill of being a bad girl.

That's all this was, no different from taking a walk with the traveling grease monkeys and gearhead farm boys at the dirt track. Not about Brian at all, no sirree. Completely about coaxing him to be a bad boy, to open up his collared shirt and give in. Once she had him, he'd be out of her system.

Thumb-punching into his phone, he leaned away from the counter. His damn grin didn't shrink a bit. "Are you going to come after me if I say yes?"

Shooting him her come-hither stare, she tossed his words back at him. "You want me to?"

* * * *

Holy fuck, those eyes. Bright as a beach bonfire, she stiffened him to attention, ready and able to serve.

"If you come after me, I'm doing something wrong." Heart whomping, he went for deadpan delivery. She'd said Thursday not to hold back on the filthy thoughts, but—

As her chin dropped, she laughed and smacked the counter. "Fair enough. Wasn't sure you had it in you to let some bad boy out to play, Brian. But maybe you do."

Foot in the door. Yes. Now if he kept that fucker wedged open long enough to win a date, he'd be getting somewhere. "You let bad boys take you out?"

"No." She twisted her lips sideways, plump and teasing. "But I let them fuck me sometimes."

Christ, she refused to budge. "And that satisfies you?"

"Depends on the bad boy." Her crossed arms pushed her breasts up and out in challenge. She raised an eyebrow. "How bad are you, Brian?"

With a deep breath, he dove in like greeting 55-degree waves on Lake Michigan in October, the cold shocking on exposed skin. "So bad I'm good. Can you handle that?"

"I'll give you persistent, that's for sure." Anchoring her hip on the counter, she sighed. Standoffish and unimpressed as Mom's favorite cat. "Okay, let's pretend you're a bad boy. Prove it to me. Tattoos? Piercings? Love for illegal street racing?"

"No to one, two, and three." More from lack of money and parlors willing to risk tatting a minor when he'd been sixteen than by choice. "But my father called me 'rotten punk kid' so many times it might've been my legal name from fourteen to eighteen."

Stories not worth telling, after he'd graduated from stupid stunts like sledding off the roof to swiping his older brother's motorbike and getting wasted with the rest of the burnouts in the boarded-up former grocer's instead of going to class.

"And then?"

"I joined the Air Force and straightened up my act." The sense Dad hadn't knocked into him with shouts and grounding and the occasional swat, he'd learned with Rob as his study buddy. Who the fuck knew he'd had an aptitude for computer science before Rob prodded his ass to tech school? Not him. He'd been too busy making his buddies laugh to worry about homework.

"You've been straight-arrow since then, I bet." She gave him the once-over.

No question what she saw—a quiet computer geek who never stepped out of line in his office-dressy leather oxfords and his I-sit-at-a-desk collared shirt. Dress pants today, too, since he'd had a teleconference presentation for the new clients in Phoenix. Not a match for her bright blue-and-gray ringer shirt, the hem flirting with the top of her jeans and the sleeves circling above those damn sexy bicep curves. Motorcycle leathers, now, those might've gotten her attention.

"So what's the stupidest thing you ever did as a punk-ass kid?"

"Surfing the lake without a wetsuit." Hands down, no fooling, the dumbest fucking dare he'd taken. Lungs had seized up on him in the first minute, and he'd been too bullheaded to cop to weakness in front of the guys. He'd paddled out and ridden the seven-foot swell all the way in, his feet not feeling the board and his chest aching so bad he'd wanted to die. He'd hardly tasted the congratulatory beer—illegally obtained—his brother Matt had slapped in his hand after.

Head tipped back, she squinted with sweetly confused intensity. Two freckles, ripe for kissing, rested at the base of her throat. "The lake?"

"Lake Michigan. Halloween weekend. The water's so cold you need a full-body suit—unless you're a dumb as fuck sixteen-year-old pissed about your folks giving a big fat 'no' to trick-or-treating and you go out blowing off steam with your brothers and friends. You can't puss out on a dare from your big brother. But you can come damn close to killing yourself when you stop shivering and your fingers go numb and your lips turn blue."

Also how you get the nickname Surfer Boy from your squad mates a couple years later, but he'd save that tale for when he had a few beers in him. Kit—*Katherine*, a whisper dancing between his brain and his balls echoed—didn't need to hear all his stories today. A handful would catch her interest, list him under "attractive potential date" in her data sets instead of stuffing him headfirst into file thirteen.

Her playful smile suggested he'd given her some secret knowledge instead of a matter-of-fact accounting of his dumbassery.

"So you're a man who can't resist a dare." Stroking a leather-bound book on the counter, she clicked her tongue. "Good to know."

Tiny nicks and burns marked her, the map of pale lines and dots a badge of honor. Skills learned and work completed. She grabbed life by the horns, his Katherine.

She tapped her fingers. "Lawn mower, you said, right?"

Freckles and scars together would take more than a full night to kiss. Wouldn't want to miss one. "Yeah, mower, but I—"

"I'm out of intake forms up front." With her burning stare, she set him ablaze. "Why don't you c'mon back with me and we'll get you squared away." She sauntered through the open doorway behind the counter.

No need for paperwork when the mower wasn't broken and he hadn't brought it anyhow. He'd been clear about his motives right up front. Hers—well, he'd have to follow to find out, wouldn't he? Her invitation, handled right, might lead him closer to winning his frustrating temptress. At least he'd glimpse how she spent her days when she wasn't ordering him around by the side of the road. "Yes, ma'am."

* * * *

Hot damn, Prince Charming owned a bad-boy streak. Curiosity, at least. Either way, he trotted at her heels into the back. Not the nice-guy decline she'd half-expected. Well hell, if he wanted to play, no point in bluffing when her throbbing clit demanded she up the stakes. A nudge, that's all he needed.

He stopped in the thin rectangle illuminated by the light spilling from the shop floor. "Holy shit, it's hoarder heaven in here."

With the overhead lights off, most of the stockroom plunged into comforting darkness. The maze of shelves stuffed with parts donors—toasters, typewriters, remote-control and battery-powered toys of all types—could've extended into infinity.

"You're racking up points with that attitude, buster." The electric graveyard stopped at three rows deep, but he wouldn't know. He hadn't grown up among the shelves, fetching pieces to bring new life to needy patients. Dr. Frankenstein without the lightning. They made their own.

"I mean I like it." He gravitated toward her workbench, breaking the circle cast by her swing-arm lamp over the latest patient. "Kind of like a server room, humming with energy, packed to the rafters. Just yours is—"

"Dead. Yeah. They come in broken and they go out whole." Except Grandpa Jake. His worktable on the far side of the room waited like he'd left it, a mess of miniature cars and trains, engines that wouldn't race again.

"So you're a surgeon." Brilliant Brian, half whited out by the work light, half sunk in deep shadow, rubbed the mixer's slender neck. "This your patient?"

A soft touch, and slow. He didn't go digging his fingers in every open bin or shift work aside. Didn't presume to take her seat and adjust the height to his liking. He treated her space with respect. He'd tracked her down at the shop, sure, normally a presumption she'd hate in a fuckee—but she hadn't fucked him yet, and she damn well wanted to.

"On the operating table. This piece here?" She sidled up easy, crowding him without touching for nothing but the charge. "It sacrificed itself to save the motor. Quick replacement and she'll be good to go again."

Nodding, he traced the decorative grooves around the head. He'd had the power last week to jack up the truck and help her seat the spare, but tonight he exposed his nice-guy gentleness. Definite love-whisperer caresses. Not a first-move maker.

He dragged a slow circle. "You cut away the wounded bit and restore the beating heart."

"The core's strong. It just needs help finding the right speed." She finger-walked over a flathead, rocking the hexagonal handle. An illicit shimmy traveled down her spine. Never at the shop, not once, and playing the bad girl to his nice guy heightened the thrill. Risky, with the shop still open, and less than smart, and yet—as her desire spun out of control, no little pieces piped up to sacrifice themselves on the altar of sanity. The screwdriver tumbled from her grip. "What about you, Brian? Are you stuck in low gear?"

"Maybe we're both stuck—me in slow, you in fast." The tool's thumpy roll ended in his steady grip. He stroked the translucent yellow-orange handle. "We could meet in the middle over dinner."

"I told you, I don't go out with nice guys. I fuck bad boys." The more she said the words, the more defiant they rang. *You chase, I choose.* "They are what they say on the label. One night, a good time, no pretending they're going to hang around." She shoved down Erin's too-familiar speeches, the years of finishing her schoolwork at the kitchen table while her sister swore off men and crossed the spectrum from ranting to sobbing the deeper she got in her beer after putting the girls to bed. "I don't need a man in my life. I just like an orgasm now and again."

The longer she talked, the lower his brows and his frown dipped. "I'm not pre—"

Grabbing his crisp shirtfront, she drove him two steps back, to the sliver of bare wall between the corkboard and the workbench, and slammed their lips together.

Hands flying, he gripped her waist. Now that was more like it. Stronger than he looked.

He opened his mouth—surprise, maybe, or to argue more—but she stroked his tongue and tasted breath mints. Nice-guy flavor. Thinking he needed to work out all the data and crunch his numbers or whatever he did before he allowed the down-and-dirty bits to get going. Sometimes you had to make the connections, turn the damn thing on, and see how she ran. Deepening the kiss, she slid a hand across his belt.

He arched his hips from the wall. Poor man had nowhere to go in his dress pants, his cock hot, hard, and grinding on her thigh. He teased in return, curling his fingers beneath the hem of her shirt. Jesus, he spread fucking flutter-strokes at the top of her ass like he meant to drop his hands inside her jeans, cup her cheeks, and haul her to him.

Better idea. She clamped his wrist and tugged. Right hand, yeah, he seemed to be a righty, and if not he'd have to make do. Dragging her mouth free, she slapped his hand between her legs. Fuck, yes, straight on the seam. The pressure overheated her in the best way.

Rubbing her with the heel of his hand, he groaned. "Christ, Katherine."

"Unh-uh." Cheek to cheek, she jostled him in her denial.

Fresh and stormy, he smelled upper-class and dangerous—a man with lily-white fingernails who never showered at day's end to scrub away his labor. A man who needed despoiling. She took him in, settled his clean scent in her lungs. The metallic tang and sweet-sour oil fragrance from the workbench would dirty him up.

"My name is Kit." She rocked into his hand. Now or never. "And I dare you to make me come."

* * * *

Christ, she pushed his buttons with her bold challenges.

Dick surging, he cupped denim-covered, squirmy woman in his palm and squeezed. "When I'm making you come, you're Katherine."

She shuddered from the feathered auburn tips of her hair to her rising-on-tippy-toes feet. Given her moan vibrating against his neck, she seemed inclined to agree.

One treacherous current navigated on impulse. Millions more, relentless and unseen, pounded their safe harbor. Turn this woman down, and he wouldn't be granted another chance. Satisfy her demand, and he still might not, not if she relegated him to just-another-fuck status.

As he went in for a kiss, she angled her chin away. "Five minutes, bad boy." Lips twitching, she teased the touch she wouldn't permit him. "Get me off if you can." She swept him with her gaze, imperious and searching. "Fingers only, and my clothes stay on."

A contest of wills. If he wanted her, he'd have to conquer her, and she wouldn't go easy on him. Fine, then. He preferred stealth mode anyway. Let her brace for a full-on war while he crept behind her lines and showed her they'd been on the same side all along. She wanted fast to deny him a connection. When he won—no, when they both won—her one-and-done rule would become a daily-with-him rule. But first he had five minutes to stop jumping the flames in her fiery eyes and feel her orgasm under his fingers.

She raised an eyebrow in cocky challenge. "Giving up so soon, Prince Charming?"

Using the wall for leverage, he locked his hands around her waist and launched forward in a two-step pivot. Her gasp brought music to their swing. She fit against him face-to-face, the perfect height for wall-fucking. The day she donned a dress, he'd hitch her leg up and over his hip, shove her panties aside and bury himself.

Positions reversed, breathing hard, she glowed with beauty fit to light the darkness. "Better."

Oh, he'd show her better. In the next four minutes and twenty-seven seconds. With a push at her shoulders and a pull at her belt loop, he spun her to face the wall and pinned her beneath his weight. They shared height, but in his wider frame he topped her by twenty pounds. Rubbing his nose at the back of her neck, he inhaled pineapple and salt. "Best."

Shivering, she pitched a shaky laugh.

"Hands only," he whispered. "I know." God forbid she worry and reach for the nearest weapon instead of enjoying their five minutes. If he meant to be long-term material, he'd seal away end-of-the-night bar thinking. Prove his trustworthiness, prove his bad-boy streak, keep her safe but let her feel endangered. Christ Jesus, give him the strength to find the perfect line to ride this wave. Impossible if she got her hands on him. "But you keep yours up where I can see 'em."

As he took hold of her wrists, she nodded. She let him guide her up, palms flat, and stop with her gorgeous muscled arms in a wide diamond framing her half-hidden face.

"Right there." In replacement for the kiss she'd refused him, he stole one from the pulse pounding in her neck. "Don't you move now, Katherine."

Fuck, her mouth dropped open and she breathed deep. Succumbed when he met her demands with demands of his own. The tiny gaps between them filled out with hot, needy woman.

Impatient and greedy for the interior tour, his dick banged at the gate. Grinding against her firm, rounded ass cushioned the ache. Her unexpected obedience left him free to roam. As righty went to work on her belt and jeans, he slipped his left hand under her shirt and cupped the warm, gentle swell of her belly. With a thumb sweep, he grazed the band of her bra.

She rocked light as the lake on a calm July afternoon, her waves peaceful, steady, and nudging the prow of his boat with relentless persistence. He mapped the curving arch of her ribs and the shallow divot of her navel. As he dragged her zipper south, her jeans fell in a gaping vee granting him access to the shadowed cotton triangle beneath.

Eyes falling closed, she ducked her chin and swallowed. "Might've worn fancy underwear if I'd known you were stopping by today."

The hitch in her chuckle found a match in his chest, a desperate urge to kiss away any embarrassment he'd caused. He nuzzled as far as her ring-neck tee allowed, nipping at the collar.

He'd cared about getting women off before, because sex was a game, a time for laughter and fun, and because he liked to win, but he'd never cared so damn much. Nothing in his life, not mastering his service skills exams, not standing by Rob on his wedding day—nothing mattered more than showing Katherine he could be a nice guy and still get her off, still satisfy her needs and be worth coming back to. He bypassed the barrier, diving through grasping curls with his whole hand. "I'm not here for the panties. I'm here for the woman in them."

Greeting him with eager wetness, she wiggled into a wider stance. Silent and breathless, she tugged her lip between her teeth.

Further still he slid, spreading his hand over the sexiest fucking curve in existence, the front swell of a woman, made to fit a man's hold. Lips silk-soft, she parted for him. Leisurely exploration would wait for another night. His woman had requested immediate satisfaction, and she'd have the best of his ability. Bad-boy talk would keep her content, turn a date into an exciting and dangerous desire. Enough to intrigue her the way she'd leashed his heart. Testing, he sank his middle finger to full depth in her slick heat.

She put the squeeze on, a jerking clench so tight he couldn't drag his way out. Positive feedback. Now to send her into a looping growth cycle, until the waves crested her jetties and carried her out to sea. He'd shown her all of slow she'd allow. Time to bring the storm.

* * * *

Sweet Jesus, she'd underestimated the charming prince. From so simple a dare, he transformed into a man bold and demanding. He cast his breath, heavy and heated, across her neck. He pressed her to the wall, here, not two feet from the place she sat daily and made broken things whole, and rubbed his cock against her as he fucked her with one finger. No—he ventured inside her with one finger. He fucked her with every circuit and synapse firing in him, from his fingernail-short blond hair to his fancy leather shoes.

"What makes you think a date with me won't be like this, Katherine?" Keeping up his steady thrusts, he stole under her shirt with his other hand. Though hooked, her bra no longer served a purpose as he peeled the cups aside and freed her. "A naughty surprise."

"You think this is naughty?" She aimed for coy, but her body gave her away with every gasp and tremble. If she had any sense, she'd tell him to stop saying her name in that damn tender-teasing tone. What right did he have for—for suggesting so much intimacy?

"I think you like thinking it is." Neither soft nor rough, he fondled her with a firm hand. Pinching her nipples, sending sparks sweeping downward, he worked her absent an instruction manual. "What if I took you to dinner?"

Dating. The first time she'd had a boy between her legs, she'd been seventeen. Too young and naïve to advocate for herself, to demand equal satisfaction. In the cramped backseat of her date's car after the homecoming game senior year, she'd put footprints on the fogged-up windows trying to work some leverage, anything to get the action near as good as touching herself.

But he'd been fumbling and sweaty, with breath stinking of the nachos and hot dog he'd scarfed in the stands, and her lost virginity had been all about his dick. As he jammed himself in, his hand might've grazed her thigh. Maybe. The flaw replicated in the guys she fucked these days, stamped in on God's male assembly line. They needed forceful, direct reminders to keep their damn attention on more than their cocks. Brian hadn't even reached to adjust his.

"And what would we"—fuck, her arching back took her breath and trapped his hands with her against the wall—"would we do at dinner? Talk?"

"We're talking now." He liberated them both and restarted his rhythm. Holding her secure as a chain hoist cradling an engine block, he delivered powerful strokes. Not a boy or a guy. A man. "You're worth the multitasking effort."

In prove-his-manhood mode, Brian remained a giver, not a taker. Flipping her toward the wall and shoving his hand down her pants—total bad boy move. Except he made bold demands on her behalf instead of his own. She hadn't moved her arms, not once, though only his words shackled them. She'd grown accustomed to giving orders. Most men lacked imagination—or the initiative to use it. In the greedy race of sex, the first-place finisher carried no obligation to bring anyone else across the line. Two bodies, clashing, in a contest she'd win first or leave unfinished.

"We'll get a corner booth, deep and dark, a cozy circle for two."

The illumination from the work light fell short of their bodies. Hidden in the shadows, he ground against her jeans. Not like a man trying to weasel his way into fucking after she'd set the terms, but one proving her arousal turned his crank.

"The waiter'll hand us our menus, and we'll order a couple of longnecks, and he'll give us a snooty look, because it's the sort of place where the women sip wine and the men drink scotch." Skillful and teasing, Brian drew out the torture with her own wetness as he pinned her in place. He understood how to work her grease into her grooves and spin her up properly. "You're wearing a dress—"

"The hell I am." As if she'd bother with frilly nonsense for a simple fuck.

"—not because women need dresses to be beautiful, but because you want me to touch you. Your choice, Katherine." Abandoning her breasts beneath her rucked-up shirt, he crossed below her navel and into her panties. Both hands, now, and not a dry, cracked finger in the bunch. "Our date is about making sure we both get what we want."

He still smelled sharp and fresh as a summer storm, but her arousal surrounded them in earthy musk. Waiting for lightning to strike. The longer their bodies melded, the stronger the sense of rightness grew. Less a dare and more a demo of smooth running when the pieces came together. Not too-tentative nice guy, and not too-controlling jackass. Just Brian, who helped her change a tire and wanted a date. A date.

"Don't you want that?" Rolling his head against her, he mimicked a nod. With his embrace, he made them one creature, his arms wrapped and snaking down her sides to his workbench. The place where she ebbed and flowed with his thrusts. "You not wearing panties and my hand under your dress in our dark little booth?"

So vivid he set the scene, cool leather caressed the backs of her bare thighs. Her loose dress bunched beside her hips but not beneath as they sat, and their foolish waiter didn't have a clue. "Say I did. What would it get me?"

"I'm sliding higher, closer, all the time, but you won't know"—he broke off and kissed beneath her jaw, deep, open-mouthed kisses as if he meant to capture her throat as she swallowed—"when I'm going to touch you."

She fought the swirling rush. No man should know her so well. He was supposed to fail. Find her dare too difficult, go back to chasing nice girls, and never again tempt her with his false kindness. Instead, he played her with his whole body. Put in service to his mind, his hands worked not harder but smarter. While his white-collar clothes wrinkled against her, he operated with a craftsman's skill.

"Will our waiter notice your rounded lips? Your widening eyes? Will he hear those breathy moans you think you're stifling?" In a two-fingered duet, he revealed the strength in his arms with each thrust from his right and swipe of her clit from his left. His shirt cloaked rippling muscle squeezing her ribs, the effort in his hands originating in his shoulders. Traveling through him the way his words did her, knotting her insides. "Does he know my fingers are inside you, Katherine?"

The tips of her fingers turned tingly and trembling. The wall offered no handholds, no yielding flesh. Indifferent and unchanging the harder she dug in. The climax he owed her—

"Is he watching you come when he serves us dessert?"

Orgasm slammed her knees against the wall, but he held on, he held on and absorbed her shaking and shuddering, burying his face in her neck. She allowed herself to release the moan she'd tried to keep from him. He'd won the race by making her win, and he cradled her in comfort beyond any her mattress or the shower offered. Certainly more than the fuckees she chose for their willingness to leave her alone after.

Nestling his cock in the curve of her ass, he exhaled a low, guttural groan around his teeth in her neck. Holding off with damned impressive restraint. After his performance, he'd more than earned reciprocation, rules of the game be damned.

She needed to taste him. Her arms dropped as she wiggled free of his fingers. She shimmied around to face him.

"Katherine?" In the shadows, his pupils swallowed the spring grass of his eyes. His cock thumped her hip.

The only chance she might get. Risking a second encounter with Brian would be foolhardy when he'd proved so adept. He almost had her craving a damn date. She followed the tail of his belt to his buckle. "Your turn to hold still, pretty boy."

Singing out in warning from the shop floor, the customer bell announced a new guest.

"Sonova—"

Covering her mouth, he silenced her whisper. Wide-eyed in the darkness, he shook his head. No kidding, he wouldn't be walking out front, not with his dick standing at attention. Didn't absolve her of her responsibilities. Fantastic finger-fuck or not, she had work to finish.

She peeled his hand away and called to the customer, “Be right with you.” Taking two good breaths, she patted his chest. Nice and solid. “Looks like time’s up. I have to get that.”

Unmoving as a monument, he stared at her.

Jesus. Straighten bra, zip jeans, resettle shirt in case he’d left marks—a million and one reminders in the blink of an eye. She scraped her hair back with spread fingers on both sides, lest the wall-flattened half give her away. A final shiver shook out her buzzing high. “See? I told you you were good.”

Jaw tightening, he produced a huffy nose-laugh and leaned in as if to kiss her cheek.

She slipped out under his arm. Rounding the corner, she left the back room with her heart racing. The harsh light blinded her eyes. She’d let him get to her. Mess her head up with desire for more than a quick release. Saved by the bell.

“Sorry for the wait.” She forced a smile for the woman approaching the counter and hunted for a stick of gum. Something in her mouth would suppress the urge to go back for Brian. “How can I help you tonight?”

* * * *

She’d reached for his belt but ducked away from his kiss.

Sucking her sweetness from his fingers, he throttled back the conclusions jumping through his cock. The thoughts going on upstairs hadn’t cycled past the rightness of her in his arms and the warmth of her tucked to his chest. Once she agreed to dating, she might spend her nights in his bed, nestled just so close. Lending the pillows her pineapple-and-salt breeze, she’d fill his embrace with her muscled curves and drop him hints of the mysteries spinning behind her secretive brown eyes.

“—and Dad’s birthday’s this weekend, so I was really glad to get the call this morning.” At bullhorn levels, the stranger who’d interrupted his pending date interrogation projected cheery and chipper feminine tones. “We weren’t sure we’d be able to get the set restored in time. I don’t think the train’s run since he was a boy.”

“My grandpa was the model train expert, but Dad’s not a bad hand at them.” Reverted to distant friendliness, Kit hardly seemed the same woman who’d moaned and shook in his arms minutes before. “You said it’s under Baxter?”

Drying off his fingers inside his pockets—one less stain for the dry cleaners to rail at him for after last week’s mud and grease—he cursed the delay. Post-orgasm, sexy-as-hell Katherine all soft and sparking might’ve granted him a night out without arguing. Customer service, business-as-usual Kit stood out front, raising her walls.

"That's right. My married name, of course. Dad's a Larson. You should have two boxes..." The woman droned on, boring as a tenth-grade history lesson.

Despite the annoyance, his damn erection wouldn't subside. The second he reached to adjust himself, he'd pop off in his shorts. So hard his dick would support his whole weight and carry a full pack besides, for chrissake. He laid his forehead against the wall and his hands alongside. Near same position he'd put her in, and damn if she hadn't loved the take-charge attitude.

"Oh sure, sure. Let me grab that for you." Kit strode into the back and passed behind him. At her desk, she settled her ass on the ledge and sat surrounded by a lamplight halo. Head tipped, she studied him as if he stored a model train set in his pants. Not damn likely, though his engine hadn't stopped chugging.

After five long-ass Mississippis he counted with dick twitches, she flashed him a smile and stood. Three soft-soled steps later, she grasped his ass with both hands.

Hips jerking, he bit his tongue. If God loved him even a little, she'd repeat that move some night when he was on top and drag him deeper.

She leaned in, grazing his back with her breasts, and nuzzled his ear. "This, I'm grabbing just for me." Letting go far too soon, she sauntered back into the light. "Oh, shoot, there they are. Sorry about the wait, Mrs. Baxter. Dad must've moved your order under the counter when he called you."

Sneaky temptress. Her entire purpose for stepping into the back room had been to tease him. Fuck, she was a bold one. Liked danger and thrill-seeking. His risky dinner scenario sure had made her come hard. And sweet.

His woman demanded an equal, one who'd meet her fire with his own. He'd be a better man with her. For her, because she deserved better. Not Brian the class clown, not Brian the fuck-up, and not coasting-through-life Brian. Standing alongside Katherine, he'd plant his feet and be the man she needed. Once he convinced her she needed him.

He flipped around, quiet-like, and rested his back on the wall. Rock-hard and stuck eavesdropping, he filtered out the customer's gabbing in favor of the rise and fall of Kit's voice in reply. She'd called him good when he'd been establishing his bad-boy credibility. Had that been compliment or complaint? Taking her up on her dare might've been the wrong move, but Christ, he couldn't regret it and he wouldn't take back a second. Scrubbing his face in his palms, he inhaled her lingering scent.

The cash register rattled out front, the drawer slamming as the women exchanged goodbyes. The bell over the door chimed. A trash liner rustled. He waited for her shadow in the doorway. Three Mississippis.

"All clear." Kit let out a sly laugh. "You waiting for me to come back there and frisk you?"

"Praying to the wall god for mercy." If winning her dare had been about getting something in return, then more time with her was the prize he'd claim. His dick would hold off until they'd straightened out her soon-to-be-gone no-dating rule.

As he entered the main shop, the bright lights wiped out his night vision. Kit wandered to and fro with a fuzzy outline, and his eyes carried her hazy afterimage everywhere he looked. No different from the way his mind had kept dragging her into view all weekend. "Thought that lady would never leave."

She stopped her flitting. Back to him, she stood stiff as a slick-sleeve at her first inspection with her proud chin raised. "Everyone has to leave sometime."

Son of a fucking bitch. He'd gotten warmer send-offs from women shoving his clothes into his arms while they pushed him out the door.

"Uh-huh. Until we meet again." With a shot of deep-breath courage, he pumped false cheer over his fears. She'd liked his style, dammit. If she wanted to throw him out now, he'd reached her deeper than she'd wanted. A step in the right direction, by his measure. "Say, Friday night?"

As she turned her head, her eyes fluttered shut and a there-and-gone smile touched her lips. "You really don't give up, do you?"

"Not on you." He'd forever believed a long-term relationship would be too confining. The death of sex arrived around the three- or six-month mark—no point hanging in for that. Short-term worked better. Except Rob was obviously still getting plenty with Nora, and Kit wanted plenty, so plenty-wanting women existed and long-term relationships worked, and they'd damn well figure one out together. "The fooling around was good, right? The date will be, too."

"Brian, I can't—" Fingers clenched back, she rubbed her palm on the side of her jeans. "I'm not going to dinner with you."

"Why not?" With them, sex was a given. The tightness in his chest came from fear of missing out on building that meaningful partnership with the woman who challenged and inspired him.

"You know why not." For a half-second, she met his gaze, and her eyes flickered wide and wild. Abandoning her stare, she exposed the graceful curve of her neck and the tightness in her jaw. "I don't date. I fuck. When and how I feel like it."

She'd have been kinder to pick up one of her screwdrivers and stick him between the ribs. Least then the hurt would stay in one place. If he walked out with a no, she'd have a stronger one for him next time he asked. She'd be a cautionary tale he told himself on nights alone, his arms folded behind his head as he practiced blanket denials. No, he'd never wanted her. No, he hadn't fantasized more with her from the moment she'd flipped him a granola bar.

Goddammit. He'd offer her everything if she'd fucking take it—and she refused to take him seriously. Might as well call him a liar. "So you're just—"

"The word 'slut' passes your lips"—four flying steps brought her right up in his face—"and you best haul your ass outside before I kick it there." Puffing sweet-cherry breath, probably owing to the pack of chewing gum on her desk, she squinched her face in tight lines. "One orgasm isn't going to melt my brain."

A harsher synonym sprang up out of spite, and he buttoned the slur down like every ill-advised retort to a senior officer. Not what he intended to say in the first place, and damn her for thinking he would. "I told you I'm not playing little-boy games, Katherine. Name-calling is the shitty behavior of a boy pouting over what he's not getting. Knowing what you want and asking for it doesn't make you a slut."

By force of will, he kept his voice level. If she had the sense and guts to ask him, she had the guts to ask any man and replace him quick as a summer storm.

Dating and sex had always been a dance, and everyone knew men led and women followed. The currents had shifted in the decades since Dad had sat him down and polished off half a case of beer before giving him the man talk in the backyard. Different expectations. Different beliefs. The changing times or the wisdom of a man who'd spent twenty-two years in the hunt, who the fuck knew anymore? He floated on unsteady ground with her, waiting for a rogue wave to wipe him out.

Dipping her head, she eased off. "No, you're right. I jumped to a conclusion I shouldn't have. I get touchy about staking out boundaries."

A fact to add to the short list of infobits he had on her. One of the great mysteries of the universe, how he cared so damn much with such limited data. Yeah, he knew her determination and strength, her grace and kindness to customers. The rightness as she came in his arms. But he couldn't lay claim to basic details. Her age. Her family. Where she lived.

She shrugged. "A lotta guys, you let one thing slide, and the world becomes fair game. I'm just—" Rolling her neck, she popped a joint. "A mite bit tense."

Eyebrow cocked, he pitched his voice low. "I thought we took care of your tension." Not his, though their argument had knocked him back to a manageable semi. Much as he enjoyed her fire and her fiery demands, what if his Surfer Boy antics doused her? Fire and water didn't mix. He might never have more than this from her.

"One kind, very well." She shot him a wry, kissable grin. "A woman who can't invent a dozen ways to think herself tense in under a minute isn't a woman at all, right? I figured a man of your advanced years would know that rule by heart."

"My advanced years?" Clutching his chest, he staggered back from her teasing barrage. "How old do you think I am?"

With her hands shoved in her back pockets, she rocked on her toes. "Thirty-four?"

"Thirty-seven. Let's go with your number instead. Dare I ask a woman's age?" Not too young, please God. "Or should I know that rule by now, too?"

Elbows bent out, head cocked, freckled cheeks shining—Christ, she impersonated a college kid but for her grown-woman skills and confidence. "Twenty-eight."

Close enough for government work. Halle-freaking-lujah. Swooping in on anyone under twenty-five came with plenty of drama and no commitment. The former he'd never liked, and the latter—well, she'd changed that, hadn't she?

She wagged a pert finger. "I'm letting your breach of the man-woman contract slide solely because I owed you for jumping to conclusions."

"This is where I take a mile, then? What about"—tapping his chin in master-villain mode, he hummed, *ta-da*—"a not-a-date?"

"Are you inviting me to fuck in your tiny car?" Cheeks rounding with a smile, she tipped her chin toward his groin. "You're packing a hefty tool. Could be a tight squeeze."

Annnd the pressure at his fly returned. Better divert her from the subject of fucking before his pants split. "Softball."

"That's a date." She tripped over him with her answer, so fast she must've been coded in an automatic loop.

"That's not a date." Lie. Bringing her to the game absolutely would be a date. "That's catching lazy pop flies and drinking beers from a cooler on a Saturday afternoon." Not a classic date where he bought dinner and she surrendered her body, but the kind where his quasi-family vetted the woman he'd chosen and she experienced the sort of life he'd offer. "Like forty, fifty people. You don't want to spend time with me, you'll have plenty of folks to choose from."

Hell, softball had worked for Rob. Why not him?

Stalking back and forth in front of appliance-laden white metal shelves, she lacked only a cat's tail twitching. Long silences and sidelong glances she managed fine. As she rocked to a stop, she swiped her knuckles across her forehead. "We take separate cars, and if you introduce me to a single, solitary person as your date or your girlfriend, I walk."

Holy fucking shit, she'd delivered a yes. Negotiating terms, not the date itself, because that was a yes. Green light on Operation Real Relationship with Katherine. A prelude to permission for waking up beside her, watching her eyelids flutter as she dreamed. Arousing her with kisses down her gently sloping nose to the rounded tip. Planting one on her sweetheart lips and nibbling to his heart's content.

She coughed. "Unless you don't want—"

"Nope, nope, I want." Christ Jesus. Standing here daydreaming while the woman at the center of his fantasies waited for his reply. Hell of a showing. "I'll text you details, and I'll tell everyone you're a stranger who followed me to alert me my taillight's out."

She laughed, thank God. Sweet and low, wrapping him in love-fog, the same substance that must've addled Rob's brains last summer. He hadn't warned the stuff would be so damn addictive. But maybe every man had to figure that one for himself.

* * * *

Rattling off her number, she rushed him out the door. Any more of Prince Charming's temptations tonight, and she'd start calling him the devil. As he swaggered out of view, he left behind an uncommon vacancy. The strange pull demanded more than his dick, though she wouldn't scrape a healthy serving of that off her plate, either.

With the sign flipped to *Closed*, she rested against the door and replayed the best five minutes of her day. Well, maybe seven minutes. The notion of timing him had flown away as soon as he'd spun her toward the wall.

The way he took control—no guy won that concession from her. Maybe the difference accounted for the surge of something-ness urging her to see him again. Micromanaged, most one-nighters got the job done, but the satisfaction dissipated in the final few climactic shudders. With Brian, the buzzing high had driven her toward more dangerous games. Grabbing his ass while her customer waited out front. Fuck, she'd lost her mind. His damn fault.

By the time she got the shop closed up and the mixer waiting in the back fixed, she'd be late for dinner again. Hung-up, moony-eyed girlfriends depended on a man to keep them company. She'd finish up on her own and like it, dammit. And stop fucking jumping back to thoughts of him. At least Mrs. Baxter provided a credible excuse for running behind. Brian's contribution would stay locked in the vault of better-left-unsaid.

A secret, gotten-away-with-naughtiness thrill.

She'd goaded Mr. Nice Guy into credible bad-boy behavior. He hadn't slunk away from the challenge, oh no. He'd owned it. Owned *her*, for those too-short minutes. The danger of a date-date with him didn't come from her giving an inch and him taking a mile. The danger came from wanting to offer him the mile. Softball would give her a people-buffer from his persuasive touch and seductive voice.

Popping the register, she fell into counting with the ease of long habit. When her first-grade homework had demanded she circle pictures of nickels and dimes, Grandpa Jake, harrumphing behind his bushy mustache, had plonked her on the counter beside the register.

"None of that piddly bullshit—now watch you don't repeat that and get Grandpa in trouble, mind—for my granddaughter. You're old enough to work the till, Kitten."

Through patient tutelage, he'd taught her the real-world skills elementary school tried to approximate. By eight, she'd been trusted with zeroing out the day's transactions and dropping the zippered bag in the bank's night-deposit box while Dad or Grandpa waited in the truck.

Nine-seventeen and change today, after setting up the starting cash for tomorrow. Not great, but not a bad take for a Tuesday. The refurbished Atari 2600—quick fix of a replacement adapter and some shine—had gone home with a new owner. The gaming console and a resurrected 1930s wood-cabinet radio stood out as the day's big-ticket items on the floor. Repair work made up the balance. She'd miss the radio, with its pointy-domed cabinet pretty as a stained-glass church window. Have to keep an eye out for a broke-down model on her next fishing expedition.

Cash bagged, she dry-mopped the vinyl and flipped the lights to night mode. A warm yellow glow, welcoming and homey, filled the display windows as the rest of the shop went dark. The penetrating evening sun fell too short to make itself known.

Surefooted in familiar terrain, she wandered into the back. Replacing the gear and closing up her patient would take a few minutes' work at the most. As she settled in her seat, her back tingled.

The wall revealed nothing of the evening. Paper, plaster, and paint couldn't return the curling smile her muscles kept forcing on her mouth. Damn thing wouldn't go down.

"Just like Brian." Laughing, she narrowly missed smacking her head on the swing-arm.

Gal chatter and dick-pill commercials insisted men got less horny as they aged and had trouble staying hard. Jesus God, in mid-argument with her, he'd sported a noticeable bulge. If anyone had been trying to notice. Which she hadn't, because—bullshit. Brian boasted a tight ass, a solid erection, and brawny arms, not qualified with for-an-office-worker, but straight-up damn fine.

Greased, the worm gear seated perfectly. The main shaft turned. Time to retrace her steps, clean as a conscientious hiker leaving no sign of her passage. Once the candy-red shell sealed up around her modifications, the mixer would work as if it'd never been broken.

Heels tucked on her foot rungs, she tapped the floor as she worked. The moves flowed easy, righty-tighty muscle memory. A small job didn't demand an overpowered drill.

Brian understood that. She hadn't believed he'd meet her dare, but fuck, he'd brought the skills and then some. Good enough to at least find out what he'd do with permission to use his sinful mouth. He talked an amazing game. Maybe his tongue had other uses. He'd had years to practice.

Thirty-seven, shit. And no wife, no kids—presumably. He hadn't said so. Not that he owed her details, because they weren't dating and they weren't going to be. Conceding to a second meet-up—third, if she counted the blown tire—didn't mean more than an appreciation for his fuckability. A little rough and a lot fast, he hadn't for one minute taken his focus off what she needed.

The man auditioned for a starring role instead of understanding his bit part in her life.

Better not to get tangled and end up heartbroken and bitter like her sister.

Family first, always.

Grandpa Jake had intended for her to take over the business when the time came 'round. Upgrade Runyon's Repairs from its post-war origins to the twenty-first century. Market the high-end vintage pieces online and simplify in-home repair scheduling. If things had gone as planned, they'd be hosting Saturday summer camp classes for tweens in basic electronics, letting them tear apart old VCRs to diagnose and troubleshoot while their parents paid thirty bucks a head for a two-hour science lesson.

With Erin fragile and stumbling from one career to another—massage therapy, cosmetology, bartending, a whole string of unfinished certifications and increasing debts—money had been tight for years. Warehouse picker fell somewhere above chicken beheader in her list of desirable jobs, and the climate and the hours sucked, but the pay came in steady. The girls wanted clothes and gadgets to keep up with their school friends. Mom needed routine eye checkups to monitor her declining vision. Grandpa Jake's funeral—fuck.

She swiped her eyes with the backs of her wrists. Brian wouldn't understand any of that. What thirty-seven-year-old man wanted to pick up his date at her parents' house, the house she'd never left, the one where Mom still made her meals and she slept in the bedding she'd gotten for Christmas at least a decade ago?

Her wildness belonged far away from home. Bad enough she'd let him get her so riled she'd brought sex into the shop. Last time she'd made a mistake, she'd been twenty-one. Young enough to excuse her stupidity in bringing a hookup home on a Friday night.

More than a little drunk, they'd stumbled through the door after midnight. She'd shushed him down the hall to her bedroom. Emery. Like a freaking nail file.

"Board," he'd said. "As in 'stiff as.'" He'd slapped her hand on his dick right in the bar, and she'd been wasted enough to find him the funniest fucking guy in existence. Hence the home-going.

Fun until she'd tried to hustle him out the door before six a.m. on a Saturday. With hangover brain, she'd forgotten the girls would be camped in front of the TV set, giggling at infomercials and God-knew-what cartoons, quiet so they didn't wake Erin, who demanded no wakeups before nine on a weekend.

Six and seven, Jess and Abby had popped their heads over the back of the couch quick as prairie dogs.

"Is that your boyfriend?" Abby studied him with animal intensity.

"Do you want my cereal milk?" As Jess held out her bowl, the liquid slopped across the rim and dripped. "It's pink."

Extra pink when landing on the living room's beige carpet.

"What the fuck?" Whispering didn't do Emery any favors. "You have kids?" His hoarse smoker voice grated as she propelled him out the door. "Crazy bitch."

Tears streaked Jess's cheeks. "I spilled. Mommy'll be mad."

"Aunt Kit?" Curling around the couch back, Abby lifted her feet and kicked the air. "Did that man give you a baby? Can we trade Jess for it?"

Seven years later, as she remembered the morning, the chill still draped her chest and the numbness attacked her fingers. The girls didn't need to witness her hormone-fueled mistakes. She hadn't brought a man home since. Backseats of cars got the job done. The occasional motel room when the guy was an out-of-towner. No repeats, no strings, and no getting personal.

She'd grown smarter. She had the strength to handle Brian without losing herself no matter how hard he tried to tangle her up. His dick hadn't gotten more than a cloth-covered cameo tonight. She owed herself one good, casual fuck with him. A man who thought himself a bad boy but acted like a nice guy—except when pushed, and then he responded with macho meet-that-dareness. She'd give him a tune-up for his next woman, his settle-down girl. As long as she didn't bring him by the house, they weren't dating.

But the way he'd said her name rolled through her head and rumbled low in her belly. A turn-on, nothing more. The fluttering lightness in her chest didn't have to mean anything but that she was late for dinner.

She left out the back, locking the door to the electric graveyard behind her.

* * * *

Sinking into the driver's seat, Brian yanked the car door shut and exhaled. Loud and forceful, he beat out the rumbling of the air conditioner competing with the built-up, sunny-parking-spot heat swirling around him.

The steering wheel roasted his hands. A purring beast, the Audi slipped down the near-deserted downtown street. Tuesday nights didn't bring the crowds even in midsummer. Too many empty and boarded-up buildings waited on urban revival.

They ought to be throwing a parade. Confetti, marching bands, the whole shebang. Kit would let her guard down at softball. Without background checks. Investigating her secrets would break the spirit of the relationship he aimed to build. Nobody stayed tense and wary through a whole afternoon of fun. Hell, he'd have settled for the nightmare of a coffee date, the will-she or won't-she of wondering whether they'd upgrade their meeting to a meal. Softball constituted a massive victory.

Almost as massive as his unstoppable erection. Fuck, his dick ached, and no litany of polar explorers sufficed, not while his fingers held her scent. The AC fanned her sweet musk around him in a dizzying lure. With his pants bunched tight, he wedged his knee against the door.

Four fucking blocks and he scanned for a decent spot. A little privacy. Seven blocks and he drove past the rusting chain-link fence into the parking lot of an abandoned furniture warehouse. Faded yellow banners sagging in the front window advertised a factory-direct clearance sale four years gone.

Forced off the road by desire for a woman he'd met five days ago. One who trusted him to finger-fuck her in the back room of an open shop but not to pick her up at her house. Swearing, he cut the engine and tilted the seat back. Riding the perfect line between being the fuck-toy she seemed to want from her lovers and coaxing her into a greater commitment, now that was a new one to stick on the aphrodisiac list.

With a slouch, he hid himself from view of anyone nosy enough to come crawling around his car, at least unless they peered straight into the windows. Getting arrested for public lewdness would have Rob kicking his ass for dumbass hijinks.

He set a land-speed record for unbuckling and unzipping. Shoved down, his shorts formed an elastic vise under his balls. He grabbed hold and stroked, the urgent, uncomfortable need a reminder of furtive after-school jerking in the bathroom behind a locked door.

A sea of crumbling red brick, a match for Kit's store, filled his windshield.

His dick didn't demand the nonstop action he'd craved twenty years ago. Hell, five years ago. Maybe Rob had the right idea. Get to know one woman.

"Katherine." He tasted her in her name, in three syllables of slamming hips and a low, trembling moan. "Katherine."

He'd memorize her sloping muscles, her rounded tits, the curve between her legs, her sun-kissed skin—and let her get to know him. The strokes he used for a quick jerk and the places where her tongue would drive him wild. None of this one dinner in exchange for one fuck. They'd practice the new math together.

This time, she'd be the one standing behind him. With her height, their made-for-each-other size, she might catch him rubbing out a quick one before work and saunter up behind him.

"I thought you wanted to sleep in," he'd tease, trying to keep his rhythm despite her enticing nudity at his back.

She brought round, firm breasts to bear as she hooked her arms around him. "I found something better than dreams."

"Yeah?" Lungs tight, he worked for breath. The cresting wave flashed up ahead, the long paddle so worth the trip. "What's that?"

"You." Clenching his shoulders, she hugged him suspender-style and rested her chin on him. "That the way you like it?"

He upped his game to a quasi-corkscrew with a twist at the tip. A surefire finishing move. "Yeah. You like watching?"

"Mm-hmm." Diving, she skimmed his chest. "But I'm a hands girl." She displaced him and took over, matching his rhythm, her grip sure and confident. "I like doing better."

Katherine grabbed what she wanted, when she wanted. And she wanted him.

He spilled over his fist and splattered his shirt tails.

As lethargy hit, he dropped his head against the seat. That orgasm, Christ. Fast and hard, a freight train rush he'd lost years ago. Even with her presence limited to fantasy, she improved on everything. Must be those tinkering skills. Loving a woman who learned his body mattered now. Emotional virtues and tenderness he'd never considered at seventeen, when a lapping wave served to get him off.

"I know you don't date, Katherine." He hunted for fast-food napkins on the floor mats in the back and came up empty. The inside of his boxers would have to do. "But last week I would've said I'd never pick one woman over the variety of staying single. People change. You can, too."

The more he demonstrated her importance to him, the faster she'd recognize the rightness in their pairing. She needed time to get comfortable and feel secure with him. Her complaint about men pretending they cared enough to hang around—a bad breakup. Anyone burned by an ex would be skittish about new relationships. The more he showed up, the more she'd learn she could rely on him.

Cursing the new stains on his shirt, he righted his clothes and tucked himself away. Dinner mandated a stop somewhere with a drive-thru. Imposing on Rob again when he and Nora had lovey-dovey baby feelings oozing out all over the place would make him a shit friend. A sad sack peeping through the window instead of taking care of his business. He deserved a life of his own, one with a partner. With Katherine. He peeled out of the parking lot.

He'd start tomorrow in the gym at work, because any idiot who'd hurt her and leave her so gun-shy about more than sex merited a pummeling, and the punching bag would make an excellent proxy. And then he'd shake the imaginary asshole's hand for getting the fuck out of his way. Katherine belonged with him, not some bad-boy shithead who didn't understand the responsibilities a man had toward his woman.

Him, voted most likely to die in a late-night TV stunt, the poster child for responsibility. Twenty years of behaving like that guy, maybe not a jerk but not a long-term catch, either, and now he'd finally wised up only to fall for a woman who would've preferred him the other way.

God had to be laughing his ass off.

Chapter 3

Driving Erin's little errand-runner, Kit turned off on a packed-dirt road with a hand-painted plywood sign reading *Ballfield* in cobalt blue letters. Some joker had hung a matching cap over the stake sticking up the back.

A passel of cars and trucks in darn straight rows for impromptu mud-and-grass parking lay ahead to the left. Families crowded around trunks. Men balanced Coleman chest coolers and pint-sized children on their shoulders in about equal measure. Waiting on a stampede of older kids crossing the entry, she searched for Brian's crimson coupe. Mid-life crisis car for sure, but he had the good sense to choose a sporty old workhorse and not a flashy dick extender.

The athletic complex where the youth leagues played, out by the airport, featured nearly a dozen diamonds. This middle-of-nowhere plot boasted two, both with chain-link backstops and sidelines. Crawling down the aisle, she spied a flash of red beyond the pickup trucks and minivans. Her sister's boxy beige Camry fit alongside at the end of the row. Shabby as all hell, but none of these folks would see her again.

She hopped out and stretched. The breeze carried shouts, laughter, and the smoky char of burgers and dogs on the grill. The clouds dotting the bright blue sky kept the heat at bay. Saturdays didn't get much better. Pocketing her keys, she joined the stream.

As she rounded a monster of an extended cab, Brian barreled into her and hoisted her off her feet.

"You made it, great." He set her down easy, kissed her cheek, and grinned. "When you didn't answer my last text, I thought you might've changed your mind."

"I might yet." Picking her up, Jesus. Treating her like a damn date. "We agreed you weren't going to make a thing out of this."

His eyes flickered, but he held steady on his megawatt smile. "No, I greet all the women I know with inappropriate displays. You should've seen the kiss I planted on Rob's wife." Elbowing her in the side, he pointed toward a couple sitting on a set of short-stack metal bleachers. "C'mon, I'll introduce you."

In the swarm of jeans and khaki shorts, Brian made an eye-piercing statement with his knee-length paint explosion. The swirling purples, yellows, and greens resembled a five-year-old's summer camp tie-dye project. He'd misstepped with the kiss, but no man seriously on a date would wear those shorts.

"Can't wait." She allowed him to drag her off to happy coupleland. No sense tanking the day in the first minute when the food and beer were free and she'd borrowed the car and driven out here. A shiny business park, the kind with mirrored buildings, sat behind a fence a few hundred yards off. "That where you work?"

"Yep. That's where they keep all the secrets." As he led her through the crowd, he offered nods and greetings to most of the adults by name and not a few high-fives to the kids. "Lot of us came over together when we left the service."

The brown-haired man broke off whispering in the woman's ear and stood as they approached. "You find her, or she find you? Your shorts are so bright the sats are tracking you from ten thousand miles up."

"My lucky shorts, man." Hands shoved in his pockets, Brian spread the wide-leg cotton and spun. "These babies are gonna bring us in at least an extra two runs. Maybe three."

The shorts absolutely qualified as a nightmare. But his ass in them? Begging for a squeeze. "Sounds like bragging to me, hotshot."

Brian pouted. "Would I do that?"

"Yes." Three voices mingled in the answer, hers and the couple's. They wore matching wedding bands. Forty-some people at softball. Not a date, he'd said. Except he took her straight to double-datesville.

"Ganging up on me already. Should've known this would be a bad idea." Grinning, he clapped her shoulder. "Kit, meet Rob and Nora. He works in encryption; she crunches numbers. Together, they—"

"Prefer not to hear the end of that sentence when Brian's the one delivering it," Nora broke in, her smile friendly and her caramel-colored ponytail swinging.

Brian dropped his head back and raised his arms in a *what gives* to the heavens. “Kit runs that repair shop in town I was telling you about. We’re not on a date.”

The man did not do subtle. Should’ve figured on brash from his red car and riot shorts. Plenty of scuff marks in the dirt as she added a few more. The divot in front of the aluminum bleacher support needed smoothing.

“Right, right.” Rob stuck out his arm. “The woman who knows her way around a flat tire.” He offered a firm handshake, short and to the point. “Rob Vanderhoff. Brian and I have worked together since he couldn’t put his cap on straight to save his life.”

As Rob spoke, Brian swung his head in wide denials. “No, no, it was a fashion statement. The angle was lucky, same as my shorts.”

Rob snorted. “The attitude was a sure shot to getting dropped. You wouldn’t believe the push-ups he did. After eight weeks, he was nothing but biceps and a smart mouth.” He gestured to the blanket-draped bleacher beside his wife’s padded backrest. “Here, Kit, grab a seat. Those first three weeks, I could’ve sworn he wanted to be recycled.”

“Recycled?” Nora cocked her head. Her plain, peachy T-shirt provided soothing relief from Brian’s misguided style.

“Like repeating a grade in school.” Rob stepped off the side of the bleachers, crouching as he landed. “Brian had trouble with authority back then.”

Confirmation of bad-boy reputation, check. These friends of his might be useful, decent folk. Getting the nod from Mr. Nice Guy, they pretty much guaranteed their likeability.

“I understand he can’t resist a dare.” Not hers, thank God. After his showing at the shop, he’d taken to invading her dreams. She met Brian’s sheepish spring-grass gaze with a smirk. “Is that how you ended up owning those shorts?”

While Nora and Rob laughed, Brian sidled into her personal space. “Oh, I take orders fine when they make sense.”

Pale, fuzzy stubble covered his cheeks and chin. A little beard burn between her thighs would scratch the itch he stirred.

“You want a job done right, with work that’ll hold up under pressure?” In his eyes, he signaled go-go-go. He dipped his chin. “I’m your man.” Deep voice. Backroom darkness, no-bullshit, vibrating-in-her-panties voice. “Isn’t that the way you run your shop, too? Clear orders, strict standards?”

Jesus. With his sharp, clean storm-scent, he sneaked past her keep-out signs and grasped bare metal. He'd fry them both to sizzling ash. And he'd almost—maybe—be worth the risk. At least once. Or twice.

Leaning forward, Nora interrupted their stare-down with her extended hand. "It's nice to meet you, Kit. I hope you brought an empty stomach and fast legs."

"I'm playing?" Shit, her old mitt lay buried in a box in the basement somewhere. She shook hands on reflex. "I thought this would be a spectator thing. League play."

A gang of noisy children scampered down the fence line and circled the bleachers to the field opposite, where a handful of adults organized a ragged line of youngsters at a tee ball setup and sent the older ones out to field.

"Intra-office. We're flexible on teams." Behind Rob, men and women clustered around the dugout benches. "You can always sub in later if you want a feel for the level of play first—or if you're worried about Brian beaning you in the head on a force out. His aim's less than stellar when he's distracted."

Thwapping Rob in the stomach with the back of his hand, Brian elicited a grunt. "Not everyone played Little League ball, farm boy."

"Your choice, Surfer Boy." After casting a glance behind him, Rob punched Brian in the shoulder. "Grab your gear, airman. We're on the first-inning roster." As he backed away, he blew his wife a kiss.

Nora captured the gift with a fast swipe and crossed her hands on her stomach.

Standing with his feet planted together and his back straight, Brian snapped a salute.

Aw hell. She refused to leave a man hanging. She sent one back.

Smile brightening his whole face, he jogged off. As he picked up a mitt in the dugout, he waved at the stands. Nora waved, which meant she had to, too. Every few feet, all the way out to left field, he spun, jogged backward, and waved.

Nora, arm raised yet again, laughed. "He's a complete goofball."

"Sorry?" Four times now, like he meant to keep checking she hadn't gotten up and left. Not the smoothest operator, but damn if she didn't wave every time. Impossible to stop herself. Wearing those ridiculous shorts, losing himself in bro-play with his buddy, ditching her five minutes into their not-date—the afternoon might actually be fun instead of a hard sell on why she should date him.

"Brian. Lighthearted optimist to the core." Nora swiveled and greeted a woman toting an infant carrier into the stands. As she turned back, she patted Kit's knee. "But after Rob, he's also the most loyal and steadfast man I've ever met."

"We're not dating." Shit. Not offering unsolicited information to a salesman was the first rule of defeating a sales pitch. Brian had roped his friend's wife into talking him up. In three words she'd told Nora the biggest anxiety weighing on her. Somehow, Brian made *nice* seductive. Surface charm. He'd show his true colors when he got bored of playing with her, unless she stopped falling for Prince Charming first.

Nora shrugged. "They're good qualities in a friend, too. He's been Rob's friend for almost twenty years."

The players scattered, and the first pitch arced toward the plate. The batter grounded out on a quick hop by the shortstop. A bevy of attaboys followed. Out in left, Brian rocked side to side, ready and waiting.

"So Brian said you run your own shop?"

"Huh?" She'd almost missed Nora's question. "Oh, yeah, with my dad." Up until last year, she would've said grandpa, too. Third-generation pride. Now she had a hard time getting the words out. "I've been tinkering since I was a kid."

Blue eyes kind, Nora nodded. "Family owned. Lot of strength in that kind of bond. The recession years have been tough on the mom-and-pops. We buttoned up the bank so tight I practically had mothballs on the loan forms when I dragged them out again."

The next batter cleared a base hit on a lucky hop past the second baseman.

Brian pounded his fist into his glove and bellowed, "Let's go, fellas, look alive out here. We got a crowd in the bleachers to impress and a cooler of celebration beers with our names on 'em."

The crowd replied with a whooping chorus. The cheers intensified as the next batter popped one right back into the pitcher's mitt.

"The lean years fattened us up." The girls had a start on college funds thanks to the people who'd put secondhand toys under their Christmas trees and the warranty repair orders. For folks with a pinched wallet, the hassle of scheduling fixes hurt less than the big-ticket hit for new appliances. "Lots of people looking to repair instead of buying new. And the scavenging was epic." For a while, they'd done fair trade in used TV sets and high-end electronics. Even the occasional electric guitar. Hell, half the time, "broken" meant a loose wire making intermittent contact. "You wouldn't believe the things people set out in their garage sales."

"How do you evaluate risk on the purchases? When I assess a new loan applicant..." Nora launched into a rundown of bank lending policies and the ever-important return on investment. Holy shit, the woman knew her numbers. Despite a clear allegiance to Brian and probable bias in getting him paired off, Nora wore her down with friendly questions about the shop.

Hashing out the economics of nickel-and-dime profit margins diverted whole substations of stress. Dad did great with repairs and people-handling, but Depression-raised Grandpa Jake had been the one squeezing the value from every penny invested. Now the load fell on her shoulders. Five other people in the household depended on her to make the right calls. "I've been thinking about adding—"

The bat cracked, loud and solid. As a fly ball topped the shortstop's leap by a foot, Brian raced in from left field. A single for sure. He'd never scoop the ball before—he launched himself forward, arm extended. With a tuck and roll, he came up on his knees. In his right hand, his arm cocked back and ready to throw, he held the ball.

"Showoff." But she hollered like a banshee, hands cupped megaphone-style, while Nora clapped with her arms raised over her head. Brian's diving catch ended the top of the inning.

"Do you like softball?" Nora waved as Rob hustled in from first base. Drifting clouds formed a patchwork of sun and shade across the field. "You should play. They're short a woman anyway, now that I'm out for the season."

"Are you hurt?" She looked healthy enough, but she did keep shuffling around against her backrest. Maybe a doctor had mandated padded cushions.

"Only my pride. Rob and I agreed no competitive sports after the first trimester." Sighing, she shook her head. But then she smiled wide. "Except maybe mini golf."

With the ease of a flipped switch, congratulations flowed from her mouth. She followed up with all the right questions—was this their first, would they find out the sex in advance—but beneath her social shell, the motor jammed.

Brian's buddy had gotten married. Brian's buddy was starting a family. Two and two sure as fuck added up to four. A thirty-seven-year-old man would be in the hunt for a wife. And he wouldn't stop at that. He'd insist on one who'd give him a kid or three to fulfill his fatherhood fantasies. She'd be insane to get involved with him. After a few years hip-deep in full diapers and middle-of-the-night crying, he'd wake up from his mid-life crisis and leave her with miniature copies of him to raise.

Brian threaded through the dugout fences and stopped in front of her. "We need at least two women in our first five at-bats. What do you say? You coming out?"

A muddy scrape decorated his shin. His T-shirt, though an aqua almost eye-searing paired with his shorts, clung in not-unpleasing ways to his chest and biceps.

"I suppose I'd better, to show up your sorry—" Whoops. A small blond boy grinned at her from the front row. "Uhh, backside." Whew. No cursing asses here, nope, not a one.

Laughing, Brian offered his hand. "If your saves on the field are as good as the ones off it, I don't doubt you'll show me up."

"Be hard to top your last performance." Grabbing hold of his forearm for balance, she clambered down the aluminum benches. Keeping things on sexual footing with him would crush any ideas he had about wedding rings and car seats. "Those are mighty fine hands you've got there."

* * * *

Hello, double entendre. As she leaned on him, he waited for her to hit the ground. Soon as she did, he ducked right up under her ear. "You would know."

Shivering, she clamped down on his forearm.

Fuck yes. He'd owe Nora a set of wingman bars if she'd coaxed Kit's guard down. Rob had made a fine partner for charming the women and exercising sober caution in their alcohol-blurred twenties, but reeling in Katherine for a real relationship demanded a whole different strategy.

"I do know." She met him eye to eye, toe to toe. "So when do I get my hands on your bat?"

"Right now." He put the devil in his voice and dragged her to the dugout. Rummaging in his gear bag, he went for the comedic about-face. "Thirty-four inches of solid maple beauty." He thrust the bat skyward. "Go give her a swing."

Her freckled cheeks pink as she laughed, she took the bat from him. "All right, smart guy. You win this round."

Seeing her relaxed and enjoying herself, he really did. An unqualified victory. His lucky shorts had worked their magic. Busting out his peacock feathers diverted Katherine's attention and let him continue his stealth campaign for her heart.

She trotted down the fence a bit. Didn't start with a shoulder-breaker, no ma'am. Like any craftsman, she eyed the barrel and tested the balance.

No added weight on the end of his bat. He swung all-natural. About the way he wanted to start swinging north as she stretched her arms behind her back.

By locking her knuckles, she pulled her faded green T-shirt tight. She rolled her shoulders and her neck. Once-white text curved *Runyon's* in a semicircle on the sweet upper swell of her breasts, cutting across the line of her bra beneath. The bottom half, an equally faded *Repairs*, smiled from around her navel. And why not? He'd smiled touching her in the exact spot. A wrench and a screwdriver crossed in the middle.

No question she'd rather their not-a-date ended with him sucking on her through every one of those letters. When the time came, he'd need a hell of a lot more than lucky shorts to remember why sex with Kit remained a bad idea. Claim the territory, lose the war. Strong and focused, icy as the lake in February. That's the man she deserved, one who'd wait to make love to Katherine instead of fucking Kit.

Level swing, steady power off her back foot, she nailed the follow-through. With a solid connection, she'd be a valuable member for their team. In a handful of practice swings, she'd adjusted her grip and her stance. Goddamn, her hip waggling would have him running to jerk in the bathroom if she went on any longer, and no man on the bench would blame him.

Trotting back, she tossed the bat at him from a few feet away. "Been a while for me, but your bat's a good fit." She stopped beside him, brushing his shoulder, and tilted in close. "How about now, Brian? Who wins this round?"

He choked the stiff maple in a two-handed grip. "Pretty sure we both do."

They stood thigh to thigh along the dugout fence as the first batter failed to get on base. Fast hands at shortstop today.

Batting helmet in hand, Rob gave Kit the wave. "You're up."

Brian passed her the bat and placed his encouraging pat in the safe friend zone between her shoulder blades. "Let's go, slugger."

On her first swing, she mistimed the pitch and came in slow. Helpful and not-so-helpful advice came from all quarters, telling her to settle down, keep her shoulders level, keep her eye on the ball—or get that second out.

As the pitch flew, she dug in her heels. She launched a drive into the gap, catching the second baseman napping. The center fielder rushed to cover as she rounded first, the base coach waving her on. "Go, go, go!"

The throw came in short. She stood safe on second, bent and huffing, as pudgy Roger from finance turned to tag her.

With a whoop, Brian jumped onto the dugout bench. "Attagirl! Way to get something started."

She raised her head and flashed him a thumbs-up. Below her helmet, the tail-ends of her pixie-short hair flared out every which way like fallen matchsticks. Christ, she needed kissing.

As he jumped down, one of the new hires rocked back and spread his knees, claiming way too much bench. "That your girlfriend?"

"Just a friend." For now. No chance she'd hear him from second base, but he'd promised her he wouldn't call her his date or his girlfriend. Doing it when he wouldn't be caught would be a bigger violation of the honor code than making an announcement over the PA. Her no-dating policy might've come from a lying ex, and no way in hell would he be that guy. When she asked for his promise, he'd deliver. "A good friend."

"Yeah, I'd like to be her good friend, too."

"No." A pop-up to the shortstop left Katherine raring to go on second. If he drove another man's face into his knee and left him bleeding in the dirt, she might have some questions for him.

"C'mon, man." Drawstring-shorts, saggy-tank hotshot drummed the bench. "Hook me up."

The company gym, though. He'd welcome a new sparring partner. One who liked hitting the mat.

"Brian!" Rob waved him in. Coaching decision or instinct to head off a brawl, good choice either way.

"On it." Serving up a dead-eyed stare for the pushy Kit-chaser, he lowered his voice. "Ask about her again, and we'll settle the question in the ring."

As he strode to the plate, the left fielder dropped back. The right fielder stood scratching his elbow. Kit waited, crouched and ready.

He tipped off foul. Looking for precision over power, he reset a half-step closer to the pitcher and a few inches away from the plate. The second pitch came in beautiful. Hardly an arc at all. He smacked low and slow, the contact solid and the ball heading for the gap Kit had found. The right fielder got off his ass, but not before Brian'd touched first and Kit rounded third. Christ, she hustled. The relay throw came in too late to stop her from crossing home plate.

The whole bench erupted with cheers. As he clapped and whistled and Rob thumped her helmet, she turned and caught him. Grinning wide, she ducked her head under the storm of accolades. But coming up, meeting what had to be the proudest fucking stare he'd given anyone in his life, she raised her hand and honest-to-God waved at him.

Ending the inning stranded on base when the next hitter popped one to the left fielder's glove couldn't take the shine off his happiness. Serious Kit could be playful Kit, too, and not limited to panty-dropping sports. Though more of those would be welcome once they'd established the exclusive, long-term nature of this relationship.

After four more innings, none so exciting as the first, he crossed them off the roster. The rematch would have to go on without them. The strong breeze carried a smoky charcoal-and-burger mix from the pavilion. "I promised you food and beer. Let some of these early eaters sweat out their calories while we fill up."

They tore through the spread, the line short, the sides on ice, and the picnic tables on the concrete slab mostly empty with the game in full swing. As Kit toted their laden plates, he snagged his half-size Coleman from the table of show-ID coolers.

Riley from HR, standing guard over the alcohol to keep out suds-seeking teens, wagged her finger at him. "Goldang, Brian, I didn't know you were playing in the intern pool. Should I card your girlfriend?"

Kit bobbled the plates. Macaroni salad slid sideways, but she recovered without spilling a speck.

"Relax, Ri, this is my friend Kit." A truth, he hoped, because fuck-buddy didn't come near close enough to what he wanted to be for her, and she wouldn't allow him to claim more. "Not my girlfriend, not an employee, and definitely over twenty-one. You won't see harassment forms on your desk with my name, thank you very much."

Bypassing the few tables with diners, he led Kit down to the cozy hexagonal table farthest from the buffet. He'd shared her since her arrival. Given her time with Nora, gotten her out on the field, kept her at a distance to help her settle in some. Now he'd get his date—a nice, casual, midafternoon burgers-and-beer date. The sky cooperated, pumping thick clouds across the sun and dimming the covered pavilion to candlelight levels. Long as she didn't think about the implications too hard, they'd be fine.

"How's the food? Good for free, right?" He jabbed the chunky potato salad with his plastic fork. Seated at adjacent wedges, he and Katherine rubbed knees the way a shoveler warmed his hands on a snowy morning. Her soft skin had him thinking hard on the teasing fantasy he'd spun for her. Maybe she imagined him walking his fingers up that road, too. "I'm a disaster in the kitchen. Hell, half the reason I come to the game every week is to give my takeout menus a break."

He tried to limit his glances as they talked, gazing out toward the field instead, but goddamn she stunned with her sweat-dampened shirt and her helmet-frizzed hair.

A post-workout woman, her cheeks pink and her blood flowing, she didn't run to the mirror and pull out a comb. She'd shown hustle on the field. He wouldn't have brought a woman playing the learned helplessness game. The men and women he'd served with, and the ones he'd met through the company, respected skill and determination. Grit. Anything less would be an embarrassment.

"You know what's great about softball?" Aside from him getting a solid grip on her temperament. Once she committed, she went all in. She would with him, too, if he made her see the value. Made himself trustworthy, upstanding, but with the bad-boy bedroom appeal she demanded. "A non-contact sport is the perfect excuse for full-contact praise. You nailed that run in the first inning. I'll have to make sure I'm close enough to smack your ass in congratulations next time, Foxy."

She burst into nose-huffy laughter and waved him off. With the back of her hand pressed to her mouth, she finished chewing and swallowed. "Okay, now you sound like every guy who's ever tried to get in my pants. Foxy? Really?"

He locked down his glee at matching her bad-boy expectations. Shrugging, he played up his hurt-feelings protest. "Foxes have kits."

"So do skunks, weasels, and wolverines." The arch in her eyebrow more than met the slow-pitch minimum-required height. With her unimpressed superiority, she came close to perfect deadpan. "You think they're sexy, too?"

Heart pounding, he slid to the end of his bench and threw his arm across her shoulders. "I'm a Michigan boy." When she didn't push him away, he chanced a hug and a friendly head-knock. "Wolverines were my first love."

Relaxed in his embrace, she dipped her head but failed to tame her smile. "You want a ferocious killer ready to rip your face off and bite through your spine?" She chomped her teeth, her ferocity closer to adorable than terrifying.

He flew back, hands up, laughing. "Let's not be hasty. At least wait until our second date." Fuck, *fuck*, no, he'd pushed the wrong button. His chest seized.

She shot him an I-know-what-you-did glance and swigged her beer. Three swallows she took, all while the condensation rolled down the bottle and across her suckable fingers. She set the bottle down and snorted. "That's a long wait, smart guy, since we haven't had one date yet."

Yet. The woman beside him was more Katherine than Kit, teasing, playful, and almost snuggly. She leaned her bare knee against his.

"Well, I worked in satellite intelligence in the service. We have to extrapolate from the existing data and form plans for every contingency, no matter how remote. So it's vitally important, should such an event occur, that I have an appropriate endearment waiting." Overtalking, throwing his hands around like an *Art of Gesture* textbook, he tried to rein himself in and failed. His mouth kept going, determined to fill the hours until sunset and the starry night after. "I feel 'babe' is a little too bro for me and maybe demeaning for you to endure. But, you know, diminutives are a traditional choice. What about Kitten? Are you—"

"No." As her voice gained a clipped edge, she lost her merry smile. Her eyes turned hard. She crumpled her napkin in her fist. The muscles in her neck stood tight and prominent.

"Whoa, Kit, I'm sorry." Christ Jesus, she might truly rip his face off. Whatever mine he'd landed on, the blast left him stumbling around blind and dumb. In one misstep, he'd blown every hard-fought inch of ground he'd gained sky-high. "I won't say that word again. Fair?"

She stared past him.

Something an ex had called her. Had to be. The asshole who'd messed up her head and turned her off of dating. Plenty of women he'd slept with preferred to keep things casual, but none had been so adamant. They'd been comfortable with choosing one night, not closed-off and defensive. Or he'd missed their signals in the static. With Katherine, he'd damn well fine-tune the resolution to peer at every pixel.

Breathing out slow, she hung her head and dropped her hands in her lap. Her knee wobbled.

Back straight and leg a steady rest, he didn't dare move. She'd hop in her car and pull another disappearing act on him. The awkward conversational fumbles he'd joked his way out of a thousand times hadn't prepared him for her.

She swayed toward the table. "My grandpa had these pet names for us."

Granddad. Not ex. Christ. Least he hadn't opened his mouth and made a bigger fucking ass of himself.

Hugging her elbows, she tugged her sleeves. "My sister was always Clover. I was Kitten. Even our parents don't use them. Just Grandpa Jake." She lifted her head and swallowed. Voice dull and eyes shiny, she radiated cracks as dangerous as ice snapping under her feet. "He died. Last summer."

Might as well've been last week, so tight the anger and grief clung to her. He ordered his hug to stand down. Get too emotional, and she'd bolt—and this sharing wasn't about his wants but hers. So no wrapping his arms around her, no dotting her face with as many kisses as freckles, and no spouting bullshit platitudes. Truth and nothing but.

He covered her fingers with his cupped hand, firm and gentle as the first time he'd cradled his youngest brother, the family oops baby. 'Bout as terrified, too. "I'm sorry about your granddad, Katherine."

Nodding, she laced their hands together and studied the interlocked result. As she squeezed, he matched her pressure for pressure until their hold turned fierce and white-knuckled.

She exhaled and let go. "He would've liked you."

Acceptance of his attempt at comfort and approval from a man she respected. They were dating. Whatever her mouth said, her heart had gotten the message. Long as he followed her lead, they'd be together when her ice cracked. He wouldn't let her spark drown.

And he wouldn't press his luck with arrogant prattle about wishing he'd met the man and what great friends they'd have been. "You must've made him awful proud."

She finished off her bottle. "Tell me something about your family. Something funny."

Quick pivot. Well all right then. S'pose the maudlin tone didn't suit the raucous fun-having around them. But he had the perfect answer to lighten the mood before some well-meaning busybody asked if Katherine needed a tissue and spooked her.

Swiping through his phone, he bypassed the clutter and pulled up shots from last summer. "Can't tell me this ain't hilarity at its finest."

He plonked the phone in front of her. Lucas and Nora grinned at the camera in mid-chicken-dance, flapping their elbows as they mocked his missed turkey. Freaking five-pin. After coming in too soft to make the third strike, he'd bought the next round for the lane.

Kit wiped her hands on her shorts. Raising the phone, she squinted. "That's Rob's wife. Who's the kid she's with? He yours?"

"Hell no." A kid. His shoulders jerked before the idea settled in place and cursed him with that bad luck. "I am one hundred percent kidless, thank God and unbroken condoms." Fuck, what if she'd— "Are you?"

The longer she eyed him, the thicker his blood grew. The more sluggishly the sludge traveled, threatening to shut down his heart. A foot-in-mouth mistake that huge couldn't be undone.

Ducking her head, she laughed. "Fastest I've ever seen the color drain from a man's face." She reached across his plate and swiped his bottle. "I'm a fan of unbroken condoms myself. They've answered my prayers so far."

His fear flattened out, a swell lapping his toes instead of threatening destruction. No kids. No accidental insult to the woman who'd come so beautifully in his hands. Hell, at least he'd made her laugh while she'd given him a heart attack.

As she dragged the rim of the beer across her lips, she made him lose his breath for a whole new reason. No beer tasting required a tongue flick so pink and sexy. A dare in the offing. One he'd best shut down before his dick took her up on it.

Ahem-ing, he tilted the phone in her hand. "Yep, that's Nora. She wasn't Rob's wife then. They'd just met." A pinch-zoom magnified Lucas until his face filled the screen. "And that smart-ass is my baby brother. I'd invited him down for the summer."

"He looks exactly like you." She studied the photo while her half-eaten burger got cold. "What is he, sixteen?"

"Twenty-two next month." Fuck. Lucas was closer in age to Kit than he was. And yeah, chicken-scrawny and young-looking. A proto-him, minus the demanding basic training regimen and boxing that had filled him out at eighteen. "Fourth of four boys. Me and Lucas scored the luck with Mom's hair."

"Aww, are you fishing for compliments, Blondie?" She waggled the phone and the beer. "I'd ruffle those golden feathers for you, but I don't have a third hand."

He pulled the slick bottle from her grip and took a swallow. Mouth where hers had been. Almost a kiss. He fucking ached for a real one, a sunset, fireworks, bonfire, laughing, full-body-press of a kiss. A perfect moment with relaxed, teasing Katherine. "Problem solved."

"Cocky." She rubbed the top of his head in a speed challenge. Probably left a haystack behind. "Your brother have trouble with authority, too, or is that just you?"

"Might could." He'd let Lucas stay with him last summer to head off those problems. Show him opportunities and job advice. Give him a break from being stuck in-between boyhood and independence. "He's bunking at home, going to community college. It's rough, being an adult living in your parents' place. A whole pack of frustration. Unnatural, right?"

She clenched the phone's protective shell as her back stiffened. "Oh?"

Hell, she wanted the bad boy. He'd have been irredeemably down that path without one goddamn miracle of an Air Force recruiter shoving literature at him.

"Think about it—you can drive and vote and maybe drink, but they're still up in your business, setting the rules." A curfew. A slam against friends who, okay, yes, ripped off the mom-and-pop gas stations and encouraged him to do the same. Pocketing shit here and there, skating by on a fucking tsunami of luck and look-the-other-way-ism because boys will be boys. "It's not like Dad suddenly believes in democracy because you turned eighteen. You're a grown man stuck in a place where everybody sees you as a kid, at least in my family. You gotta have respect for anyone who can hack that mission. I couldn't. Partly why I blew out of the house and enlisted the day after graduation."

The travel. Fucking Hawaii in the brochure the recruiter handed him, and visions of warm sand and perfect waves had him signing his name without a second thought. Nobody mentioned they'd be sending him to Texas for basic first, hours from the gulf and no leave time to enjoy the summer swells at Padre Island.

"Respect, yeah." She passed him the phone and rolled her shoulders. "You and your dad didn't get along so good?" Elbows on the table, she settled in with the rest of her plate. "But the military turned you around?"

"The military kicked my ass. Sherwood—Rob—turned me around." The good influence scraping off the barnacles of his older brother's bad habits. The wiser-than-eighteen man who'd slammed the books open on his desk and demanded he learn the goddamn material because no way would the class leave him behind, no matter how hard he tried to prove himself a fuck-up. "I owe him for that. Huge debt."

Like the one he'd paid on his first visit home. Dress blues neat and clean, shoes polished until they glowed, and three crisp hundreds, straight from the bank, in his pocket.

The two-pump gas station on the corner had been their favorite spot to hit. The owners were old, the cashiers young, and the unblinking security cameras for show. The old man had been behind the counter. Good, because he hadn't had to ask for him with his throat screwed tight. Bad, because the confession reminded him of every time he'd taken advantage, and the apology couldn't set things right. The money covered the financial loss, but nothing excused his callous behavior.

* * * *

"I dunno if you remember me, sir. I used to come here a lot with my friends."

The old man scanned his uniform, his eyes dark and sharp in a face crisscrossed with the grooves of age and experience. "I remember you. Pack of young hooligans. There's no trouble a boy can't find if he goes looking for it. But you're not dressed for trouble today."

"No, sir." Fuck, this'd be easier with Rob at his side, being the stand-up guy so he could laugh the whole thing off as clowning. The rows of candy bars and packs of gum mocked him. He'd taken a fucking eyeglasses kit once, because it'd been small and slim and easily tucked in a pocket. Didn't wear glasses, but he'd still ripped off the old man and his wife. "I'm here to apologize. For the things I took."

"Less than your friends did." The old man's stare came down as heavy as a superior officer's. He stood tall despite the bow in his shoulders and the faded gray of his hair. "I remember that about you, because you stood lookout. Chatted and joked to hold attention while them boys loaded up their jackets. Studied your feet a lot, like you're doing now." He swiped the counter with the side of his hand. "You were already ashamed of yourself, son. I figured you for a boy who didn't have nothing else." With one pointed finger, he waved at the single row of color decorating the left breast of Brian's uniform. "Looks like you do now."

As he pulled out the hundreds, his hand shook as hard as the old man's. "For everything we took, and the trouble we caused. I'm sorry, sir."

"You were a troubled boy." The old man clasped him with both hands before he accepted the bills. "You're a better man. And you and me? We're square."

* * * *

As she finished off her burger, Kit reclaimed his beer. "Maybe you owe Rob a debt, sure, but no amount of support'll make someone do something they don't have it in them to do."

She took a slow sip, her head tipped back and her throat exposed and vulnerable. Same as she'd look straddling him, except she'd be bare and moaning and he'd have her breasts in his hands. Fuck, not a good thought. Later, later, later—when he'd made clear sex belonged in a package deal, inseparable from real dating.

Offering him the bottle, she eyed him sideways. "You might've played at being bad for a while, but you're a good guy at heart. The Air Force—and your buddy—gave you an excuse to be that man." When their fingers grazed, she laughed and shook her head. "Sorry. That's not my business. I don't know you now, and I sure as hell didn't know you then. Beer talking."

"No, you're right." He refused to grip the bottle when her fingers fit so perfect inside his hand. She might not know him yet, but she sounded like a woman who wanted to, finally. "The service wasn't what I expected, but it was what I needed."

"To prove you could be your own person. Nobody controlling you or waiting for you to mess up your life like—" As she slid her plate away, raindrops pinged off the pavilion roof and splatted in the dirt beyond. "Jesus, that's stupid. Not you, me, I mean. It's the fucking military. You had nothing but people controlling you."

"Orders, yeah, but proving to myself I was capable of being a man? That's the best thing basic taught me." Better by far than learning that one-handed pushups impressed uniform chasers, which he'd definitely believed the most valuable lesson at eighteen. "I pulled a ton of stupid shit as a kid because I wanted to be liked. Keep up with my big brother, impress my little brother." No dare turned down. He flashed her a grin. Her sort of dare, he could get used to. "Now I do stupid shit just for me."

"Ohh, so that's why—" Palm out and forward, she mimed a circle over his face. "I thought you'd forgotten to shave. But clearly you lost a bet."

"I'm growing a beard." He scrubbed his face. Still scratchy. Approaching scratchy, at least. Theoretically over-the-top attractive to a woman who liked bad boys. "This is my badass scruff."

"This?" She touched him. With gentle fingers, she danced across his cheek and down his throat. "Fuzzy and blond is not badass scruff, Prince Charming."

Feeling up his face and giving him cutesy nicknames. Forget dating—they'd jumped to sickeningly sweet honeymoon coupledom complete with gagging bystanders. Their next date, first date, whatever the hell he called the damn thing, was an absolute lock.

"What you have is sweet cottonball fluff." She ran her short nails up under his chin and let go too soon. A few seconds more, and her fingertips would've been in kissing range. "Maybe give it a few days before you try calling it a beard. Or scruff."

"This here is five days of primo beardification." He hadn't taken a razor to his face since she'd come in his arms. Endured the good-natured ribbing of the rest of the chair jockeys in data analysis all week. Worth every minute to get her hands on him. "It'll be more impressive when I dye the beard to match my lucky shorts."

Collapsing into giggles, she landed with her forehead pressed to his shoulder. A sweet sound and a sweeter weight. He'd carry both a mighty long while, see if he didn't.

* * * *

As thunder boomed, the skies opened up. The ping of sprinkles on the pavilion roof surged into a roaring downpour, drowning out conversation.

Good thing, since Brian's so-called beard lacked the substance to survive the teasing. Hell, the minute he stepped out in the rain, the hair would rinse from his face like so much Magic Marker.

Men. Brian. Ridiculously proud of his scruffy face and his color-riot shorts. God. He'd make her life simpler as an out-of-shape hound dog with a sagging belly and a balding scalp. If she didn't want to fuck him, he'd make a great friend.

He smelled different today, musky and male under the sharp storm and fresh with grass stains as spring green as his eyes. The swirling mix of comfort and arousal called for his arm around her as much as his shirt peeled from his back and dropped to the floor.

"You all using these?"

Kit shot up straight. Draped on Brian like a lovesick puppy, ugh.

The shouter, a smiling guy in a soaked tan T-shirt, waved at the four empty benches filling out their table. The rain had driven two score players and families onto the covered concrete slab. The crowd, hemmed in and adding to the humidity, pressed closer on all sides.

"Not a one." Raising his voice, Brian piled their trash in a small stack and snapped his cooler shut. "Looks like tables are going for premium prices just now, but I'll let you have the rest of this beauty for an overnight sat shift sometime when Daniel's in Prague and wants a morning briefing."

"Shit, that price might be too high for me." But he swung into a seat and extended his hand as Brian flipped the trash into an open-barrel can. "Aaron. You're the gal who got a double off my slow scramble in center, but I won't hold it against you. Next time you come to the game, though, I won't be sleeping."

"Kit." She shook extra-firm. Next time didn't scare her a bit. Wouldn't be a next time anyhow, because she'd fuck Brian tonight and get him out of her system. That'd be the right play. A shame, because he—but absolutely the best option. "I might have to stay off the field so my victory isn't ruined."

"Oh, now that's an unfair move." Aaron bounced his fist off Brian's forearm. "C'mon, Surfer Boy, manly pride on the line here. Tell your girlfriend she's gotta give me a chance to even the score."

His friends needed to stop fucking calling her his girlfriend. The easier the word rolled off their tongues, the better the idea sounded circling in her head. The better Brian looked. Not the entitled white-collar office jockey she'd imagined him, the college guy who played racquetball in a sweatbox or golf on manicured lawns and drank imported shit for the prestige of the fancy names. A regular guy who'd made mistakes, fixed the ones he could, and tried to put his little brother on a better road. A man who cared about family.

"No can do." Brian swatted his buddy away and flashed bright eyes toward her. His blond fuzz would be gentle on her thighs. "I don't tell Kit her mind. She's her own woman. No labels."

Goddammit. The pit in her stomach belonged to a lovesick fool. Exactly the situation her rules avoided. Wanting and not-wanting twisted up the guts until the springs popped and the gears bent. Every stuck tooth jabbed in a sore spot. No shortage of those.

Aaron launched into some story half-drowned by the growing buzz of nearby conversations and the deep-voiced thunder rumbling through the heavy gray clouds. In a clattering shuffle, a foursome claimed the remaining benches.

More people, more labels, more pressure to know what the hell she was doing with Prince Charming. Would an uncomplicated fuck in his car while the rain beat down around them be so much to ask for?

"Hey." Brian slid up against her, their shoulders forming one broad bulwark. No shouts to be overheard, just a solid nudge and a low tone meant for her alone. "Sure is getting stuffy in here, right?" He clasped her fingers in a quick squeeze, gone before the full hold registered. "Must be all the hot air trapped under the roof."

His lips shaped each letter. Syllable. Whatever those things were called that no one gave a damn about after middle school because boys with mouths and lips and teeth and tongues grew far more interesting. A soft kiss, for his sweet rescue. A hard kiss, for the way she'd taste him before she let him fuck her. No kiss at all, because they sat surrounded by his friends and colleagues, who undoubtedly figured them for calf-eyed new lovers.

She followed his thumb up the curves of his knuckles to the back of his hand and traced the tendon to his wrist. "You wanna get out of here?"

A glance for the roof and its driving beat, and he set his level gaze on her. "Make a run for it? My gear bag's in the dugout. We'll get drenched."

Reason enough to strip off their clothes and warm up together.

"A little water isn't going to break me, Brian." Hell, the rain shower might wash away the muddiness in her head until her thoughts ran clear again. She gripped his arm, and he flexed under her palm. She'd hold his biceps when he braced himself over her, when his nice-guy manners insisted on not crushing her and she dragged him into the abyss beyond manners for a night he wouldn't forget. "Is it going to break you?"

Swallowing, he stared at her hold on his arm. "No, ma'am. Lead the way."

She snatched his little cooler off the table and threaded through the crowd with his hand tucked away in hers. He stayed at her heels, so close they rubbed together as often as a grasshopper's legs in a mating song.

Same reasoning, too. She ought to fuck him before she grew more attached to his sexy-sweet stares and his ridiculous shorts. Hell, imagining he might understand her living at home because he took pity on his baby brother's situation. As if she wanted his pity. A quick fuck had no reason to know a thing about her, and a long-term prospect would be an unwelcome hassle.

Thunder boomed over the chattering crowd as she reached the edge of the concrete slab. Run-off sleeting from the roof pooled and streamed through the grassy area behind the bleachers.

"Ready to run?" She flashed him a smile, her best mischief-making grin, and crossed the line. "Let's see you hustle."

The storm devoured her shout, but Brian plunged into the riot with her all the same. She sprinted for the dugout with the six-pack cooler banging against her knuckles. The rain infiltrated her clasp on Brian, turning their skin slick. Easier to let him go, but a rebellious no fought simple logic. She clamped down until her fingers ached.

As they rounded the bleachers, the packed dirt churned into mud under their feet. The earth sucked at her tennis shoes, threatening to pull her out of them. She lurched forward.

Grabbing her shoulder, Brian yanked her upright. "Watch your step. Ground's muddy."

The storm had soaked them to the skin. Water ran down his face and across his T-shirt collar in rivers, unable to saturate the fabric any more.

"Oh, is it?" She raised her face to the sky and swept the plastered hair from her cheeks. Tempting to lick the water off his neck and see what he made of that move. "You think that might have something to do with all the rain we're getting?"

"Might could." As he steadied her, he brushed a ticklish spot beneath her ear. "Be right back."

He trotted around the chain-link and snatched one of the waxed canvas bags lying in the mud.

The water beat down with the warmth and pressure of a showerhead. Brian still owed her for the interrupted shower orgasm. She didn't dare glance down. Her shirt, heavy and sopping, clung every time she moved, and her hardening nipples undoubtedly gave him a barometer on her thoughts.

Wait 'til they reached the cars, at least. Families with kids milled under the pavilion, for chrissake. Out toward the parking lot, a few other brave souls ran for their rides. A line of cars crept forward, each pausing at the walkway between the barbecue pits and the cinderblock bathrooms. Passengers rushed out from under the roofed picnic area and dove into seats.

No point running, aside from the fun of splashing in the muck. Kicking through a puddle, she splattered mud clear up her legs. She hit Brian's, too, as he sauntered up with his bag slung one-handed over his shoulder despite the weight of multiple bats and gloves.

"Playing dirty?" He tsked and clicked through his smile. "Somebody likes to stir up trouble."

Somebody sure as hell did. She stomped, one-two, and splashed more mud his way. "Come and stop me, then."

As he reached out, she darted back. She jogged just enough to stay ahead of his advances. With his arm extended, his hand clenched in a claw-grip, and a shambling gait, he chased her movie-monster style. All the way to the parking lot, her leading and him following, she giggled as he swiped and missed and mock-growled at her.

The happy, carefree moments came few and far between in adulthood. This, with Brian, felt more like childhood. Fun. With a man. Without sex. Somehow, the drive to fuck him fell second to the joy of playing with him. She'd lost her fucking mind, and madness was glorious.

He'd had all afternoon to play Mr. Nice Guy. Maybe he'd like to spend the night as a bad boy. Loosening up her rules more for Brian would be all right if he made concessions, too. A summer fuck-buddy. Still casual, with no guarantees except a good time. But how to ask him in the middle of rain-monster tag?

Brian stopped his pursuit. Their cars waited a dozen more down the line. Water-filled tire ruts with squishy-slop sides created an obstacle course.

She hopped across one. "I guess I win this round. Too big a leap for you?"

He nodded toward the next row of cars, over the low hood of a sporty coupe. "Married life."

She followed his cue to the couple standing behind an old pickup. Brian's buddy Rob held a wide umbrella over his wife's head.

Brian switched his grip on his bag to his right hand and resettled the weight. "Sherwood's Mr. Careful these days."

Mr. Overprotective, more like. With one hand on Nora's back, he kept her under shelter and guided her around toward the passenger side.

Nora shook her head and danced out into the rain. Twirling, she extended her hand.

Her husband closed the umbrella and chucked it into the truck bed. Then he took his wife's hand, reeled her in, and started a slow dance. After three spins, he pulled open the passenger door, scooped up Nora, and set her gently in the seat. Laughing, she leaned out and kissed him.

Jesus, he'd better not be the same sort of man Erin had married. Skip town and leave his wife juggling car seats and diapers and questions about why her kid didn't have a daddy. "Yeah. Married life."

* * * *

The allure of the rain must've worn off. Kit stood wringing out the bottom of her shirt in a two-fisted grip, the cooler shoved under her arm.

"Getting somewhere dry's not a bad idea, though." He hustled past her, digging in his pocket for the key fob. The sooner they stowed the gear in his car, the faster they'd get on to something else. Dinner, with a heap of convincing. Sure, they'd dragged out lunch for the last hour, but they'd both need time to shower and change. Easy enough to pick back up for dinner and a movie. He'd play up the apology angle—a friendly makeup non-date to compensate for the rain. She might let him get away with that.

Shoes squelching, she strode across tire ruts and trudged through the muck. She'd been kid-at-recess playful running into the rain and all girlish giggles and squeals when he'd chased her. Hints of the Katherine inside had peeked out all afternoon, a string of small victories. But every time, she reverted to a more distant Kit.

As he popped the trunk, the downpour eased into a steady shower. Kit set the cooler inside.

Fuck, she shone even when the sun hid from nature's fury. Her clothes, pasted to her with rain, and the mud streaking her legs made her more beautiful still. Sleek and curving, she leaned her hip on the car.

With a quick drop to his knees, he could push up her thin shirt and suckle the soft skin of her belly beneath. Lick the rainwater from her forearms when she reached for him.

She squelched those plans with a stern brow and a finger-tap on the bumper. "You planning to stow your equipment, or are you using the trunk as a rain barrel?"

Right, the reason the trunk yawned and waited. Flashing a so-sorry smile, he swung the gear bag.

His leg slid out in the muck. As the bats thudded on the trunk lip, he tucked his head and went down.

Splat.

He'd missed the bumper by an inch. Real close to giving his teeth a good clacking and his head a bump.

"You okay?" Clanking bats and a solid thud gave her voice a background track. "Brian?"

Was he okay? Downside, he'd be an absolute mess when he got up. On the plus side, the bag hadn't fallen on his head. She must've heaved everything the rest of the way in.

Belly flopped in the muddy tire tracks, he rolled over.

She'd lost her stern expression. She bent over him, eyes wide and lips parted, her breasts rounding in her tight T-shirt. A vision.

Raindrops pelted his face. "Right as rain."

High and low, their laughter mingled. His new favorite soundtrack. When he was with her, clowning wasn't a plea for attention. The ability to make her laugh was a gift he gave himself.

He patted her ankle. Soft, smooth skin in his palm. A leg he'd drape across his shoulder when he knelt and tasted her. Fuck, not helping divert blood flow from his cock.

Releasing her, he left muddy fingerprints behind. "Mud's some expensive skin care shit, right? Lookit all I'm getting for free."

Covered, head to toe. The mud camouflaged his lucky shorts. He spread his arms wide and grinned, eager for a new round of her amusement. Her joy in him.

She dropped on top of him.

Arms flying, he caught her waist as she straddled his stomach.

Cool mud slid between them. With strong calves, she gripped his sides. She leaned forward and folded her forearms across his chest. "Now we're both filthy. Do the skin-care benefits work through the clothes, or should we take them off?"

Whoa boy. He tamped down the urge to flip her over and find out. "Probably not in the parking lot. Kids and whatnot."

She nodded, her face rearranged into faux-serious lines broken by her twitching lips. "You have a shower big enough for two?"

If he didn't, he'd swing by the hardware store for a sledgehammer and a tarp on the way.

No—bad, bad, bad idea. Once he let his balls leapfrog ahead of his brain, he'd be nothing more to her than a quirky weekend in a long summer. Fuck that. He'd be every damn weekend. And winter, spring, and fall besides.

"We could squeeze in." He grabbed hold of her hips, gorgeous and flaring, to appreciate her gasp. A little incentive never hurt anyone. "But once you get what's in my shorts, you'll be off to the next conquest." Exaggerating his sigh, he added a pouty droop and jostled her seat. "Unless you're gonna put a ring on it. Can't walk away then."

Her face hardened faster than a mud mask.

"Fuck you, Brian." Jamming her elbows into his chest, she wrenched herself upward. "Fuck you."

Christ Jesus. Two divots burned holes in his chest, and still the coiling wrongness in his stomach outmatched them. He always pushed the jokes over the edge. Shit, shit, shit. "What did I say? I'll take it back."

Her foot caught and dragged his shirt. She lurched forward, arms outstretched, and thudded against the bumper, his scrambling intervention too goddamn slow.

"Katherine? Are you—" Fuck, no, she wasn't okay.

Cradling her left arm, she kicked mud toward him and stood on her own. A wince cut through her glare. "Leave me the fuck alone."

"Let me get a medic." He scanned the lot. Anyone in shouting distance would do. They'd have the kit under the pavilion until the last person packed up. "Or drive you to the hospital. We should get you looked at."

Backing from him, she circled around his car to hers and dug keys from her pocket.

"At least stay and let me ice that." He gave chase. "You're hurt. You shouldn't be driving."

She opened the door in an awkward backhanded grab. "Tell me one more time what I should and shouldn't do, Brian. Who the fuck do you think you are?" Dropping into the seat, she hissed air between her teeth. "I'll tell you what you are—nothing. We're done. Don't text me. Don't call me."

The door slammed. The engine started.

He pounded on the window with the flat of his hand. "Katherine, wait. Please. I just want—"

She reversed past him, too fast.

"—to make sure you're all right."

Spraying mud and rattling through the bumps, she zipped down the aisle.

His whisper fell short of her retreat. “I want to fix this.”

Impossible, standing in waterlogged wheel ruts. Mission outcome: utter failure. His date idea had shifted her farther from him than they’d started. And for his next trick? Wooing a woman who actively loathed him.

“Good talk.”

Chapter 4

Tucked away somewhere on the backroom shelves, a perfect replacement knob waited. Kit pushed aside the more modern parts-donors. The radio carcasses held a wealth of useful materials, but her current project demanded 1940s styling.

Holding the pristine exemplar from the client's vintage set, she searched for a match. Wood, smooth, with a basic round-shiny-button look. No frills. The owners would be getting their radio and record player combo—a wedding present way back in the day—returned to them in brilliant restored and playable condition for their sixty-fifth wedding anniversary as a gift from the granddaughter who'd smuggled the poor neglect victim out of a damp basement.

Three weeks ago, the machine had been a wreck. Now, the degunked insides and refinished outsides waited on her worktable. She should've had the whole project done by now, but Monday afternoon had been busier than usual.

Couldn't complain about good business, especially not when she'd offloaded a classic early-seventies pinball machine to a collector who'd driven up from Omaha to take a gander. Could complain about the damn just-in-case brace on her left wrist and the shoulder sling. Take it easy, let the sprain heal for three or four days. Right. Great advice from people who didn't have deadlines to meet. An extra pair of hands would be heaven-sent. The woman would be in tomorrow to pick up the radio, and the restored grand dame still needed to be assembled and given a test run.

But first—ah, perfect. "What a beauty you are."

She plucked the knob from a basket of loose parts. The dark lacquer under the thin dust-fuzz would match the piece in her hand with some spit and polish. She gave the wood a quick buff against her orange tank top.

As she rounded the shelves, Grandpa Jake's desk leveled an accusing stare. Dust shrouded the surface. Particles drifting down since August formed a snowy film over the train set he'd been tinkering with. Nothing for a specific client, just a set they'd picked up together at a junk sale. He loved working on miniatures. His magnifier waited for hands to swing the lens from the cradle and extend the arm over the tiny engine.

He'd called before he left the shop that Sunday. Extra time on the projects he loved but rarely indulged, always finishing just one more job for a friend, or a friend of a friend, or a stranger he'd made into a friend in five minutes of talk. She'd teased him about the train never regaining its spark.

"It'll keep. We'll get her running tomorrow. You tell your mom I'll be over in time for supper, Kitten."

But he hadn't.

He'd had a heart attack behind the wheel and driven into a drainage ditch in front of a minivan whose driver had called 911. The paramedics couldn't have arrived in time. The doctor had said so, in her short but kind condolences about how Grandpa Jake hadn't suffered.

The shop bell chimed.

"Be right with you." The desk would keep. The dust would keep. The anniversary radio wouldn't. She hustled to her own workbench and set the knobs amid the lineup of parts beside the empty cabinet.

The wall clock showed five-thirty as she reversed course, empty-handed, and headed out front. Probably a post-work customer, though nothing waited to be picked up tonight. A drop-off or a walk-in.

She dug deep for a smile. Her loneliness would keep, too. "Hey, if I can help you with any—"

Brian stood before the counter. He hoisted a picnic basket, an honest-to-God woven basket with dual handles, onto the top. "I brought an apology."

"Why the hell are you here?" She clutched the stress ball tucked in her sling. Stretching exercises to work her wrist without overworking it. The doc hadn't seen her crush the squishy foam into ball bearing size. "I told you not to contact me."

A persistent man didn't have to be a bad thing, but she'd driven off and left him standing in a parking lot, for chrissake. Her tantrum-throwing skills rivaled a toddler's. One with a driver's license.

“You told me not to call or text, and I didn’t.” Frowning, he tracked the strap of her shoulder sling down to the fist sticking out. “No matter how bad I wanted to know how you were. Doesn’t look like nothing.”

“It’s only a sprain.” An aching nuisance slowing her down all day. The way Brian frowned, best he hadn’t shown up during one of her frustrated fits, when she’d balled up the sling and flung it into the corner where her desk met the wall. Impossible to properly hold small parts and degunk with a bristle brush one-handed. Or to wipe down and pat them dry after. “Work’s still gotta get done.”

“You’ve got to be the one to do it? Your dad or somebody—”

“My responsibility.” Dad ran himself ragged with the house calls for the large appliance repairs. Erin slept half the day away after working late shifts at the warehouse. Mom kept everything running at home. As if she could hand the shop over to the girls, who were supposed to be enjoying their summer break but had picked up babysitting and lawn-mowing gigs. Nobody to mind the store and get the orders done except her. “We have a reputation to uphold, you know. Sixty-five years since my grandpa opened the shop. I can’t skip out and do whatever the fuck I want. People depend on us to keep our promises.”

The stress ball bounced free and rolled across the counter. Past the picnic basket, the neon green slipped over the edge.

Brian scooped the ball up as it fell. “You keep your promises.” Holding out his hand, he offered her the ball on his flat palm. “I believe you. Let me help you do that.”

“You don’t know how to rebuild radios.” She snatched the ball with her good hand. She’d meant to be quick, darting out and back, but he curled his fingers in a teasing brush, and she scraped him with her nails as she clenched. She yanked free. Distraction, distraction—“And your dinner will go bad.”

He patted the basket lid. “Cold packs inside. The food’ll keep.”

She jerked back from his smile and his certainty. So, so ridiculous to imagine Grandpa Jake had sent him. Working his ghost magic from up in heaven. Believing angels existed at all, let alone meddled on Earth, belonged in the minds of little kids and insane people. Kids, crazies, and schmaltzy movies. “You’re crazy, you know that?”

“Okay, I don’t know how to do what you do. So tell me.” Charming grin well in place, he shrugged beneath his collared dress shirt, the top two buttons open but the fabric still stiff. “You say what to do, and I do it. You direct, and I’ll tinker. I know how to take orders.” He leaned in, elbows on the picnic basket. “Worked for changing a tire, didn’t it?”

Who the fuck was this guy who ignored her rudeness, who acted as if they could carry on some hybrid relationship of friendship and romance—fucking romance, Jesus, not even lust relief but picnic dinners. He had to be a trick. He had a game, or an angle, and she hadn't plucked loose his motive yet. "I ran out on you Saturday. I just swore at you. Why are you still trying to help me?"

* * * *

Because his heart beat for her.

He stuffed the true answer down deep. Telling her he'd never felt this intensity with another woman would upset her. Drive her further from him, to where she pretended their connection meant no more than cock-hardening, pussy-wetting hormones.

He packed his hopes into a shrug and a headshake. "I told you I'm not giving up on you, Katherine."

Even though she trusted him so little—or feared their attraction so much—that he hadn't been allowed to check on her over the weekend. Wasn't allowed to know her home address, though that'd been easy to remedy. He'd granted himself only the superficial background snooping available to any idiot with a computer and a rudimentary knowledge of Google. No re-tasking sats.

She lived with her parents. No shame in it, but he'd run his mouth off about Lucas on Saturday and she hadn't said a word. He couldn't apologize for his speechifying without admitting he'd checked up on her. Maybe her folks needed the help, or her granddad's death had drawn them closer, or she'd been running from a bad relationship. Hopefully not a situation where she'd ended up with her arm in a sling often. He'd sure as fuck nailed worst way to end a first date.

"I'm sorry about Saturday. You being hurt, that's on me. Let me make it up to you tonight. Put me to work." Too close to begging. He dialed back the pleading before his fear of her rejection brought the boogeyman to life. "Look, I wasn't always a guy who meant what he said. I chased the biggest laughs. Maybe you were hurt by a guy like that once upon a time." An asshole he'd cheerfully hunt down and beat the shit out of. "But I won't let you down."

Her mouth dropped open, but otherwise she stood still as a poster hung behind the counter. Her navy blue sling cut a swath across the front of her tank top. Orange today, the shirt somehow brought out the glow in her eyes and the deep reddish hues in her hair without clashing.

He held his tongue. Telling her she looked beautiful when he dumbfounded her would be pushing things.

She turned away.

No, no, no. He reeled under the weight of a full-gear pack slamming into his chest. Mission Picnic Dinner: a plan turning out more clusterfuckingly worse than taking her to softball.

"You coming, or what?" She glanced over her shoulder as she disappeared through the doorframe. "You can't be my left hand from way the hell over there, Brian. Bring your basket. We'll get to the food when the work's done."

Salvation. He snatched up the handles and barely stopped himself from vaulting across the counter. Standing outside, he'd donned imaginary cold-weather gear for the frosty reception he'd expected.

Their connection mattered to Katherine. She always left him room for convincing her—first softball and now dinner—and she let herself be convinced. With coaxing, her sharp edges were softening into curves molded to his hands. Her heart would follow. Time, patience, and not holding back so far that she went looking elsewhere for satisfaction—those would be the keys to success.

Shoulders rubbing, they sat on tall work stools with the patient laid out before them. A radio, she'd said, but every delicate bit had to come together from her neat spread of coils, wires, tubes—hell, even an old, swing-arm turntable—and fit into a refinished wood cabinet.

Hampered by her sling, chafing under what she repeatedly called damn-fool restrictions, she directed him in brisk, bossy tones. But she prized kindness, too, despite her irritation and haste. With gentleness, she adjusted his finger-holds when he misunderstood her directions as she rebuilt the guts piece by piece. Showed him what she wanted while she repositioned things this way and that. The whole time, she talked about what she did and why. Not so much about herself, though he sneaked in a few questions. Her short answers leaned heavily on her granddad's teaching, a sore spot, judging from how quick her smiles turned wistful. Missing the old man.

Whenever she rolled her shoulders, he stopped digging for personal details to store away. They had time. He'd learn eventually. If he pushed for emotional intimacy as hard as she pushed for the physical, he'd send her running. So he soaked up her voice and her faint hint of pineapple amid the grease-and-solvent odors under their noses, and he held his tongue.

Going on seven, the turntable lid lowered into place. No thuds or clicks, thanks to the thin felt bumper around the edge.

"I bet that baby didn't look half so good the first time it came off an assembly line."

Stroking the side panel, Katherine smiled. "It's a beauty." She fiddled with the knobs, and static crackled. "Can't tell now how broken it got, shut up in a basement all those years."

A classic rock station twanged and drummed into existence. The tuner translated nonsense into signal. Fading chords shifted into a new song—longing and love floating on a slow-moving guitar river. Perfect for dancing.

He extended his hand. "May I—"

"It's after seven." She scurried back from the worktable. "I need to lock up the front. Don't touch anything."

Not touching a thing. Especially not her. And not the wall five feet away where she'd rocked against him, her ass thumping his cock while she rode his fingers. Six days ago. Closing his eyes, he added the soundtrack of her gasps and moans to the radio.

"Daydreaming?" She spoke beside him, almost in his ear. "I'll have to dock your pay for that, apprentice."

His cock stiffened, but he maintained his cool. Tough to sneak up on a man trained to stay alert, even when said man took a desk jockey analysis post. The tease in her voice, though, fuck. Irresistible, despite instincts reading her move for a deliberate counter to anything deeper than sex.

"Consider the labor free—in trade for you sharing dinner with me. You don't want to go out, so I brought the food to you." He patted the picnic basket with overzealous enthusiasm and flashed slapstick comedy eyebrows. Hell, he'd throw in a fake glasses and nose routine and chomp on a cigar if burying his heart under more layers of laughter helped put her at ease. Whatever she needed to realize and accept that he wouldn't be going anywhere.

Her squinting suspicion lost ground when she gave in and chuckled. "Set up your dinner, then. I need to make a call."

She lifted the old-fashioned phone off the wall-mounted base beside the door and dialed. Push-button, not an old rotary, but the handset was the clunky kind from his childhood with the long corkscrew cord perfect for strangling brothers in the kitchen.

Twisting the cord around her fingers, she swayed in the doorway. "Mom?"

He set the basket on the cleared space in the center of the floor. Blanket first, a blue-and-gold plaid he'd picked up three aisles over from the deli counter. The checkout gal, old enough to be his grandmother, had thrown herself headlong into helping when he'd sheepishly explained he needed a last-minute picnic.

Shaken out, the thick blanket covered as much ground as a king-size mattress. Waterproof backing, padded fill layer, soft top. He might've gone overboard.

Katherine stood with her back to him, rubbing her toe against a worn spot low on the door frame. "No, don't hold dinner for me."

Seemed like she'd grown up in this shop. Maybe she'd played jump rope across that coiled phone cord while grown-ups talked. Dragged over the battered metal-and-rubber stepstool to answer the phone in a little-gal voice weighted with big-girl importance.

"I'm going to grab something and eat in while I finish up." She twirled, slowly, winding the cord around herself. "Oh, from the drugstore counter up the block, I think."

Busted. He laid the cold-cut subs beside the container of macaroni salad—two forks—and bottled waters. Made fresh today, all but the water, and the label promised it'd come straight from a mountain spring. As close to a homemade picnic as his skills allowed.

Katherine folded her lips over, tucking away the smile filling out her cheeks. "They have those ready-made deli sandwiches. And pasta salad, maybe. I'll make sure I eat something filling."

He moved the basket off the far side of the blanket to hide his own smile. Bristly surface, soft-center Katherine would be slow to admit liking his picnic, if she admitted it at all.

"I promise, I will if I need you." She drifted toward the wall hook. The cord untangled as she spun. "Uh-huh. Love you, too. See you tonight."

The phone clicked into the cradle. The radio station played a low, rocking beat.

He patted the wide, empty fabric. Plenty of room for her to sit as far away as she liked. "Hungry?"

"Famished." She dropped into a tailor pose, crossing her legs as she sat. "We're not dating, so you know. This is not a date." Her furtive glances between the food and his face made her seem spring-loaded. "I'm eating this food because I told my mom I would."

"Of course." Her excuses slid right off him, not least because of how she kept checking his bullshit meter. She'd broken the mechanism with her last whopper. "We're not dating." Never mind he'd made history by bringing her a picnic at her office, a first-time event in the annals of Brian's Guide to Getting the Girl. "You're just not lying to your mom. I respect that." He nudged the plastic salad container her way. "Better eat up."

She unsnapped her sling and laid it aside. A blue brace supported her left wrist from her knuckles almost to her elbow. "Points for the stylish way you're trying to get in my pants, though."

"What?" Maybe he should tell her to keep the sling on. Or offer her an ice pack from the picnic basket. "Not trying to get in your pants." Well, fair enough, he did mean to—just not yet. Not until when he did, she promised the first time wouldn't be the last. "Besides, you're injured."

Bite by bite, she devoured a third of the turkey club. She swigged her water and smiled at him. "I can lie back and think of endorphins."

He coughed through swallowing macaroni salad. Christ, she delighted in tempting him to step across the lines he'd set. Sex with her would be one dare after another. "I'd like our first time to rank a few rungs higher than tolerable. At least not registering on the pain scale."

Watching him, she chewed through a few more bites. "You say first like there's going to be a second."

"I'm an optimist." That he wouldn't choke to death trying to eat a meal with her. The ham and Swiss on rye went down easier than the slippery pasta.

Katherine picked at the salad. She raised her fork with a single noodle and wrapped her mouth around the plastic, overlooking the less-than-full serving. "I haven't."

Backtracking gave him nothing. "Been an optimist?"

"Been hurt by an ex who lied to me or broke his promises." She laid her fork tines-down on the lid. "That's what you think, right? Some guy broke me and you can fix me. Because you're a nice guy. Mr. Fix-it."

"I don't—" *want to fix you.* He wanted to understand her. But maybe, kind of, yeah, to fix her. To ride in all white-knight and be the hero like Sherwood instead of the Michigan Surfer Boy. Shit. No wonder he'd avoided relationship complications before. "I want to get to know you. Why you are the way you are. Is that so bad?"

"Why I am—" Her laugh echoed to the metal crossbeams in the ceiling. "Jesus. A woman can't enjoy sex just because she does?"

"No, you can, I want you to." Nope, making things worse. "I, not that I'm giving you permission, or—fuck." Taking a deep breath, he reached for the calm center of the shooting range. The peaceful pause before the punch in the boxing ring. "You're angry about sex, or dating, and I want to understand what makes you so defensive. Secretive."

With a quiet snort, she tipped backward and lay with her knees up and her arms folded across her stomach. "Yeah, because the reaction from society is so fucking positive. A woman who likes sex is still a slut." She snipped the "T" in a hard bite. "Even people who don't say it are thinking it." She stared at the ceiling. "You are."

Christ, he'd done more than given her the wrong impression. He'd landed in the lump of sad sacks who cast judgments while they sampled the forbidden fruit. "I'm not, I swear I'm not. I just—the guys you've been with, none of them hurt you?"

"No." She sighed, and the snap in her voice softened. "I've always been in control. They were my choices, Brian."

He pushed the food aside and settled on his elbow beside her. "Then I don't care who or how many. They don't matter to me or change what I think of you."

"My sister…" She flinched. "She married her high school sweetheart. Two weeks after graduation, both of them eighteen and dumb as fuck."

Ouch. Her bitterness stung sure as a smattering of BB pellets on unprotected skin. He'd received the full blast more than once, courtesy of his older brother's teenage stupidity. Katherine's brother-in-law could've gotten the marriage version from one angry dad. "Shotgun wedding?"

"I wish. At least then we might've seen the end coming. But no." Her breaths lifted her arms in a rolling sine rhythm. "I was twelve, and their marriage seemed like a fairy tale. The heaps of flowers, the yards of fabric on Erin's dress—so extravagant it had to be true love, right? He was her perfect husband for three years. And on his twenty-first birthday, he walked out and never came back."

She didn't deviate from her cynical tone as the wave crashed in his head. The blue of her wrist brace, the slip in the mud, the anger that had driven her to swear at him and run. He'd cracked a fucking joke about wedding rings. About guaranteeing faithfulness and forever.

"My sister had a one-year-old and a nine-week-old. She and the girls moved back home. My nieces don't remember having a father."

He'd been half-right, at least. A guy had broken her trust. He just hadn't been her guy. "You know you're judging every man for one asshat who couldn't hack responsibilities, don't you?"

Huffing, she rolled her eyes, as rebellious as any teen. "You know not every woman's dying for a big wedding and a bunch of babies, right?"

"Good. I don't want a houseful of babies, either." Just her. They'd rewrite her fairy tale with a woman who didn't wait to be rescued and a man who wanted commitment, in whatever form it took. "And a piece of paper wouldn't change how I feel about you. Signing on the dotted line just tells the state where my assets go and who gets to visit me in the hospital."

* * * *

Holy—marriage.

In his casual, offhand way, he'd yanked happily-ever-after from the scrap heap and set to tinkering. He seemed to think he'd stick out a commitment without a ring and a legal obligation. As if he believed in keeping promises, too.

Heart racing, she turned liquid. Flooded with heat for a man who might stand by what he said, and—"Do you mean that? About not wanting kids?"

She prayed to God his answer would stay yes.

Propped on his elbow beside her, he squinted beneath lowered brows. "Do you?"

Ah. He hadn't been serious. He wanted one or two, the same as most guys, enough to keep up with his married friends. He'd fallen behind on the life track. Not the future she wanted for herself. Thanks for playing, folks.

Still. Fucking him once without keeping him remained a solid option. With her good hand, she gave his shirt a teasing tug. So formal in his tucked-in button-down. The tails ought to be out. "You know how babies are made, don't you?"

He clasped her wrist and curled her fingers away from his stomach. "Yeah, but I don't want one."

"Seriously?" Some kind of thing between them might just work. Without kids, without commitment, but more than a backseat fuck in a deserted parking lot.

"I'm thirty-seven." He rocked forward and back. "I like my space." Dragging her arm along for the ride, he gestured in wide swings as his voice picked up speed. "I like not having kiddie shit all over the place and demanding munchkins deciding what I can do and when I can do it."

A quick shove would roll him on his back. His belt might take two hands to unfasten, but she'd be nimble despite the brace. Her jeans, though. She'd need to shimmy out of them for the main event. Lying down or stand up and give him the full ass-wiggling show?

As he caught his breath, he clamped his mouth shut and watched her with wide eyes. He peeled strong, gentle fingers from her wrist. "Sorry, I—"

"God, that's hot." Fuck, too much daydreaming and she'd left him wondering.

"It is?"

Yikes, he must've met way too many baby-hungry women. She should take him off the market, make him hers on her terms. And when he someday changed his mind and wanted a settle-down gal, she'd cut him loose.

"Nice guys always want babies." She sneaked back to his shirt and restarted the undressing effort. "They're all, 'Oh, boo-hoo, I'm missing my chance at fatherhood.'" Spreading beyond the bottom button, his shirt slid out of his dress pants in a vee. A sexy patch of pale curls filled the gap. "I half-raised my sister's kids. I don't need my own."

"Being Geezer Dad at graduation isn't a dream of mine." He ran his knuckles across her shoulder and down her bare arm to the edge of the wrist brace. "Besides, Rob and Nora plan to fill their farmhouse to the rafters. If I get a yen for fatherhood, I'll borrow one of theirs for a day, and that'll cure me." On the return trip, he kept going, tickling her neck and ruffling the hair above her ear. "I didn't look at you and say, 'Wow, what a baby factory.'"

"Yeah? What did you say?" With a tug and a push, she freed his shirt button. Peek-a-boo, solid wall of abs.

"At first sight?" He arched toward her, resettling his hips.

She dared a hand inside. "Uh-huh." Closed buttons above and below gave her enough wiggle room. She scraped her nails beneath the edge of his ribs. "Tell the truth."

"You were bending over to look at your tire." The front of his pants rippled around his cock.

Too hard to hide himself now. His inner bad boy wanted what it wanted. Convincing him to take it would be her job.

"Uh-huh." Fuck, his outline deserved a mouth around it. In a minute, she'd toss good-girl restraint aside and go after him right through the fabric.

As redness tip-toed through his cheeks, he ducked his head. "'Wow, I'd like to get my dick in that'?"

Perfect. Bottling up her moan, she gave in to laughter. Underneath Brian's nice-guy surface lay the darker instincts she needed from him. The desire to fuck for no other reason than incredible pleasure.

"But then we talked, and it was more than—"

"Nope." She shushed him with a finger against his lips. "I asked for honesty and you gave it to me. Don't go backpedaling now."

Not when she had plans for him. She owed him the blowjob she hadn't been able to give him last week. No customers would interrupt them this time. All closed up tight, the two of them in secluded bliss. She owed not only him but herself. Her mouth had been watering for the taste of him. She'd given him his five minutes to play with her body. Tonight, she'd take hers.

Fingers spread, she caressed down his neck and across his stiff collar to his breastbone. Her firm push sent him onto his back, a move impossible without his complicit cooperation. Good boy. This would be her show, not his.

He breathed harder, his chest rising and falling beneath his half-open shirt. As he tracked her movements, his gaze followed her, and his hand clenched at his side.

With a roll and a wriggle, she knelt between his thighs. Too bad she didn't have a pillow to stuff under his head. Fuck, she wanted him watching her. Desperate to see her going down on him. Palming him through his pants, she savored the satisfying flex in his hips as he rose to meet her. "I don't think I've ever sucked an honest guy's dick. This'll be a first."

He blocked her reach for his belt. "What?"

Had he misunderstood her? Hard to believe he'd missed her intent. She snagged the black leather and pulled the tail through the buckle. "Blowjob time. Let's go, Prince Charming."

Hoisting himself on an elbow, he held her off with his other hand. "I'm not some sex-crazed beast, Katherine. I'm a man."

A man with a cock tenting his pants. She worked her fingers under the waistband and teased the top open. The zipper slid. As he moaned, she smirked. "Same difference."

"No, it's not." He poured an insistent edge into his voice. The blushing comedian had vanished. "My dick doesn't make decisions for me. Not with you."

Sonovabitch. She rarely offered blowjobs to the guys she fucked. Aside from the power struggle, putting her mouth on them would've been more…intimate. Not that she wanted intimacy with Brian. The blowjob was a thing for a thing, her mouth for his fingers, that's all. What guy wouldn't be happy to take that trade?

Unless he—

She yanked her arm back. If he didn't want her, fuck him and his dating runaround. "Look, if you aren't interested in me, say so. I don't need to waste my time chasing a man into bed."

Brian growled through tight-pressed lips. "I am interested. In *you*." Sliding his knees high around her, he squeezed her sides. "Not how warm and wet your mouth is, but you, Katherine, the damn stubborn woman who's making me argue against my own blowjob." He chased her gaze until he pinned her down with pale green persistence. "Jesus, who does that?"

A guy who wasn't truly interested, obviously. One who didn't fully desire her. She didn't entice him enough to make him lose control. But she aroused him. His hard cock proved that much. She rubbed the ridge thrusting out of his open fly, covered now only by blue-gray cotton boxer-briefs.

Watching her without argument, he arched into her hold.

"I'm not making you." A gentle stroke, two fingers along one side and her thumb against the other. Light enough to tease, hard enough to feel him pulse. "You could just agree." She circled his tip. Plucked the elastic waistband of his undershorts. Why wouldn't he let her give him the lone tie they had in common? Nothing but lust bound them together. "We both know you want this."

* * * *

Of course he wanted to. In no world was his interest questionable.

But grabbing what he wanted would be going back on his word to take things slow and show her she meant more to him than sex. Yeah, he'd be the only one who knew, but that would be one too many.

"I could agree." He curled his hand around hers, and her forearm tensed. Slender strength wrapped in a dotted layer of freckled skin. Her hand felt more than good enough through his shorts. Imagining her mouth—Christ save him from temptation. "And maybe I do want this. But if I said to you I knew what you wanted and told you to lie back and take it, we'd be drifting into pretty dark corners."

Losing her sexy smile, she ripped her hand free and sat back on her heels. "You think I'm trying to rape you?"

"No." Fuck. His vigorous headshake failed at erasing her open-mouthed horror. He tapped his knees against her sides and tried a soft smile. "I think I've said slow down, and you aren't listening, because you want our connection to be only about sex."

She angled her head like old-fashioned rabbit ears picking up a fuzzy signal. Receptive to his message, if he stopped shoving his feet in his mouth.

"Seems like so far, that's worked for you, because you pick guys who'll happily walk away after. Nothing wrong with that." Shit, he'd been the easy and available one day, gone the next day kind of guy for years.

Those surface games wouldn't fly with her. Hadn't since he'd first watched her stride to his car with the same no-nonsense purpose the handful of women in basic training had worn like armored jumpsuits. Katherine would make a hell of a commander. Strong and capable, she'd muscled through her own tire change and delegated jobs as if he'd been her hop-to right-hand man for years. She was chock-full of get-the-job-done grit. The two of them together, they worked.

She hadn't seen the truth yet. He needed more days and nights together before she'd trust him to keep his word.

"But I'm not that guy." Not with her. Not ever again, because from now on he'd be the steady man she deserved. And still put his foot in his mouth half the damn time. "If that means I don't get blown but I do get to take you out, I'll take that trade."

Leaning against his upraised leg, she wrapped her injured arm around his knee. Her speculative gaze, darting between his face and his gaping pants, pumped him harder. "But you'd rather have both, right?"

"Fuck yes." As if he'd been hiding his unrelenting desire for her. Fine, she hadn't seen him jerking off to fantasies of her every night. Arching his hips, he grabbed his pants and shorts and shoved them to his thighs. His cock sprang free. "Does this look uninterested to you?"

She gasped, a mewling half-moan, and her arm tightened around his leg. Her tongue, pink and pointed, flicked her lips.

Between her stare and the air flowing across his tip, he might come quick as a kid with his hand on his dick for the first time. Clamping the base of his shaft, he wagged. "Soon as I walk outta here, I'm gonna end up jerking off in my car. Again. Am I only a man if I jam my dick in you every chance I get?"

Sparks flew in the fiery orange centers of her eyes. "Maybe it's the only way I'm a woman, damn you."

What? No, impossible for her to believe—

"Maybe I want to be desired." Her voice loaded with righteous fury, she shook beneath a blazing halo of auburn hair. "Maybe I don't want more baggage and expectations. Maybe I want guys to be available and uncomplicated."

Her breasts heaved with her breath. Her muscles ran in taut lines from her neck down. She knelt trembling between his legs, her face an angry mask demanding he let her fuck him.

His delays, fucking hell, his delays read like rejections in her book. The signals he meant as "I value you most" came through on her end as "I don't value you at all." A blanket no now to all fooling around would do him more harm than good.

He stroked her fingers, trying to uncurl her clenched fists. "Katherine, if you're determined to keep believing a man can't be worth more than one night of meaningless sex, nothing I say will stop you." Swallowing, he picked through the minefield in his head. A safe route with her existed, and he'd damn well find the thing. "But I won't be your proof." Please, God, don't let her call his bluff. He couldn't give her up any more than he could give up breathing. "You want to fool around? I want another day out. It doesn't have to be a date."

Every moment he spent with her was a date. God would forgive him those white lies.

Resettling her hips, she rocked sideways between his thighs. The tension in her shoulders eased. She narrowed her eyes, drilling him with laser precision. "If I say yes, are you gonna shut up and let me suck your cock?"

His dick jumped. Eager bastard had been leaping toward her for days now, but never while naked in her presence. "Yes, ma'am."

Hell yes. Dropping his head to the blanket, he let his arms fall. He knew an order when he heard one.

* * * *

Heat danced through her as she scrunched her toes tight, a hidden outlet for the exhilaration of his surrender. Every day, she fulfilled a dozen roles—dutiful daughter, understanding sister, doting aunt—but the days when she fit all the pieces together into a woman with needs and desires of her own arrived few and far between.

But Brian would let her be that woman tonight. Flawed and hungry, aching to own all of him her way.

"Fine." She surveyed her territory. Hints of solid chest flashed in the gaps of his tangled dress shirt. His pants spread across his upper thighs. In between, a masterpiece waited for her mouth. "I'll take you out Saturday."

Bending over his bunched-up pants, she puckered her lips and blew across him. The twitch in his cock echoed inside her. Pure power hummed louder than the radio playing its low serenade from her worktable. Her fingers had rebuilt those connections. They'd configure these wires, too. "You sure make a girl work for your dick."

His eyes glowed, soft and grounded. He shoved one hand beneath his head in a makeshift cradle, his elbow out. "Watching you work gets me hard. Fuck, thinking about you working gets me hard. You." He swayed from head to hips. "You get me hard, Katherine. Morning, noon, and night."

Lowering herself over him, she braced on her right hand. Her left wrist wouldn't stand the backbend and support her weight, but her fingers held enough agility to deal with his pesky buttons. Her jeans rasped against his pants. She laid her hand in the gap at the top of his shirt.

Adam's apple bobbing, he otherwise stayed still. His collar stood stiff, buttoned down tight. As she teased the vee between the two buttons he'd left open, he hissed in a breath. His outfit screamed professionalism. Office-serious, minus one crucial element.

"Did you wear a tie today?" She nestled her knees against his ass.

His chuckle dipped into a moan. “It’s, uh, in the car.” He grazed her good wrist in a fingertip caress. “Seemed a little formal for a picnic.”

He’d loosened up for her. Ditched the tie. Opened his shirt. Tingles spread up her arms as she slipped the rest of the buttons free. “You’re still kind of overdressed. A good picnic offers a nice view.”

Fuck, he qualified. With his shirt pushed wide, he showed off the toned layout of a man who worked for a living. Maybe he came by his in the gym, but he put his time in. Firm flesh under the hood as she laid into him, dragging her fingers in furrows that rose again in her wake.

Catlike, he stretched and pushed into her heavy caresses. Owning a Brian-cat wouldn’t be too much work. A sleek, independent fuck-buddy who came around when he needed help scratching an itch. Flashing his coiled muscles as he paraded in front of her until she pounced.

Bending low, she flicked her tongue against his nipples. Back and forth. Building a line of teasing bites between. Not kisses. None of that soft romantic bullshit.

He hissed and groaned as he rippled beneath her and the blanket backing scratched against the bare concrete floor. Their rough symphony rivaled the radio still going strong, a testament to her skills.

Well—and their teamwork. He deserved a smidgen of credit.

Thick muscle wrapped his abdomen, curving in from sides she squeezed and nipped. No patch of flesh left untouched.

And he chased her attention, Jesus, begged for her hands and mouth with his rocking. His low swearing rose like pleas to his god for mercy.

But she was his god tonight. She’d choose when to offer mercy.

The heat in his cock warmed her neck, his stiff erection tucked beneath her chin while she built anticipation nuzzling his stomach. As his legs closed in around her, she pushed them back. Spreading his thighs, she ignored the twitch in her left wrist. Leaning into him, forcing him to stay open for her, filled her with fire. Her nipples, hard points under her tank top, ached for his mouth.

Twisting temptation into power, she swirled her tongue around his cockhead.

His fingers curled beside her face as he gasped. He dug his hand into his hip without touching her.

On the rare occasions she’d gone down on a guy, she’d told him to keep his fucking hands to himself. One goddamn tug at her hair, and she’d be done. No second chances.

She sampled him again, flicking his tip and tasting salt. The start of a rich, slick coating she’d give him to let her take him deeper, to help him slide over her tongue so his soft skin and musky-male warmth filled her senses as much as his hard cock filled her throat.

Covering his cockhead, she sucked in tiny pulses and pressed her tongue against him in counterpoint. Simple men, stupid men, figured blowjobs were about their pleasure. Wrong.

He rocked his hips and uttered nonsense syllables, maybe her name. Helpless and obedient, he gave in to her demands.

The real joy of a blowjob: power. Hers over him. Her ability to command his entire body on the point of her tongue. In the firm suction of her lips. All of his desire focused on her, and he had no say in what she'd choose to do about it. Satisfy him or leave him hanging.

She took him deeper, in steady strokes, his gaping pants tickling her chin. No man would ever control her. But as he laid his hand against her head, resting his palm in her hair, she burned with the unprecedented urge to order him to pull harder. Her body tightened, a twisting screw catching hold, as she imagined a bossy Brian.

With her hand slipped between his thighs, she cupped his balls and squeezed.

He bucked into her mouth. "Fuck, Katherine. I'm—you're—fuck."

Heart racing, she pulled back. Too close to gagging. Or to coming herself. He'd gone deep, and the thrill tingled like fingers on her clit.

Palming her cheek, he trembled. "Fuck, did I hurt you?"

She covered his hand and dragged him back into her hair. "Don't you dare apologize. Just hold on tight."

Letting him go, she bent her head. She'd brought him to the edge. This time, she'd push him over. With one hand to hold him, so she wouldn't have to stop no matter how enthusiastic he got. He'd damn well better be enthusiastic. Hell if she'd be the lone participant enjoying this blowjob.

He gripped her hair. Tight, not tentative, thank God. He didn't push, but he held on.

Perfect. She swallowed his cock. The salt flowed faster, stronger. She'd taste all of him in a minute. She sped up her strokes. Soon he'd surrender in this contest of wills. Nice-guy Brian would be her bad boy, coming in her mouth and spilling over her lips because she was impossible to resist.

* * * *

A lifeline, her hair in his fist. Auburn and shimmering under the lights, Katherine rose and fell with the beauty of the sun setting across the lake. Enticing, luring him to paddle out to meet her, to dive into her glowing fire and lose himself.

Fuck, she'd nearly made him come already, the way she wrapped herself around him. Kneeling between his thighs and bending over his dick. Her tank top dipped, and her breasts flashed between light and shadow. Her mouth gleamed, her lips impossibly wet.

She treated him like a dessert she meant to devour down to the last spoonful and lick the bowl after. Amazing. An amazing woman he wanted to see again. Every night. Every morning. To lie naked in bed with her and roll over and kiss her mouth—

Hips jerking, he tugged her hair. "I'm almost—"

Christ Jesus, fuck, she worked her tongue up his shaft and moaned, fucking *moaned* as if she might come when he did.

Choice. He ought to say something before he got too far gone to warn her. "You don't have to sw—"

With a hard, fiery stare and a slow, deliberate suck, she silenced him.

So goddamn gorgeous. Bold. Unflinching. She spread her arms across his hips and held him down with her weight. One hand clamped around his dick, she lowered her mouth to meet her knuckles again and again. Watching him, fuck-fuck-fuck, watching him while she swallowed him down and dared him to come.

Heat rushing through his cock, he gave in. His hips bucked. His eyes tried to close, and he forced them open. He refused to lose Katherine, to deny his connection to her. Their gazes locked as she drank from him.

Fuck, he loved her.

He slammed his teeth shut on that confession. Best case, she'd take it for the addled ramblings of a post-orgasm mind. Worst case, she'd throw his picnic at him and order him out the door.

Lifting her head, she gave an exaggerated swallow and licked her lips. "My show, my rules. If I wanted you to come somewhere else, I would've handled the arrangements."

Her smile said she'd won something, but no obvious answer presented itself. He'd gotten to come, for one thing, and she'd agreed to his condition for another date. Two wins for him. And fuck, she gave a fucking fantastic blowjob. How many men had she practiced—

He shoved the worrisome flicker aside. Whoever she'd been with before, however many, didn't matter. She was with him now. Wasn't she?

"Lady's choice, that's fair." Hell, she could pick where he finished as often as she liked. He unknotted his fingers and stroked her hair, his aching knuckles welcoming the stretch. He'd taken control with most of the women he'd spent a night with, but sharing the lead with Katherine heightened the excitement. "Do your rules let me do something for you, too?"

He wouldn't be a gentleman if he didn't ask, but he'd thrown the question out there because his mouth watered for her. The salty tang of her on his tongue and the strength in her thighs clamping around his face when she lost control. Even though reciprocating might be moving too fast for his own rules. She wanted his desire without the emotional ball of wax.

She knelt between his thighs, her weight no longer balanced on her arms across his hips. With a speculative tilt to her head, she slipped her gaze sideways.

If she pushed for sex, he might lack the strength to say no. He needed to hold back enough to keep her interested in the rest while she grew comfortable with the whole not-just-fucking, long-term love they deserved together.

Scooting free of his legs, she shook her head. "Not tonight."

A-fucking-men. The sad twist of his tongue for the lost opportunity didn't sour the air-guitar and drum-frenzy cranking out solos in his head. She hadn't said no—she'd said not tonight.

As in, on another night, the answer might be yes. Because they'd have another night. More chances to demonstrate her importance to him and lead her deeper into the big, scary sea of coupledom.

"A hug at least?" He crooked his finger and his smile, aiming for a light tease. A snuggle those bad boys of hers wouldn't deliver. "Have you seen my arms? I hide 'em well in my sleeves, but they've got some serious power."

"Yeah, I've felt your grip, tough guy." Chuckling, she ducked her head and smoothed down her hair. She stretched out alongside him. "Peak performance."

An encore would be in order if she threw out more compliments. Fuck, what he wouldn't give to kiss her right now, roll her under him and eat her for dessert until his dick returned to mission-ready status.

He managed a one-armed hug. Landed a kiss on her temple, maybe because she hadn't expected the move. She hadn't avoided him like she had when he'd gone in for a true kiss the first night.

She squirmed away after a few minutes. Not close enough for snuggling, but maybe she'd never been an afterglow kind of woman. Her emotional progress would be measured in fractions of an inch.

The foot of space between them would have to stand, tonight. He raised his hips and wrestled his clothes back into place. As she lay on her side, facing away and propped on her good arm, he risked a graze against her back. "So, where are you taking me on our not-a-date Saturday?"

"Unh-uh, nope."

The tease in her voice held his heart suspended. If she backed out on the deal—

"You surprised me with this picnic thing." Craning her neck, she rolled toward him. "I'm not telling what I've got planned for you." Her sparking eyes challenged him while her barely-there smile seemed half-shy. "But dress down. I'll pick you up."

A dare. If he dismissed the instincts barking at him to command the situation and instead let her take control again. Made himself the one who waited and wondered, who got picked up at his door and whisked off on an adventure. Probably a place out in the boonies where she wouldn't run into anyone she knew, folks who might fuss at her about having a boyfriend. Hell. One step closer to a true date. Stealth mission. Whatever Katherine needed to feel comfortable with him for more than one night.

"I got no problem with that." He shrugged, putting effort into nonchalance. "Your show, your rules."

Chapter 5

Idling outside Brian's swanky apartment complex, Kit texted him from the driver's seat of her sister's beater.

Tonight wasn't a date, so why pretend with door-knocking formalities and all. Brian would tag along to her usual Saturday, same as she'd hitched a ride on his afternoon softball wagon last week.

His return text chimed back. *On my way.*

Good. If he'd been Perry, she would've honked at him to get his ass moving. Of course, Perry rented an attic apartment from an elderly couple downtown who let him play handyman in exchange for cheaper rent. No chance a hundred people would peek through the curtains on their fancy windows and ask about the unmannered trash waiting in the driveway. And being friends since elementary school bicycle-fixing days granted a lot of leeway.

Brian emerged in jeans and a black T-shirt with a faded white logo. Thank God he'd taken her fashion advice to heart. White-collar office jockeys stood out in a crowd of farm boys and gearheads.

As he strode down the sidewalk, she leaned over and popped open the passenger door. The finicky outside latch remained on the list of unfinished projects.

Swinging into the seat, he ducked toward her.

Jesus God, he meant to kiss her.

He froze, reversed course, and yanked the door shut. Coughing, he palmed his still-patchy beard. "Hey."

"Hey." She let him skate on the near-miss. Thinking he'd kiss her like a date would. No, worse than a date, a boyfriend, because a date waited until the end of the night to lean in for a kiss. Habit for him. Nice guys trained for serious girlfriends, not random hookups. “Seat belt, mister.”

He buckled up as she backed out. His shirt celebrated some band from before her time. “Vintage tee?”

“You know it.” He drummed his knees and rapped the dash. “Saw them play in my bad-boy days. Sixteen. Didn’t breathe a word to my folks.”

“Illicit road trip?” She hesitated at the turn. Left would take them to the night she had planned. Beers and gears. Right could lead anywhere. Keep driving until they ran out of road and she spilled out all the things that scared her, the dreams she’d never live, the terrifying happiness she maybe wanted to grab hold of with Brian and not let go.

She turned left.

Oblivious, Brian nodded along with the rock on the radio. “Seven of us crammed in somebody’s grandma’s Caddy, a real old boat, skipping out of town to catch them play. Around the lake to Chicago. Three-hour drive. We sneaked back in as dawn hit.”

Laughing, she steered them down the highway. Green-light luck stayed with them. Less than ten minutes to the track. “Perry’s gonna love you.”

“Perry?” Brian flashed deer-in-headlights at her before he wiped his face blank and chased it with an insincere smile. “You’re not setting me up for a blind date with one of your girlfriends, are you?”

Oh God. She pounded her palm against the steering wheel to stop herself from punching him in the shoulder. “You think I’m so scared of dating you that I’d pawn you off on a friend? And I’d tell her what, ‘Meet Brian. I’ve road-tested his dick with my mouth, and I think you’ll be very satisfied’?”

He jerked in the seat. “Shit, you’re right, that was a stupid—let me pull my head out of my ass and my foot out of my mouth—”

“You must be built like a pretzel.”

“—and start over.” He cleared his throat, fake-fluffed his hair, and turned toward her with an evening-news anchor smile. “So, is Perry a friend of yours?”

“My buddy.” Closer to brother. Bonded for life with welding torches and countersunk bolts. “He’s an A-1 mechanic and a concert fiend. He crews for one of the local boys who runs hobby stock. He’ll get us into the pits. You ever been to the dirt track?”

“Nope.” Brian stretched his legs as far as the car let him go, which left his knees riding the glove box. Cracking his knuckles, he pushed back in the seat. “Dirt track virgin here.”

His warm tease curled around her like an arm across her shoulders. Fuck, she'd shaved her legs to the top in case he loosened his nuts and agreed to some real sex. A taste of backseat action. The bulge in his jeans suggested he was toying with the same idea.

Pulling into the sports park, she played off her excitement with a laugh. "Don't worry. I'll be gentle when I pop your cherry."

* * * *

"I'm gonna hold you to that." He'd pop a seam if he didn't stop teasing with her. "Save the rough stuff for after we know our way around the curves."

Fuck, he failed at following his own advice. As she drove through the gate, her skinny jeans and tank top clung to the places his hands ought to be. Especially when she introduced him to some dude whose name made her smile.

"Don't sell yourself short." With an underhand grip on the wheel, she turned in and snagged an open space. Her flexing forearm revealed a long stretch of pale, freckle-dotted skin in need of kisses and caresses. "You know your way around a few nice curves."

Maybe this Perry guy did, too. Kit didn't give much weight to sex—to fucking. She might have slept with her concert-loving mechanic buddy. But she didn't make friends with those guys after. Claimed not to drink from the same well twice.

She hopped out of the car. "C'mon, slowpoke. The time trials are already running. You hear 'em?"

The low-pitched buzz settled in his bones as he climbed from the passenger seat.

She came around and gave the door an extra bump with her hip. "Has trouble keeping a tight grip."

Not like its owner. She'd clamped around his fingers when she came, fierce and shaking, in the back of the shop. And her mouth, fuck, her lips wrapped around him and her fiery eyes danced when she owned him at their picnic. His cock begged for a repeat. Bad idea on his hard-won date night. Ten minutes at her side, and he needed to turn down the heat.

He spun and scanned their surroundings, the grandstand, lawn seats, and chain-link fencing plonked in the middle of tall grass meadows. Looking anywhere but at irresistible Katherine. The parking lot sat mostly full. "Popular place."

"Uh-huh. Let's get a move on." She grabbed his hand and pulled. Her low-heeled boots gave her a touch of height on him, and her pursed lips shone with a hint of glossy red. "We can watch a few races before we visit Perry."

Hand-holding. In public. Holy fucking—he lurched forward, near about to lose his balance, as she dragged him along between the cars. Two quick steps saved him from a world of embarrassment. The gleam in her eye, the giggle slipping free of her mouth if he'd had to explain that one?

Well, see, a man can keep his wits about him even when you're so beautiful his blood flow's going straight to his cock. He's used to that. But you taking his hand, on your own initiative? Grinning with little-gal excitement? Fuck. You make my heart skip too many beats, Katherine. You steal them away, and I don't want you to ever give them back.

She bought beers and dogs, smacking his hand when he reached for his wallet. "My night, my rules. Besides, you paid for the picnic."

He throttled back his instincts and swiped the molded cardboard carrier. "Whatever the lady says. You cash, I'll carry."

Dutch treat smelled of paybacks. She considered their last night together a debt, and she meant to settle the score. As if she didn't want to owe him, didn't want to accept a gift from him. If they ran a tab together, she'd have to acknowledge their continuing connection.

They watched awhile from the stands, sitting knee to knee and sipping on overpriced beer. As the sun sank behind them, the overhead ultra-bright lights clicked on. The air hung heavy with exhaust, hot rubber, and grease. Dirt flew in waves on the banked turns. The first races featured heavily modified machines halfway to being dune buggies. When they rubbed and rolled, the side panels ripped off like so much thin-sheeted foil.

Katherine leapt to her feet and issued full-throated yells, exhorting No. 87 to pick up his pace and No. 34 to stop babying the transmission. She dropped back into her seat smiling or shaking her head and never failed to lean in and offer him some clue to the action.

The crowd and the roaring engines made conversation a heart-pounding, cock-thumping challenge. He placed his lips against her ear as he poured out unimportant questions—any fucking one his mind conjured, from the fence height to the dirt-surface depth—between her whooping encouragement and jeers to the drivers.

When she replied, she laid her lips to his ear. Skin brushing skin. Circling her nose in his hair.

She seemed alive. Exhilarated and not afraid to reveal her enthusiasm, grinning broadly and bouncing to her feet. New raw data for his Katherine puzzle.

As the showcase stock car race of the night started, she grabbed his hand, tipped the plastic cup inside, and finished off the last of his dark amber lager. "You ready to get out of here? I want to take you behind the scenes and show you off—" Squeezing him so hard the plastic buckled, she flushed. "Show you *around* before Perry gets deep in repair mode and zones out with his music cranked."

Show him off. A sweet, telling slip of the tongue. He'd done the same, dragging her straight to Rob and Nora. Looking for approval from the closest thing he had to family in town. And now she meant to do the same in her own way. Not driving him across county lines and hiding him away. From her family, okay, but not from her friend. Closest friend, maybe.

"Yeah. Yeah." He jumped to his feet. Fuck, he'd better make a damn good impression on the guy, or Katherine might drop him faster than a hot corncob at a bonfire. "Show me your secrets."

* * * *

The track gated the pit area to looky-loos once the real racing started. No more autographs and amateurs shooting the shit about the time they almost had a shot at the big seat but wouldn't have wanted to go anyway. Too commercial, shoveling bullshit for sponsors with a smile. A third of the guys here told the same story. Another third pretended the phone was gonna ring any day now. All of them thought their talk would drop a woman's panties. The smart ones—the third who loved their hobby but kept a tight grip on their day jobs—knew when to shut the fuck up.

Kit lacked a registered badge to flash, but Perry'd left her name scrawled on the attendant's clipboard.

Poor kid sitting the post came within spitting distance of fourteen, fifteen at most. "Kit Runyon, yes'm. It says 'plus one.' And—" Flaming red, he rubbed a hand over his acne-spotted face and dragged his ballcap low. "Aw, jeez. That your plus-one's got to show he's man enough to carry you past the gate."

"Oh, Perry's so in for it now." Having fun at her expense. Smart-ass. See if she ever spent another Saturday afternoon fixing his landlords' dishwasher. "Not happening, kid."

Ignoring the teen, who yanked his hand down about two seconds before she'd have run smack into him with her breasts, she charged through.

Brian followed at her heels. "I would've carried you. Easy scoop and run, right across my shoulders." His smug needling sang out loud and clear. The smirk smacked of overkill. "Simple matter of weight distribution, really."

"Keep talking, smart guy." Standing at the edge of the soup, she scoped out the rows. The team Perry crewed with flew a neon purple skull banner with dice in the eye sockets. Hard to miss. "We'll redistribute your weight in the weeds and gravel."

"Nope, not for me." He feigned a limp, bent over, and rubbed his back. "At thirty-seven, I can't be lying on my back with stones stabbing and pinching." Crooking his neck, he winked at her and touched her knee. "Or taking a beating from those boots."

His slow calf-stroke raised her heel, had her tapping on the stones. Fuck if he didn't have more in mind than talk tonight. She stretched on her toes and caught a glimpse of purple in the lights. "I see the flag. This way."

He released her leg and straightened up. "Guess I'll have to be a good boy, then."

Not all night. Just a smidge longer. But he let her lead him. Most of the guys she met fought her on that count, at least a little. Brian never bothered.

Irritating, for a man to be so passive and intimidated—no. His lack of intimidation made the difference. Other guys got their hackles up and snarled to pretend they weren't embarrassed. Feeling smaller when a woman took charge, they acted bigger.

Bigger fools, anyhow.

Easygoing, affable Brian—he knew himself. He didn't puff up and cock-crow, because her being in charge didn't faze him. He'd wait for an opening and take control back when the shift suited them both.

Fuck. Rubbing her thighs together as she walked, she overshot comfort and intensified the ache. Time to go soon. They'd limit the meet-and-greet to one drink with Perry, and she'd steer Brian out to the car. Late enough that the early-birds had left, early enough that the die-hards would stay in their seats.

She'd be busy stripping out of her jeans and straddling Brian in the backseat. Maybe she'd let him dictate the pace, his hands digging into her hips as he drove himself into her. Heat flashed in her belly. Thoughts to save for later, or she'd need a dry pair of underwear.

"Kiiit! My gal." Down the aisle, Perry shouted and jumped on a two-stack of tires. He spread his arms as the perch wobbled beneath him, turning the gesture into an elegant bow without losing his balance. "Am I tall enough for you to see me? Hear me? I know you giant-folk have trouble with us regular-sized humans."

"Who said that?" She threw her hand up, visor-like, and cut the glare of the work light. "Is there a talking mouse in this joint?"

"Was. We roasted him for supper." Perry hopped down, his five-three frame putting his eyes just above her chest. "Nice view. You borrow that tank top from some girl my size?" He sidestepped her joking shove, going toe-to-toe with Brian. "This the new muscle?"

"In the flesh." She wiped her hands on the seat of her jeans. Sweaty palms, Jesus. "Brian, meet Perry. He's a scrawny son of a bitch, but his tiny fingers make him half-decent at tinkering."

Standing military-straight, Brian shook hands with stiff professionalism.

Perry went in for the guy-bump, trapping their hands and knocking his shoulder into Brian's chest. "Shit, man, where'd you get the Scarecrow Creek Hanging tee? I've got the official-unofficial bootleg from the Chicago show they played in '94, but those shirts are super-rare."

Absorbing the hit on steady legs, Brian smiled at her. His scruffy near-beard gave him a wicked shadow. Almost a bad boy. "Saw that show in person. Worth every damn minute of trouble it took to get to the club."

"No shit?" Perry pivoted and flung his arms around her. "Kit, I love him already. This guy's got way better taste than the rest of the fools around here." Tipping his head back, he pulled her in tight. "Seriously." He dropped the teasing tone, his harsh whisper of the don't-do-something-stupid variety. "You keep this fucker. You see how he looks at you?"

He danced back without leaving her time to respond. The energy at the track got him frenetic and buzzed. At least his hyperactive delight didn't land him in detention here. The guys at the nearest setups paid him no mind. They had their own mini-parties, the low music and loud laughter from most, the swearing and kicking and metal-clanging from some too bullheaded to let a loss go. Tent lights glowed along down the line, dark gaps marking where the odd few trailers had pulled out early.

"Drinks?" Perry waggled six-shooter fingers at her and Brian. "You guys want drinks?" With a nod to himself, he shoved his long-sleeve tee up to his elbows. The short-sleeve tee layered overtop featured another obscure band with a faded orange horse skull logo. "You need a nice ice-cold beverage. Extra hands, extra hands—Brian, my man, come take a dip in the cooler." Swiveling, he tracked a skinny straggler beating feet to catch up with a loud roving party down the aisle. "Kit, don't let anybody put their pristine mitts on my dirty machine. My boys done off and left me to chase some short-skirted siren."

Brian flashed her a double-eyebrow raise as Perry herded him around the work tent toward the front of the hauler. But he smiled, too, and his easy stride made his ass a joy to watch until they disappeared past the trailer.

"Non-alcoholic for me," she shouted after them. She'd finished her own beer and half of Brian's watching the races. Too much yelling—and, okay, maybe sitting pressed up against him for a couple of hours—had dried her throat. "I'm in the driver's seat tonight."

She circled the car. The purple nightmare—dubbed Ghost of a Chance by the driver-owner—had finished fifth in a field of seventeen. Surface damage, looked like. The rub rails had done their job on the side panels, taking the hits and the scrapes. The cracked and twisted bumper would need a replacement to keep the judges from disqualifying them for sharp edges next time out, but Perry would tweak every detail tomorrow anyhow.

A beer run to the cab couldn't possibly take this long. Two minutes, max. The neighbors' music killed any hope of eavesdropping. Jesus God, if Perry interrogated Brian—no, worse, if Brian interrogated Perry. Witness to God knew how many mistakes she'd gone off and fucked. Thank Christ she'd mostly stuck with out-of-towners to limit the awkward run-ins later. She must've been drunk when she'd decided to introduce Prince Charming to her best goddamn friend in the world. The stories he could tell.

But Perry made up half the reason she'd brought Brian to the track on this not-dating, non-relationship outing for two people who probably-definitely wanted to fuck and maybe-someday wanted other things. She'd brought Brian to meet Perry and learn a sport she loved like he loved softball or surfing. He might take her out on his lake someday and show her his waves. Not a date. Two potential friends with fucking privileges?

Getting over-tipsy would blur her memory of the night if they did end up littering the backseat with condom wrappers. Brian was a man worth remembering every moment with. So when she cut him loose, or when he found his settle-down gal and they had to strangle the desire humming between them to keep some kind of friendship, she could relive the way he touched her. How he made her squirm. How he made her arch and flex and—

Smack. Someone grabbed her ass. "Here's a bumper I'd like to ride again."

She slammed her boot on his foot and followed up with a kick at his knee. Missed the inside angle to truly make the dipshit howl, but he dropped his hand off her as she spun. "Back the fuck up, asshole."

Mr. Handsy sported a silver double-bead nose ring. A familiar trying-too-hard twisted tattoo gave his neck a barbed-wire smile. Fucking fuck. Mooning over Brian, bent and eyeing the race damage, she'd let a swaggering bad choice from last September sneak up on her.

A not-quite stranger whose name she'd forgotten. He traveled with a crew. Not a mechanic. Somebody's useless relative pretending to be a big shot. Aggressive jerk had been her goal back then, and she'd sure as fuck found him.

And now he'd found her.

* * * *

Brian ambled through the short weeds behind the crackling energy Katherine called friend. The guy bounced around more than a pinball on Friday night at an old-school arcade. Talked like he'd emerged from a year under monk silence and meant to make up for lost time. And he'd thrown his arms around Katherine without fear of getting shoved away. Hugged her, touched her, teased her.

Fuck. Blaming the burning in his chest on the concession-stand dog, much as he wanted to, would be a flat-out lie. Envy sat striking matches against his heart. "So, Perry. You and, uh, Kit, you've known each other awhile?"

Perry slapped his hands on the pickup and heaved himself over the side with inches to spare. Wiry for a short guy. "You care about her, Brian? Like you're gonna give a shit tomorrow morning, and the day after, and the—"

"I do." Katherine. With all her hopes and dreams, and the fears she let hold her back, and the boldness she held in check only because he'd forced her to slow down. He hadn't found their speed yet, the one to keep them from missing the wave or wiping out. "Every day. Every goddamn day."

Plastic scraped on metal as Perry hauled a cooler from the far side and popped the hatch. He leveled his gaze, dark eyes with pinpoint sparks in a face shadowed by the travel trailer blocking most of the light behind him. "Then ask the questions you really want to ask. We've got a couple of minutes before she'll be over here busting my balls to hide how worried she is about this conversation."

Well shit. That was honest. And telling about how well the guy knew Katherine. "You two ever date?"

Perry snorted and shook his head. "Figured you'd go straight to that one." Rooting in the cooler, he pawed through crunching ice and sloshing water. "Not a chance in hell. I kissed her once, at a birthday party, in eighth grade, because the rules of the game shoved us in a closet together." He held out a dripping can of light beer. "We both made sour-lemon face and agreed our lips should never touch. Too much like kissing my sisters. Ick, weird, and unsexy."

Thank God. As he gripped the cold can, the tight heat in his chest fizzled. "I've got all brothers. We do less kissing, more punching."

"Same for me and her. Love taps, man." Perry beat his chest Tarzan-style, flicking icy water. "Kit could break me in half. Time we hit sixth grade, she topped me by a foot. I never caught up. I'll stick to the cute shorties." In his black jeans and layered black tees, with a spooky-shit skull logo on the trailer behind him, he crouched in the truck bed like a demonic gargoyle. "You spar with Ms. Badass Amazon. She'll only let you in the ring once."

The chill traveled up his arm. Worse than the heat. Jealousy over Katherine's friendship with this guy, improved data would quash. But the worry she wouldn't let him close to her heart? The fix for that trouble had to come from her, and she might choose the status quo over change. "Yeah, she's said that. She's really never had a long-term guy in her life?"

"Not even a high school sweetheart." Ducking his head, Perry sloshed in the cooler long enough to have dug to China. "She is fierce, man. Independent as all hell, and the best damn friend a scrawny guy could have to make it out of metal shop and vo-tech alive with his fingers and teeth intact, but falling in love is way the fuck outside her skill set. You want her to reach peak gooey-eyed awe, you're gonna have to teach her one step at a time. Practical demonstrations." He thrust a ginger ale over the wall. "Here. Bro-time's up." He swung down with his own beer in hand and wobbled the landing. "Fuuuck."

Brian juggled a fingertip hold on two chilled cans. "What fuck? You roll your ankle?"

Following Perry's gaze, he swung around and stepped wide of the trailer. Down the end, at the lit-up tent, a hulking SOB slapped Katherine's ass and held on.

Not. Happening.

He flipped the cans toward Perry and took off. Twenty-five feet. A solid charge would knock the fucker on his ass for his beating.

But Katherine—strong, sexy-as-hell Katherine—put the intruder down with a boot-stomp and a knee strike. The right placement would've made the move crippling. Even minus the necessary precision, the brawny fuckwit hopped backward and grabbed his shin.

Brian skidded to a stop a few feet shy. The way Katherine glared, she'd as likely snap at him as at the real problem. If her moves had dissuaded the guy, he'd leave well enough alone.

Flashing an insincere smile, the ass-slapper stuttered into a laugh. “Dishing out pain for foreplay? If that’s the way you want to play it this time, I won’t hold back. Should we go right here or take a trip to my place?”

Katherine drew herself up, the boots granting her extra height, and raised her chin. “Your place?” Her voice slid smooth as river stones despite the crackling fire in her eyes. “What, a rusted-out hunk of RV junk in the parking lot?”

The smug fuck leaned in, his stringy brown hair swinging across one eye. “Whatever winds your crank, Kitten.”

Brian launched forward.

The coward flinched, wide-eyed in retreat.

Katherine slammed her arm across Brian’s chest. “Brian—”

He muzzled trained instinct before his reflexive grab became a broken joint.

“—ignore him.” Flexing in his grasp, she threw glances between them. “This jackass isn’t worth the time or the bloody knuckles.”

The tatted-up jackass eyed her top to bottom. “Baby, you thought me worth the time in September. The parking lot was good enough for you then.”

“I was wrong.” Voice sour, she lost her there-and-gone smile. “Thanks for proving it again.”

“What, like blondie there—” Punk-ass nodded. “He’s gonna make you cream your panties? Slutty Kitten’s so hard up—”

“Watch your mouth.” With a reassuring squeeze, he lowered Katherine’s arm.

The punk smirked. “You think you can make me?”

“You think a cheesy tat and a nose ring make you a hardass?” He sidestepped to draw the fight away from Katherine. Perry, well clear, leaned against the car, and the three fellas watching from the neighboring tent didn’t seem inclined to jump in. “I’ve put down bigger guys.”

“Brian.” Katherine spun, her back to the damned enemy. “I can handle this. Grandpa Jake boxed, and he taught me. If anyone’s breaking their knuckles on this asshat’s smug face, it’s me.”

“Like any of you could—”

Clasping Katherine’s shoulders, he shut out the idiot’s whining and nudged her ’round toward safety. “You box?”

Her I’m-warning-you expression dissolved into a startled laugh. “A little.” She formed loose fists and pulled a pair of short jabs a hairsbreadth from his chest.

Fuck. Her knuckles needed kissing, her just-healed left wrist protecting from overzealous use.

"Fuckin' pussy." Sure as shit, Nose Ring lacked the skills to back up his mouth. "That what you are, Br-eye-an? Old pussy, standing by watching a woman fight for you?"

His fists had dropped him into the same sort of trouble, as a teenager. Rob had shoved him toward boxing, told him to lead with brains over brawn. But this guy—close to Katherine's age. Mid-twenties. A goddamn juvenile bad-boy poseur. What the fuck attracted her to that?

With a sly fucking smile, the punk leered at Katherine's breasts. "You planning to stand by and watch me bang her after, too?"

He forced himself to relax, to resist the urge to drag Katherine against him, hoist her onto the car, and demonstrate exactly who the guy fucking her would be. For the rest of her life. "When she says she can knock out one punk-ass bitch, I believe her. And if by some divine intervention she's wrong, you'll be licking oil off the gravel when I drop you anyway."

She'd get pissed at him for the jealous boyfriend routine. Rights she hadn't granted. Hell, if she decided to fuck jackasses as obnoxious as this one, he lacked the clout to cast a no vote.

"Don't think you're special. She's fucked half the guys at this place."

Accept her as she was or walk away. Fuck. He shouldn't have tossed Perry that beer.

Kit exhaled a bitter laugh. "When every guy comes up short, a girl's gotta keep looking for one that doesn't."

"You were singing a—"

"Hey, enough with the short jokes." Perry slung a beer at the punk. "Take this and schlep your ass back to your own bay. I know you're here snooping at my exhaust manifold. Carson's dying to get his hands on my setup."

Beer in hand, glancing from Kit to Perry, the fuckwit shrugged. "Nobody's looking up your tailpipe, little man." He cracked the can and guzzled.

Perry studied the two drinks he had left.

The ginger ale came flying in, and Brian snatched the can before it would've smacked him in the chest. Love at first sight walloped harder. How the fuck he'd missed recognizing the feeling—and this damn punk hadn't even appreciated her when he'd had her.

Kit grabbed Brian by the forearm. "Great to see you, Perry. Next week, okay?" She stalked down the aisle and crossed into the next.

Brian wrenched his arm free before they reached the gate. Fuck if he'd be dragged home like a tantrum-throwing child. The fuck had she been thinking, bringing him to her hunting grounds.

Every smiling face they passed, every gut-busting laugh bellowing from the guys gathered around the racecars—potentially a man who'd fucked her first. Who'd fucked her at all. She'd never ask him for more than a single night. And he'd thought she wanted him to meet her friend, for fuck's sake, not show him how little he meant to her. More fool he. Dashed hopes stung as sharp as the stench of burnt rubber.

They crossed the parking lot. A long walk to the back. Empty spaces dotted the rows. A wasteland of spilled soda cups and program books. Nothing left but the trash.

"Did you bring me here to wave all these dicks in my face?" Fuck. Those words, fuck, they shouldn't have left his mouth.

The car keys fell. She chased them to the ground, her head bowed. Scooping them up, she scraped her knuckles across the stones.

"So what if I did?" Crouched and still, she kept her face hidden and her voice hard. "You want to drop the damn celibacy idea now, Brian?"

Fuck, fuck, fuck. Rein in the boiling anger and the stupid fucking little-boy hurt.

She shot to her feet and unlocked the car. Yanking open the back door, she waved with auto-show model flair. "You want a go? I'm a backseat girl, doncha know? Quick and dirty, and never the same guy twice."

"You—" He snapped his teeth shut on his tongue. Just his luck to fall for the most frustrating woman on the planet. Maybe that's what love was—frustration and determination. When walking away wouldn't work and you had to commit your whole heart or forever be a coward and a failure. Except he had to convince her to commit hers, too, or his wouldn't be worth shit.

Katherine stood trembling. A pane of glass about to shatter. From her hand on the frame, her overly tight top-grip, an invisible network of cracks spread across a too-brittle surface.

She'd told him. A hundred times, a hundred ways, she'd told him the fantasy of a relationship he'd pinned to his heart wouldn't happen.

And he'd pushed, and he'd pushed, and now he'd broken her. He ached to pull her into his arms, wrap himself around her, and promise her more didn't have to be scary. He'd be the wax, or the duct tape, or whatever the fuck she needed to smooth the edges and hold her together until the repairs grew permanent.

He reached for her. To cup her cheek. To soften her wide-eyed stare. "Katherine."

Gasping, she flinched away.

His chest ripped open and stopped his breath. His heart's fantasy shredded. She didn't trust him to heal instead of harm.

As he backed up, she guided the door shut. The latch clicked.

"Front seats." She looked everywhere but him. "I'll take you home."

Silence filled the car. Like he'd pulled the cord on an emergency float and the thing kept expanding, stealing the unused space and the air besides. He sat with an unopened can of ginger ale on his knee as she drove and the pavement droned.

He had ten minutes before she shoved him out the door. Less, the way she tore down the highway toward his place. They'd have lights and sirens after them at this rate.

She clenched the steering wheel in both hands. They'd lost the easy laughter. The knee brushes. The ear-grazing proto-kisses. She should've been enjoying a drink in a camp chair under her buddy's tent, the three of them kicking back and talking shit. They'd have walked away with smiles. A deeper friendship, a better appreciation of each other—a basis for more.

Instead, he had fresh images of hell. Katherine shaking and moaning while that smug punk used her without giving a damn about her. Her calling his name when she came.

Except—she hadn't. Not once had she said the guy's name. She might not know his name.

He ought to adopt Sherwood's old motto: looking for love in all the wrong places. They'd been drinking to the end of Rob's relationship with—fuck, who could remember names?—with that woman who'd cheated on him years ago. Rob had sworn to steal his attitude the next time around, and he'd said his was—

Get in, get off, get out. Never the same girl twice.

Oh God. Queasy stomach-taste hit the back of his throat. Swallowing hard, he popped the ginger ale open. He nursed the drink with slow sips.

A hypocritical fuck, that's what he was. He'd told her he didn't care about the guys in her past, and the first flipping second one showed up, he'd made a liar of himself. Laid a double standard across her shoulders. She went out and fucked who she wanted when she wanted, and if she'd been one of his bros, he would've cheered her.

She glanced over three times. Little looks as he sipped. "Are you okay?"

He would have to be. Accept what she felt able to share with him now, if she still wanted to have any contact with him, and stop pressuring her for the commitment and certainty he craved. The down-the-road when he'd wake up beside her every morning for the rest of their lives. When. Not if.

He raised the pop can. "A toast."

Eyebrow flitting skyward, she tipped her head.

"To a woman who knows what she wants and won't stop until she finds it." He watched her over the can as he drank.

She slowed, taking the turn-off from the highway, and reached for the drink when the road straightened out. Her gentle tilt screamed polite sip. She set the pop in the console cupholder. "You're a nice guy, Brian."

Here it came, the parade of reasons why they'd forever be wrong for each other. He choked on his laugh. "Why do I think every time you say that, you don't mean it as a compliment?"

Twisting her mouth, she almost managed a believable smile. "Because you're too smart by half." As she lowered her window, cool night air rushed through the stifling atmosphere they'd built between them. "Nice guys are more dangerous than losers. Charm hides a lot."

Arguing with her defined a no-win situation. Be a loser, and she might fuck him but discard him. Be a nice guy, and she'd imagine devious calculations going on inside his head. Forget boxing. He should've studied for the damn debate team. Reframing the issue would be the prime strategy to get anywhere with her.

She acted as if she'd never met a truly nice guy. Bullshit.

"You pigeonhole all guys as deadbeats and losers and say the 'nice' ones hide the lies better, but what about your dad?" They ran a business together. She had to have bonded with him over work, at least. "He's still around, still with your mom, and teaching you after how many years?"

She started shaking her head long before he'd finished talking. "Different generation. People were different then."

"Oh, so not all guys are dicks—just all of them under forty." Great. In three years, he might qualify for not-a-dick status.

Speeding up, she cruised beneath a light turning red. "Fifty."

Should've seen her smart-ass retort coming a mile off. He dropped his head to his chest. Busting his knuckles on the glove box wouldn't solve a damn thing.

"You are the most combative woman I've ever met." And the first—second—*first* he'd loved with his eyes open. He sucked in a hard breath. "Your sister got handed a shitty deal, but other options exist. Different outcomes. Better ones."

She turned into the driveway leading up to his sprawling apartment complex. Seconds left at best. Another outing, another failure. The definition of insanity, taking the same actions and expecting different results.

Slamming her hand on the wheel, she jammed on the brakes in front of the walkway to his building. "How can I know the difference? Fall in love, get married, have kids and then, what, if the guy's hanging around five years later, he's not an asshole? Lucky me, I picked a good one from a random, blindfolded drawing."

Arms outstretched, nearly touching the windshield, she bowed her head.

"Katherine." Fuck. He didn't have a satisfying answer for her. Cracking a joke about her knowing he didn't want kids would gloss over her pain. The weighty undercurrent of defeat beneath her anger. He'd reached her, rattled her, and he had no goddamn plan in place to steady her world again.

Unmoving, she sat with the engine running and her eyes closed.

The seat belt tightened across his chest. Stabbing the damn release, he freed himself and banged his knee on the gearshift trying to get closer. "Talk to me. Please."

"I need you to go." Hollow-voiced, she raised her head and stared out the windshield. "I'm not—this conversation—I need you to go."

And he needed her to stay. His throat burned.

He pulled the door latch twice before the metal and plastic let go. The door creaked out an invitation to end whatever the thing was between them. Killed before they'd been able to name it. He swung his legs out and grabbed the roof handle. His shaky bones demanded the support.

"Brian?"

He froze.

Her breath hitched. "You're more than a condom wrapper on the floor mats."

Her quiet, wobbly words rearranged themselves into *I love you* in his heart. Big, scary words fixed to drop them into another argument or send her fleeing faster than she already was.

Staring across the well-kept lawn and the trimmed hedges, he saw nothing but the woman behind him. The one he dared not look at. "You're not a backseat girl, Katherine." Fuck, how long since he'd prayed—a true prayer, a plea for God to make her believe in him. "You never were. You're the driver. You deserve to be the driver."

He launched out and closed the door without looking back. A glimpse of her and he'd lose it.

One foot in front of the other, all the way to the apartment. *Keep walking, airman.*

* * * *

Straight-backed, he disappeared into his building.

Her legs refused to ditch the car and follow him. Her throat rejected her order to open and call him back. Her fingers insisted they didn't know how to compose a text.

Not a backseat girl. His words, his truth, but not hers.

After ten years of being nothing else, she wore the name with pride. Didn't she?

"You let a habit go long enough, and it becomes who you are." Her voice came out rough and raw, a whisper yearning to become a shout.

She threw the car in drive and left with less haste than she'd arrived. She'd wanted the passenger seat empty anyway. A fool's wish. The silence accused as much as Brian's persistent picking away at her beliefs. At her.

Even if she wanted to be the woman he imagined her, she wouldn't know how. Her control systems locked out the capabilities for happiness and trust in a relationship. Accepting he operated the way he claimed to without cracking the case and testing his wires for herself would be impossible. Easier to classify all men under sex-only. Simpler.

Northbound on a rural route, she escaped the lights and traffic of the populated outskirts where the twenty-four-hour conveniences lived. The darkness, cut by no more than the twin lines of headlights, embraced her.

Saturday nights belonged to her alone. She didn't pick up a disposable guy every week. Hell, not most weeks. But some nights, a woman needed to be touched by hands not her own. To be surprised and delighted by unpredictability.

Brian touched her with that spark. He made her feel desired. Her, not a set of boobs and a hole to fuck. He saw more than a faceless body. Wanted to be more than a pair of strong hands and a filling cock for her aching, thumping need.

Sex as more than stress relief when the demands of the world got to be too much. With the men she fucked, she took control. Brian brought his own needs and creativity to the table. Sexy and furtive, he turned arousal into a partnership with his capable hands and his hot breath.

She hit a stop sign, finally. Silly to roam so far, to blow the gas budget on aimless wandering to nurse her Brian hangover.

He'd left the ginger ale, the open can at her side. Warm now, and going flat, with the rim leaving a hint of metallic aftertaste. Jesus. She sat at the fucking crossroads in the dead of night sampling the memory of his mouth like her nieces giggling over boys on their phones. Middle-school mentality.

But driving home, she touched her lips again and again. Rubbing with her fingers, she imagined the taste of him.

She showered away the clinging scents of exhaust and oil without dallying. Muted and melancholy, her faded desire lay like an ache beneath her ribs and flared as she crawled under the covers in sleep shorts and a cozy tank top. Sleep wouldn't come, and neither could she.

The room where she'd lived her whole life. Her closet, stuffed with nuts and bolts going back to childhood. A place Brian would never belong. Safe. Comforting. Stifling.

She retreated to the garage, to projects lying piecemeal in neat rows on bleached rags. But the rhythms of work, too, failed to drive away the emptiness and wondering.

The living room couch offered safe haven, as soft as the blank TV screen was silent. The cable box kept the time creeping forward in blue-white numbers. The hour crossed past three, past four, into five. Pre-dawn light filtered through the shades.

As a door closed in the hall, she slouched into the cushions. Since the spots had invaded Mom's vision, she liked to be the first to rise. She started her mornings with the sun, watching the parade of pastels crest the horizon. Storing them up, just in case, for the eventual day when the blackness consumed her.

The toilet flushed and the sink whistled. Ought to check the washers again, maybe replace the valve stem this time. Mom walked soft on the carpet, but she trailed her hand along the wall as a hedge against falling, and the skip-rub-rustle led into the kitchen.

Unseen. Kit hugged a pillow to her chest. Brian would be a spooner, for sure. All cuddly and sincere. He didn't dwarf her, either. They might share the big-spoon duties. Trade off for fairness.

As the coffee maker kicked on in the kitchen, she slid sideways and tucked her feet up. Back wriggled into place against the cushions, she evaluated. Brian would be firmer, and not only in his pants. He took care of himself. Boxing might have given him his toned abs and muscular arms. He'd sure seemed surprised when she mentioned learning a few moves. Before the night had slammed into the wall and burst into flames.

They'd saved themselves at the end, though, hadn't they? Another chance, if she dared to keep playing with fire.

The thing he'd said about Dad staying. Mom had made a choice, and she'd chosen right.

A fresh direction for her restless energy. She rolled off the couch, pitched the pillow into the corner, and went to learn the secret.

The patio door stood open, the screen pulled shut to keep the bugs out. A second mug waited on the frosted glass tabletop. Cushioned chair angled east, Mom held her coffee below her nose. "I wondered if you were going to admit you were awake. If you stayed up all night, you'll want the caffeine."

Of course, Mom would've noticed. The couch slouch maneuver always failed. Kit dropped into the open seat and cradled the ceramic warmth. They sipped in silence as the clouds turned lavender, then pink, in thick bands racing each other to the edge of the world.

"How did you know Dad was the right man for you?" The last time she'd started such a stilted, awkward conversation with her mom, she'd been eleven years old, and Erin had her half-convinced she'd bleed to death in seven days if she didn't learn to flip over and walk on her hands.

Head tipped back, gaze on the horizon, Mom smiled. "He danced with me at my cousin's wedding."

"Mo-om. I know the story of how you met." A thousand thousand tellings she'd rolled her eyes and turned up her nose at. Love. How disgusting when parents held the starring roles. "I want to know how you knew."

"I'm telling you." Mom sipped slowly. Settling unevenly, her coffee mug clanked against the table. "We talked to each other. Face to face, not through screens the way they do today. We found common interests and shared values. Long before he worked up the nerve to ask me out, I knew I'd say yes."

Dew glittered on the grass between the concrete patio and the dark soil of the garden. Created in the night, the sparkling carpet disappeared in the morning. Fleeting beauty, burning off under the sun.

"But how did you know he'd stay?" Some sequence of events must have revealed Dad's worthiness. His honesty, his commitment. If Mom had traced all of the wires back to their sources and found them sound, she could use the same method to search out Brian's faults. "That he'd keep his promises?"

Mom twitched. She stared at Kit, not quite straight on, but with the sideways tilt that said she was really studying her. She wore a soft expression, the outer corners of her eyes and mouth sloping down.

"Oh, honey." She snaked her hand across the table, found Kit's fingers, and squeezed. Strength. Mom still had it in spades, though her hands carried lines now, and her knuckles had grown more prominent. "I didn't."

Nobody would take that bet. Her heart pounded. "But—"

"Love is a risk." Mom nodded, slow and thoughtful, her gaze distant. "A big, scary risk. If you take it, you might get hurt. But if you don't, you'll never grow." Rocking their clasped hands, she swayed in the warming air. "Do you remember, you were just four—I found the kitchen stepstool dragged to the counter and the toaster missing. The door to the garage stood open, and out on the dirty slab you sat, half your father's old toolbox scattered next to you, and a pile of plastic and metal in front. Do you remember what you told me?"

God, that morning. She'd clamped the machine between her feet and twisted the screwdriver in both hands to crack open a box of wonders. "I wanted to see what made the toast jump."

Matching smiles dissolved into giggles.

Mom had called the shop. Dad had brought home a working toaster. The parental talking-to about not destroying things from the house had been completely undercut by Grandpa Jake.

He'd perched her on his lap after dinner, with the toaster's remains spread out on the table, and given her her first lesson in repair, tsking at the screwdriver scrapes around the holes. "We leave things prettier than we found them, Kitten. The best parts, the parts that do the hard work, are on the inside where no one else sees them. But you'll know."

Mom patted her hand. "You've always been my bold baby. Taking chances, adventuring because you needed to know. You grew closer to your father and your grandpa, and I let you go because you loved the work so much." The breeze carried her sigh toward the sun. "But maybe I should've taught you more about the things a father has trouble explaining to a daughter."

She'd been daddy's girl—grandpa's girl—since that day with the toaster. Mom and Erin had their female bonding stuff, and she hadn't pined for the lack of girl talk all those years. "I never asked. I never needed to."

Not before Brian.

Raising a speculative eyebrow, Mom flashed her I-know-you've-been-in-the-cookie-jar face. "Love is an amazing gift, honey. If you think you've found it, don't let fear stop you. A bruised heart is no different from a skinned knee or a blistered finger. It heals."

Erin's hadn't healed. Her heart had grown callused and bitter. But maybe she hadn't let the wounds heal. Love might not always end in disaster.

Trying to avoid painful complications hadn't helped with Brian. Arguing with him hurt. The churning questions in a sleepless night stung. Not seeing him again would slice through her. She took a deep breath. "You'll put a Band-Aid on and kiss it better?"

"Always." Mom pushed herself to her feet and waved her in. "Kissing things better is on the first page of the mom contract."

Kit took the hug on offer, clutching tight. Moms did make everything better, no matter how tall daughters grew.

The sun, strong and bright, rode the horizon. The long night lay behind her. Something new and unknown lay ahead.

"C'mon and help your old mother in the garden." Mom tugged her down and dropped a kiss on her forehead. "The weeds need a strong, young back to clear them out so the seeds worth nurturing can grow."

* * * *

As the rhythm settled in his muscles, Brian moved with mindless instinct. The speed bag rebounded against his gloves, the force it delivered as measured as his own.

The office stayed open 'round the clock, seven days a week, and so did the gym. Sunday afternoon didn't draw much of a crowd. A few guys down the other end worked the weight machines, filling the room with the clanking white noise of unhurried reps. The pair in the ring sparred with laughing taunts broken up by the occasional thud and groan.

He had the bags to himself. On the speed bag, the power and timing of each punch had to be spot-on. Too little, and the rhythm would never come together. Too much, and he'd send it careening in unpredictable arcs and lose their equilibrium.

He hadn't found Katherine's balance yet. He moved too slowly for her liking. But she wasn't tethered. Hooked in. If she went bouncing off in an unexpected direction, he couldn't clasp her in his hands and steady her for another try.

She might never come back.

His arms ached. Every time she darted away, he tried to hold on tighter. His brilliant strategy landed him nowhere but the gym, working out his frustration. Saturday—Christ. Last night had been a clusterfuck. He'd demanded a date, and he'd gotten what he deserved for pushing her.

He should've turned down the blowjob last week. He shouldn't have turned fooling around into a transaction. The intimacy he wanted with her couldn't be forced, not in one date, not in a hundred dates. She either felt the connection or she didn't.

His phone vibrated through the ass pocket on his gym shorts. Text message. Maybe a plea for help from someone upstairs who'd seen him logged in on the intranet roster and needed a second opinion for a time-sensitive project. Data mining would take his mind off Katherine. Better than boxing was doing, anyhow.

He stilled the bag and stepped back. With teeth and elbow grease, he stripped off his gloves. A nice, fat project to work on. Perfect. He slipped the phone from his pocket.

Katherine looked out at him, her photo capturing her mid-laugh from their store picnic. *So our night out didn't go how I thought it would. Maybe you can pick the place next time? Say, Saturday?*

Holy fucking—his gloves smacked the floor. A do-over. Yes, thank Christ, yes. He scrambled to compose an answer, fingers flying across the screen. Maybe their talk in the car had touched a nerve in her. Maybe she'd felt the *I love you* as much as he had. Enter and erase. Too goddamn eager. Too standoffish. Fuck fuck fuck.

"Hey." One of the guys in the ring bounced his arms on the top rope. "Hey, I know you."

Not well enough to interrupt the most important minute of his day. "We work for the same company, and we're in the company gym." A friendly note, but without sounding desperate. Katherine respected strength and confidence. "That's not mind-blowing, buddy."

I'm happy to pick the place. Saturday sounds great.

Send. Too late to call his words back now. Maybe he should've admitted last night had been a disappointment to him, too. Or reassured her the whole mess hadn't been her fault. But he'd wanted so bad to punch that asshat hassling her. Riling her up, calling her names as if he had any right to judge. Fuck, his fingers clenched into a fist thinking on it.

"Hey, man, you wanna go?" Feet dancing, boxer boy swung his arms toward the opponent rolling out under the ropes. "This dude's pussying out, and I'm good for another beatdown."

"I'm busy." Waiting on a reply to—shit, he hadn't asked a question. Maybe she wouldn't acknowledge receipt without a question. He tapped one out and hit send in a hurry.

Should I plan to pick you up?

She'd have to hand over her address for that. Dammit. Too much, since she apparently didn't like guys knowing where to find her. Good reasoning, for dicks like the one from the track. A policy she'd change, someday, for him. When she felt comfortable.

"Your phone giving you a good workout?" The lone boxer paced along the ropes. Six feet, maybe one eighty, brown fade. "Fucking pussy. S'what I thought. You were all chickenshit at softball, too. Walk away, man."

Fuck, that's where he knew him from. The mouthy new-hire weasel from the dugout. He still deserved a good whupping, and the ring made it nice and proper.

"I'm talking to my girlfriend here." One word with a goddamn truckload of meaning. She might not agree on the terminology yet, but the classification rang true in his heart. "I'll give you a beatdown in a minute."

"That sweet piece? Thought she wasn't your girlfriend. You nail her yet?"

He ignored the bravado and bluster from the ring, waiting on his phone to vibrate. The screen refreshed before the shake came.

I'll meet you at your place, and you can drive from there. Let me know when.

Not a total victory, not a true pick-her-up-at-home date, but her willingness to put herself in his hands for a night sure as fuck wasn't a loss.

You got it. Let's say 8.

Early enough for whatever plans he might hash out between now and Saturday. Her agreement came swift. He scooped up his gloves, laid his phone on the bench, and climbed into the ring. "You ready for that beatdown? I've got time now."

More mindless, easy physical exertion would be a fine distraction while he processed his new problem.

The perfect first date.

Something spectacular, amazing, to make Katherine understand her importance to him. Big and flashy, a real knockout with a message impossible for her to miss.

New-hire asshat dove in with a swing hard, swing fast approach. Blind with the frenzy of inexperience, he must've figured the more punches he threw, the more likely one would land.

Brian took his time. Watched his footwork. Waited for the opening. When the moment came, he got in close, absorbed the body blows, and launched a low uppercut square to the solar plexus.

The cocky-as-fuck kid dropped to the mat. Gasping, he kicked his legs in a defensive retreat and hugged his chest.

The guy last night would've deserved a boot-stomp follow-up. This idiot, though—not worth the time.

"Crouch, kid. Deep breaths. You'll get your air back." He ducked under the top rope and gathered his shit, keeping one eye on the kid. Not likely he'd damaged a rib, but he'd hang back another minute to be sure the new hire didn't panic and pass out. After that, though, he had plans to make. Crucial, rest-of-his-life plans. "You need another lesson, you know where to find me."

Chapter 6

Using the guest passcode Brian had sent to her phone, Kit slipped into his building at five to eight on Saturday night.

Swanky, inside and out. The prairie tech boom had brought modern glass-and-steel high rises to compete with the water towers and grain silos. At seven stories, the place was one of the tallest in the county after the vacant hotel downtown.

She rode the elevator to the fifth floor. One more way Brian outclassed her. The damn dress she'd borrowed—okay, outright stolen—from the back of Mom's closet had better be good enough for whatever romantic night on the town he had lined up. The girls had gone nuts, ooo-ing and ahh-ing with way-too-knowing teases about her dressing up for a boy as she hustled out the door.

Tight jeans and a camisole top had always formed the basis for her seductions. Tonight, though—the sleeveless copper-brown dress, tasteful but sexy. The sling-back black heels. The stockings, Jesus. Sheer black and thigh-high, they left a gap of bare skin below her panties. If he meant to make his restaurant booth talk a reality, she'd be ready, aside from the underwear. No telling what Brian would've said if she'd actually gone without and he'd discovered them missing.

She rapped hard below the ornate fifty-seven on his door. The silver numerals complemented the hallway's dove-gray walls, a subdued, high-end hotel look as soothing as brushed metal. She might as well soak up the comfort now. Once he whisked her off to dating hell, experience told her the night would turn into a pointless chore of hidden agendas—the nice-guy subterfuge designed to land her in his bed. Except he refused to fuck her, so his insistence on wooing her made no sense. She made no sense. Together, they made even less sense than that. But she couldn't stop coming back for more.

The door swept open.

"Welcome to Chez Brian." He'd shaved off his patchy blond beard. Smooth face frozen in a grin, he eyed her with the concussion-victim blankness he'd shown the moment they'd met. "Christ, you look amazing. I mean, you always do, but—" He shook his head.

If she'd known then he'd been knocked out by her and not the accident, hell. They might've been fucking in his backseat before the last rays of sunlight sank under the horizon. She could've managed the tire by flashlight. Part of her wanted the missed opportunity back. But the rest of her, the scary and growing part, promised they'd have another chance. Maybe many chances.

As her feet flexed in the tight shoes, he waved her forward. "*Entrez-vous, entrez.*"

Bowing as he backed up, he flashed a multicolored nightmare of non-seduction. His lucky shorts formed the centerpiece of an otherwise formal outfit.

Holy fuck.

He'd tucked his white dress shirt into the elastic waistband and tied the drawstrings in a neat bow. The rich, deep plum shade of his tie almost made the whole crazy ensemble match. Or would have, if he hadn't pulled black dress socks up over his calves to match his shiny black dress shoes.

Laughter bent her near in half as she gripped her stomach. Oh God. She struggled to stand up. What a ridiculous man. Bare knees and all.

"We have a short wait for a table this evening." He kept his poise with what had to be military training, because no fucking way would any normal person hold a straight face so well. "May I offer you a beverage from our extensive drink menu? Would the mademoiselle care for a glass of water before giggles become hiccups?"

The slurring buzz he seemed to think turned him into a credible French maitre d' intensified the unshakeable laugh attack. Closing her eyes to avoid glimpsing the riot shorts got her nowhere when his teasing assaulted her ears, too. She landed a hand on his shoulder in her blind search for support to stay upright.

He curled his arm around her, his hold sturdy and warm. "You sound happy." So did he. Accent dropped, he reclaimed pure Brian. "You want to cross the threshold? I can carry the table into the hallway if you want, but it's probably a fire hazard."

Deep breaths got her laughter under control and wrapped her in his crisp rainstorm fragrance with its ozone-sharp edge. Trust Brian to concoct a date that circumvented all of her expectations. "So I guess we're staying in?"

As she stepped into the main room, his hand fell from her back. The missing warmth left a cold spot behind.

"Staying in, yeah." He rubbed his hair from the back of his neck up. "I thought it'd be more comfortable with just us. No awkward small talk about restaurant menus and whether the waiter's still in high school."

Takeout containers and empty plates stood stacked beside a bag from Mancini's, the fancy bistro down on Fifth. His kitchen hardly merited the name—more a nook than anything. But the rest of the living-dining room sprawled to a wall of tinted windows, beside which he'd set a table for two. Beyond the glass, a fat bend in the river separated them from the downtown lighting up as dusk stretched in the valleys where sunset's slender fingers couldn't reach.

She gravitated toward the view. Home had never looked so serene. "It's beautiful."

"I tried to get the sun to cooperate, but the eastern exposure wasn't so accommodating." As the door thudded into the frame, Brian's voice grew louder. "My neighbor across the hall refused to switch apartments for the night. Would've upset her cat, she said."

"Can't have that." The table boasted a cloth with embroidered scroll edging thrown over the top, far fancier than the quick-serve places she hit up most often. A man's dinner jacket hung across the back of one chair. She rubbed the stiff shoulder between her fingers. Fresh from the dry cleaners, neatly pressed. "At first glance, this restaurant seems pretty high quality. But I have to tell you…"

She waited for him to get closer.

The hint of panic in his eyes exited his mouth. "Tell me what?"

Leaning sideways, she whispered, "I don't think your host is French. I think he's faking the accent."

With a jerk, he shook loose a handful of chuckles. "That scoundrel! I'll fire him right away and serve dinner myself. Does that work for you?"

"Sure does." The wall above the couch boasted a surfboard as colorful as his shorts. Maybe he'd share more stories about his adventures on the lake. Brian's late-season surfing had to be at least half as crazy as Grandpa Jake's annual insistence on ice fishing from Christmas through the spring thaw. But they'd dined on a chest freezer full of walleye, crappie, and bluegill every year until this one. "What are we having?"

Brian clapped his hands together and hustled into the kitchen nook. “Well. You have your choice of main dishes.” The plastic lids unsnapped with two pops. “We have steak and pasta—” He managed a decent drum roll on the counter. “Or pasta and steak.”

With his legs hidden behind the low cupboards, he impersonated a proper date. One who might have dress pants on below his collared shirt and subdued tie. But those guys, the ones who wouldn’t grin the way Brian did as he scooped pasta between two forks and dropped it on plates without pretending in the least that he’d made the meal himself? Those guys bored her. Brian sometimes pissed her off, scared her, surprised her, impressed her, and touched raw nerves, but he sure as fuck didn’t bore her.

“I’ll take the pasta and steak, please.” The furniture lacked the flair of his shorts and board. Maybe the neutral ivories and grays of the couch and chairs had come with the apartment. “I’m feeling that more than the steak and pasta.”

“Excellent choice. Coming right up. And I wasn’t kidding about the drinks—I’ve got four kinds of beer in the fridge, plus hard cider and water.”

“Beer’s good.” The coffee table held an odd assortment of clutter. Framed photos. A yearbook pinned open beneath a shot of what had to be a younger Brian with his arm around his friend Rob’s throat, the two of them in dark blue uniforms. A stuffed tiger missing an ear.

Brian ahem-ed. Spinning a fork in one hand, he waved toward her with the other. “Thanks for taking tonight seriously, Katherine. I know you weren’t sure about—” Squaring his shoulders, he dropped his arms to his sides. “About all of this.”

How a man who stood so solid and unyielding carried his heart in his eyes remained a mystery. Fuck. This Brian, sweet and vulnerable and ready-to-serve, somehow coexisted with the Brian who’d finger-fuck her into oblivion in the back room. With the one who’d allow her to pin him down and tease him to explosive heights, but not until after he demanded a date in exchange. A smart man, a canny one, and a joker besides.

“You’re welcome.” The engine driving this non-relationship had room on the wheel for both of their hands. She steered toward safer waters, ones where he didn’t look like a man about to spill dangerous confessions. “And thank you for taking it not so seriously. With the shorts, and the takeout. You make me laugh, but in a smart way. Not a clown way. You’re—”

A good man. More than a fake shell.

Her pulse leapt ahead, pumping her full of something more potent than the simple mechanics lust set in motion. Far beyond what she wanted to talk about with him on a first date.

The coffee table clutter offered a conversational escape route. She snatched the closest photo frame and gripped for dear life. Fuck, the filigreed metal edge would leave an imprint in her palm. "So, what's with all the—"

A skinny little boy straddled a Big Wheel. Blue and gray streamers hung from the handlebars he gripped with preschool intensity. His jeans bore an army green patch across one knee. In an oversized denim jacket, he came as close to badass biker as a toddler with blond ringlet curls and a wide grin ever would.

"Oh my God, is this you? Your hair is so curly." The curls tumbled across his forehead and over his ears. He would've been the baby getting his cheeks pinched by a parade of aunts, family friends, and strangers at the grocery store.

"Yeah, that's me." He paused and glanced over her shoulder before waltzing past with salad plates. "Right before my big brother Matt dumped my ass off and hogged the trike for the whole afternoon."

She and Erin hadn't fought over toys much. The six years between them cushioned the overlap, so by the time she wanted something, Erin had already disdained to play with it anyway. Erin's girls, though. Jesus. Mom and Dad still sent them to separate corners at least once a week. "Your folks didn't stop him?"

"Naw." He headed back to the kitchen empty-handed. "We got shooed out the door and told to play nice. Dad worked long days at the plant, and Mom had my younger brother to mind."

"Lucas?" That couldn't be right. Way too young.

"Nope. Lucas was the surprise baby." He snatched the entrée plates and made another pass to the table. His shorts swung above his bare knees, and his dress socks slid down his calves with every step. "Long before him, it was Matt, me, and Jason. Two years from Matt to me, and another year from me to Jason. We ran Mom ragged."

"You, obviously, were the adorable one." She laid the frame down gently and picked up the tiger. A man sharing his baby photos while wearing the ugliest outfit on the planet shouldn't be so fucking sexy. And yet. Every time he walked by from delivering another piece of dinner, she fought not to grab his tie and drag him against her. The heat throbbing in her breasts had permission to stop anytime. Now would be great.

"Golden wheat good?" Shouting from the fridge, he lifted the bottles over his head. "I've got a trendy chocolate stout to go with dessert."

"Golden wheat, yeah." Ruffling the tiger's rust-orange fur, she snorted. "Matches your hair, ringlet boy."

"Ohhh, direct hit." He carried the beers over and stopped behind her, dangling one across her shoulder. "Now you know why I don't grow my hair out. Toss a sailor suit on me, and I'd pass for one of those historical society photos of little lord so-and-so."

Especially without the beard. He had nine years on her, but he gave off an electrical charge of smooth-cheeked youth. She spared one hand from the soft tiger to take her beer. "So what's with the trip down memory lane?"

"First date, right?" He shrugged and sipped from his bottle. "My mom's not here to do the honors, so embarrassing myself is a necessity."

"I think your socks have that covered." Nice. She flashed a smile to sell the distraction. Forcing herself to see goofy Brian instead of fuck-me Brian might let her survive this without ruining his desire for a no-pressure, non-sexy night out. Or in. Or in and out. Fuck, no, desire belonged to her, not him.

Leaning back, he studied his legs. "You're right. I should've worn the sock garters. It's falling-down amateur hour over here." He eyed her legs and rolled the lip of his bottle against his mouth. "I don't suppose you have a pair you can loan me. Your stockings hug you the way the water hugs the shore."

"In lapping waves?" The words flew out faster than her lips closed to stop them. Too much, too soon, too *her*.

He flicked the bottle with his tongue. "If the stockings are that good, I'll have to up my game to compete."

Thank God she'd worn the panties. Her body refused to separate silly-shorts Brian from demanding backroom Brian, and both seemed determined to get her wet. Hadn't he wanted a sex-free date, though? For her to stop looking at him as a single-use sex toy. Memory teased, coy and elusive.

"Anyway, my mom got a notion last year to clean up the house." His voice lighter, easier, he reached across her and rubbed the tiger's head. "She boxed all the shit my brothers and me had left behind and shipped us the results, along with copies she had made of the family album for each of us."

"And this fierce fellow was your best buddy?" Neat orange stitches marked the ragged line where the left ear should have been. The kind of patient work a loving mom would do. "He looks like he tangled with a closet monster or two."

Brian snorted. "I did manage to lock Matt in a closet once or twice, but no. Stripes lost the ear in a car tussle." He eased the tiger from her hold. "Matt got his hands on him and bit down. Ripped the ear loose and spat it out the window. We had a bumpy rivalry, a lot of one-upsmanship." Rubbing the ear scar, he bent and set Stripes on the coffee table. "But I idolized him for a long time."

He might as well have sighed. The hint of pain floated in his voice. The ache in her chest urged her to find the source and soothe his hurt. Not her usual skill set with guys. "So that's your big tragedy? A chewed-off tiger ear?"

Smooth. Total fucking classy nurturing-woman move right there.

"My what?" Well, confusion was a start.

She elbowed him in the side. Fuck, he didn't give an inch with his solid wall of muscle. "C'mon, you mean you don't have a dark secret you want to confess to make me feel all sorry for you and drop my panties? You know, your 'getting laid' tragedy."

Every guy had one. She tried to cut them off before they opened their mouths, because their scars weren't hers to fix. And they were bullshit anyway, the calculated move of a guy aiming to score sympathy points from a wishy-washy date who either didn't want the sex or wouldn't admit that she did. The upfront, wanna-fuck approach eliminated the need for lying and posturing.

"What, like my mom died or my uncle molested me? Or I was the sole survivor of a post-prom car crash that killed my one true love?" He took a long swig of his beer. "Is that the crap you expect to sit through? No wonder you hate dating."

"Good start." She nodded and waved in a firm command, the sort she imagined he'd been trained to follow for years. "Go on."

She actually wanted him to share. Fuck, now she needed a deep drink.

"Sorry, nothing like that. I'm your average fucked-up human, not deeply tormented."

She sucked down a third of the bottle. Still didn't change the curiosity gears clanking into motion, flaking off rust and shaking loose dust in her head. Something about Brian merited more consideration than her typical sexual conquests. He'd tweaked her settings somehow when she wasn't looking.

"But." He unwrapped his index finger from the neck of the bottle and pointed at her. "My mom did lose me in a department store once. It was incredibly traumatic." He nodded with solemn dignity, his eyebrows raised and his lips narrowed. "For her."

She'd wandered off more than her fair share of times, but she'd been easy to find—playing in the hardware aisles, building piles of junk the clerks would have to sort out later. "For real?"

He burst into laughter. “Not that bad. We made it home in one piece. I’ll tell you over dinner.”

“I’m not done yet.” Leaving her bottle on a coaster for safekeeping, she dragged out the open yearbook. “Class photos?”

A teenage Brian Hendricks stared out at her from beneath a faux-hawk, the sides of his head almost fully shaved and a two-inch-wide strip of springy curls on top. His shirt, a black tee with half a logo showing, sported a finger-sized hole under the seam at the neck. Of course, the hole probably went unnoticed by most people, given the fat bike chain draped around his neck.

“Yeah, that’s me, senior year. Complete stud, aren’t I?” He tugged her arm. “You hungry? We wait too long, the food’ll get cold. I don’t know a lot about cooking, but I know some about eating.”

“Hang on.” She flipped the pages in a fat heap. Pictures were fun, sure, but everyone knew the messages from friends held all the secrets. The kids in her class had fought the move to digital yearbooks and won. The hardbound copy with its cryptic notes still brought back memories. “I wanna see what your friends said about you.”

“The usual. That we’d hang together all summer. That we’d never forget.” Folding his hand around the top edge, he laughed. “Stupid kid stuff from twenty years ago.”

Stupid kid stuff didn’t explain why his laugh sounded nervous. He’d confessed about his bad-boy behavior, his truancy and risk-taking and shoplifting. And his punk phase immortalized forever in the photo didn’t bother him, either, maybe because he’d met Perry, but something in this yearbook bugged him.

She scanned the inside cover. Nothing weird or shocking. The usual, like he’d said. Back cover, then. She flopped the weight, dropping the pages on his hand.

Jackpot. On the inside back cover, a huge black scribble blotted out the center of the page. Like he’d taken a Sharpie to erase the message, but the pen lines dug deep enough to shine through anyhow. Mushy love talk from some girl named Becca.

“Ouch.” She closed the book, gently. As she pulled his hand free, she curled their fingers together. “Bad breakup?”

“You could say that.” He tapped his bottle against the yearbook. “First steady girlfriend. We dated all through senior year, right up until the weekend before graduation.”

She left the book behind and grabbed her beer as he tugged her toward the dinner he'd laid out for them. "She pull the whole going-off-to-college routine? No long-distance strings?"

He set his beer on the table, and hers too, and shook his head. "Nope. She pulled the whole 'fucking your older brother up against the back of the cabin during your last-hurrah camping trip' routine. After eight months of, 'I'm saving myself for marriage.' Turns out, marriage is named Matt. She thought, anyway."

"Your girlfriend cheated on you and married your brother?" Jesus. His older brother truly had stolen all of his toys. Maybe changed the shape of his life the way Erin's marriage had changed hers. Fuck, and he didn't think that counted as a panty-dropping tragedy?

"Tried, I guess." He shrugged and pulled out her chair. "He'd ditched her by the time I finished basic training and visited home. It was a long time ago. Have a seat, miss?"

She let him have the victory. He could tell his lost-in-the-department-store story instead and avoid the frayed nerves. Because however much he pretended not to care, he sure as hell hadn't meant for her to go snooping down the ex-girlfriend path.

Helping her settle in the seat, he smoothed his fingers across the back of her neck and out to her bare shoulders. As he rolled his thumbs in tiny circles, her memory finally wiggled loose.

"What makes you think a date with me won't be like this, Katherine? A naughty surprise."

Brian's tender, teasing tone as he fucked her with his fingers a few feet from her workbench. She'd happily take more than his fingers right now, as he sank into his seat across from her. But the whole dinner-date thing? Knowing Brian-the-person? That wasn't so bad, either. Having both might be feasible. Desirable.

* * * *

Hell, dating Katherine wouldn't be nearly so tough as he'd feared. They'd sailed through the first three-quarters of dinner and polished off a pair of beers apiece. She'd settled in fine with his get-to-know-me strategy. Asking questions about his childhood, she must've been thinking of him as someone to get to know and not just something to fuck.

She hadn't run far and fast when he told her about Becca, or dug up old hurts to watch him squirm. The more he made himself vulnerable to her first, the more she'd open up to him. Like when she'd talked about her granddad at softball or how entranced she'd been by her sister's wedding during their picnic. Those moments had been real. They'd been the Katherine she tucked away inside her Kit-face.

He'd be able to take her out somewhere next time without her getting all self-conscious and riled about romance. In the integrated datasets, friend and lover would overlap to be more than fuck-buddy. He'd take her out next Saturday, or maybe sooner, but he wouldn't ask her now, not when she had a ways left to go on her plate. End of the night would be soon enough. When he gave her a proper kiss, lips on lips and tongues tangled, and she didn't turn away from the intimacy.

A stray smear of salad dressing lent her mouth a sheen as bright as sunlight flashing off waves. His cock heartily endorsed a proposal to kiss her now. The cozy dinner table wouldn't be much of an obstacle.

Pausing in mid-fork-raise, she released a quiet laugh. Her cheeks flushed. "You stopped eating. It's a nice meal, even if you didn't make it yourself. Maybe better because you didn't." Her smile turned wry, but the pink stayed in her face. "You should enjoy it."

The food, right. He'd almost cleared his plate without tasting a bite, and then he'd lost himself in her. The best kind of evening. His risk had paid off. "So a date with me's not as bad as you thought it'd be? It's okay, you don't have to tell me I was right about us being perfect for each other. Just nod, and we'll both know."

She jerked backward. As her fingers tightened, the cherry tomato perched on her fork tumbled to her plate and rolled over the lip onto the table. She pierced the skin with a vicious thrust of the tines. "Date's not over yet."

God fucking dammit. He hadn't meant to needle her. But if one tease went too far, she'd never let him into her heart. He'd forever be circling her defenses in some exhausting dance. If he found the machine playing the music, he'd yank the plug from the wall and smash the electronics on the ground. They needed the silence to be together. To just be. And they never would until she'd drowned the tune repeating in her head—the one trapping her in one moment. If she wouldn't stop the music, he had to try.

"Katherine." He waited for the flicker in her eyes. Being careful with his words, seeking the perfect line, hadn't worked to get through to her. Christ, don't let her hate him for this. "Every day, you wake up and your sister's husband walks out the door."

"No." The way she tugged her lip, she might be gnawing off more words with her teeth. "Every day, I eat breakfast with two girls who don't have a father."

Her tomato burst, juice and seeds spurting over the sliced-open pillowcase he'd turned into a tablecloth in a last-minute rush.

"I bet they're dealing with it better than you are." Fuck, now he'd done it. Words no amount of apologizing would take back. None of his business.

She sat as frozen as the lake in the depths of February, her surface cloudy and the goings-on below murky and sluggish. The ever-present fire around her pupils, once a safe haven, seemed too dim and distant now to warm either of them. Closing her eyes, she shuddered as she exhaled through parted lips.

"I'm not saying this to hurt you, Katherine." He had hurt her, though. Tired and defeated and out of options, afraid he'd lose her by staying silent or by speaking up—but the words had been necessary. The conclusion of all of his data gathering and analysis, his formal summation of her. Painful because no one had spoken to her so bluntly, maybe. But he loved her fiercely, and she refused to fucking look at herself, to see how she tore herself up every damn day and how her self-harm wounded him along with her.

"Can you guarantee you won't hurt me?" She sat hunched in the dress she'd worn for him, her body a compact bundle with her arms tight at her sides and her hands shaking. "We go out and you disappear a few months later, after you've made me care about you."

The embrace he ached to offer wouldn't be a comfort until she wanted it. Wanted him. Or didn't hate wanting him. Fierce hurt, sometimes. "I'm not him. You keep trying to force me into the framework you've got in your head, and it doesn't fit me, Katherine. If I did what you're doing, I'd assume every girl I met was using me to get my brother in bed because he's the popular one and I'm the fucking clown. Second-goddamn-best every time."

"Are you sure you aren't doing just that?" Her voice vibrated. As she leaned across her plate, the fire back in her eyes, she curled her hands into fists. "Going through women the way I go through men?"

Sonovabitch. Her cracking ice dumped him into the chilly, churning waters. One-night stand after one-night stand, and he'd never questioned why. Boys-will-be-boys. Keeping score, bragging with the guys—normal. Not some dysfunctional reaction to one shitty weekend at the end of fucking high school, for chrissake.

Shaking her head, she laughed. "And now you're testing me. I was wrong, Brian." She stared him down, her jaw tight and her trembling fists thudding on the table. "You're not a nice guy. You're a selfish, manipulative ass trying to make me love you so you can finally one-up your big brother."

Losing his first steady girl to his brother had stomped his heart into pulp. Losing Katherine to his own stupidity would hurt a thousand times worse, and it felt just like this. Like she'd torn his heart from his chest and sat deciding whether to let it beat again.

"Fuck, Katherine, I don't know what the hell I'm doing any more than you do." As if he had all the answers. Not a one, not since a chunk of shredded rubber had whipped past his windshield.

She pushed back as if the tire had nearly clipped her, too. Her shoulders dropped, smoothing taut muscles. Under drawn brows, she studied him. "You don't?"

"I was doing the same damn thing, living the same day over and over. Keeping my distance so I couldn't be betrayed." He'd always known he'd never be the star athlete like Matt. He'd worked hard to be the one who made women laugh and relax. Pleasant, fun, and fuck-worthy. And he never, ever, wanted more from them than they wanted from him. Until Katherine. What a sorry pair they were. "Then I saw you and I didn't want to do that shit anymore. I wanted to move forward instead of running in place."

She squinted with the gorgeous pixie squinch she used at her worktable, her nose wrinkling and her lip disappearing between her teeth.

Waiting for his pulse to return ached, but a clean restart depended on her. "I want us to move forward together."

"But why me?" Loose fists falling open, she implored him with her palms spread wide. "I don't understand what changed for you. I'm not some glamorous woman who mesmerizes men, Brian." Waving at herself, she flicked auburn strands from her forehead. "When smudges land on my face, they're machine grease, not mascara. I fuck when I want to, who I want to, and I'm comfortable with that."

Bullshit she was. Her words and actions didn't line up in the comfort column. But what had changed for him, well—"You liked me."

"Of course I like you, that's—"

"No, I mean the day we met." His thoughts jumbled and unfocused like the pixels in a low-res satellite image zoomed into incomprehensibility. He dove deeper, hunting for the words to make him transparent to her. "I was so far off my game, knocked on my ass and impressed by you, playing fetch-and-carry for you—and you still liked me. You didn't look at me like Brian the fuck-up, or Brian the class clown. You saw me, and I saw you. Changing that tire together, I felt comfortable, Katherine. I finally understood what the hell Sherwood rambles on about, because I could've spent hours kneeling on the damn roadside just to be next to you."

He had been testing her, except not the way she thought, and not from some all-knowing plan. Making her wait for the sex—making himself wait—he'd been testing the friendship, not the romance. A did-she-care-about-him test.

She did. She fucking did, or she wouldn't keep breaking her own rules to spend time with him, whether they labeled them dates or not.

"Yeah, and I felt comfortable up against a wall with your fingers inside me." With her shrug, she shed his love the way she did whenever their talks veered too close to real depth. "That was a good time. Uncomplicated. More than that is messy." Sweeping the room with her gaze, she rambled in all directions but his. "We fight every time we try for this 'more' that you want. What's comfortable about that?"

Everything. Every goddamn thing, because they weren't fighting against each other. They were fighting for each other. If he had the least chance of showing her their truth, he'd fight to the last breath in his body. "I dare you."

She tipped her head, as sweetly confused as if she'd cracked open a radio and found a toaster's guts inside. Beautiful, kissable confusion in her pursed lips. "What?"

"I dare you to step out of your comfort zone and take a fucking chance on me." His heart pounded. A sign of success for sure, because she had to be squeezing it in her hands, bringing him back to life the way she did a dying motor. God, if only his love would do the same for her. "You think you're some kind of rebel, but you're a coward, Katherine."

* * * *

Fuck him. Fuck him and his fake nice-guy act and his judgment. His Prince Charming romantic dinner with his ridiculous tie-dyed shorts under his formal jacket. With his upfront confession about the takeout and his so-obviously-a-pillowcase tablecloth. Fuck.

"I like sex, Brian." She'd ruined the fabric. The split-open tomato stained the ivory linen with splashes of red. At least nothing had been real. The damage wouldn't matter. "I'm not going to be ashamed of that."

Laughing through his nose and shaking his head, he knocked his knuckles against the table. "Do you hear yourself? If you aren't ashamed, then why do you hide your sex life from your family?"

Jesus God, his eyes. He begged for an explanation with a sad smile and pale green tendrils of new life rising from once-frozen earth. He piled his hopes in her inadequate hands, as if she knew the difference between the seeds to nourish for strong roots and healthy growth and the spoilers to pluck out before invasive weeds choked their dreams. Her hands didn't know nurturing. They knew hex wrenches and offset gears. Percussive maintenance, rough and dirty.

Clean-shaven Brian, smooth-cheeked and pristine, would forever be too good for her.

He spread his fingers wide, one palm up and inviting. "Why no dates? Why treat guys like an ugly secret you can't take home?"

She would ruin him. Her sister's bitterness had soaked into her soil. Those first two years of terror, when she'd been unable to imagine dating anyone in high school because love landed you on suicide watch in a hospital bed, your cheeks drawn and your voice thin when you spoke at all. When the big sister who'd once let her stay up late and watch scary movies together, and soothed her nightmares after, no longer lived behind those hollow eyes. When two little girls crying for their mother had to make do with their sixteen-year-old aunt instead. Love did that.

"Maybe I am a coward." She abandoned dinner. Brian's stuffed tiger with its ragged ear stump watched her from the coffee table. She'd have to pass the silent guardian to reach the door.

Brian had shown her his tender underbelly tonight. The boy who'd grown up to be the man at the table now. Not a stranger, not blank and faceless the way she imagined the men she fucked, because who they were never mattered so long as they gave her the escape she sought for an hour or two.

Needing the sex didn't make her ashamed. But wanting more, tangling lust with the wires of love and loss and regret dead-set on strangling her when he walked away—she shivered.

"Maybe I am." No maybe about it. "But I still want to fuck you. I would've fucked you weeks ago if you'd let me." And dropped him before he became a real person, one with feelings and desires she'd have to consider. Jesus, she should be ashamed. "You think I move too fast. That I'm a disgusting—"

"No. Fuck, Katherine, no, that's not what I'm saying." Brian launched himself up. His chair tipped to the rug. "I would never tell you to be ashamed of wanting sex. I don't divide women into Sunday school virgins and lying whores. I'm trying to show you *you* do, or at least you act like you do."

The girls didn't need to meet the men she fucked, to have their aunt's example of how not to find love. Her parents didn't need to see the Kit who cavalierly plucked a man from the crowd for his broad hands and his smile filled with sharp, dangerous thoughts.

Creases lined Brian's forehead, and behind them lay nice-guy thoughts she didn't deserve. The man who'd nearly turned down a blowjob because he wanted to know all of her, not just the skills that made him come.

He eased toward her, his slow steps as gentle as his voice. "You have a good-girl life around your family, and then you treat your desire like it's something filthy you can't take home with you."

More than her desire. All of her, stained, torn, and unstitched. The way she'd always be. Because Erin, fuck, she didn't need to see the opposite—a goddamn genuine nice guy, a man who stayed when he said he would.

Bringing a happy relationship home, she might as well hand her sister the pills all over again. *"It's just a headache from the girls crying, Kit. Would you toss me that bottle from the counter and watch them awhile? I need a nap."*

And then not being able to wake her. The frantic calls and the begging. The lights and sirens competing with the girls' wailing. Her fault for missing the signs.

For so many years, she'd put everyone else's needs first. Pinned herself in a vise between fulfilling the bare minimum of her own needs, but only where no one would see her, and rejecting any hope of something better, because her sister's dreams had crumbled.

Brian twined their fingers, his right in her left, and raised her hand. "You treat yourself like something filthy. Unworthy." Kissing the bare underside of her wrist, he locked gazes with her over the top. "It burns me up, because you are so incredibly beautiful, all of you, and you refuse to see it."

His soft kisses stung. He wounded her and healed her in some simultaneous impossibility, teasing away with lips and tongue the injury she'd gotten in the softball parking lot. When his crack about wedding rings had hurt more than the throbbing pain of wrenching her arm.

Swift and sure, he stitched her up now with his mouth. The hurt fell away, leaving the happy memory of them covered in mud and laughing together. The kind of fun she never allowed herself with the guys she fucked. She lusted and she took, but they weren't men she liked. They weren't men she wanted to talk with. Laugh with. Love with.

Clasping her bare shoulders, he rubbed the wide straps of her borrowed dress with his thumbs. Under his steady gaze, he inhaled and exhaled with unhurried calm. "I want you to be one woman, whole and complete, not just for me but for you. Because you should love yourself."

His lips, pale pink, called to her. Her favorite piece of him, because he delivered so much kindness with them, even in his cruel challenges to be more. To be better. To be his Katherine and allow him to be her Brian.

"I'm—I want—" Throat closing, she choked on nothing. What he wanted for her, she wanted for him. Whole and complete. The risky love, the one where you had to love yourself first or the rest wouldn't fall into clockwork rhythm. Real love. Fuck, so much bliss should be joyful and together, not damn scary. "I'm afraid you'll break my heart."

His exhale skipped into a shaky smile. "I'm afraid you'll break mine. That you'll let fear hold you back."

He cradled her cheeks with the delicacy of a man holding an irreplaceable part. Without her, unbroken and ready to work, the machine would never run. And their awkward contraption might turn with grace and precision if she found the courage to let it.

He swiped beneath her eyes. God. When had she started crying?

"I don't know how to make the scariness disappear all at once. I would if I could." Pushing tears into her hairline, he trembled. Braver than her. He stood with his innermost pieces exposed and vulnerable. "I think maybe the fear fades over time. Until someday you realize you haven't worried in years, because we've been showing each other day in and day out by still being here. I love you, Katherine."

Warmth flooded her, warmth and urgency to move with him as a unified whole. To taste his mouth and the promises on his tongue. He nestled his heart in her hands. A trust she hadn't known she'd needed until she felt the comforting weight. Whatever tinkering she did would have to be her best work. A new challenge, a new dare, but one they would solve together.

Bowing his head, he clenched his jaw and nodded half sideways. "If you can't believe the words yet, if you can't hear them, then tell me how I can make them real for you."

"I hear you, Brian." She gained strength in each whispered syllable, driving through the thick wash of fear remnants. "Show me. The things you've wanted to tell me all these weeks and I haven't let you say. Show me, Brian. Talk to me in a way I can understand."

She sought his mouth, to finally kiss the lips she'd watched from the day they'd met. No more denying herself. No more cutting herself in two and leaving half to starve. From now on, she would be one woman who feasted with the man who loved her.

* * * *

She kissed the way he'd imagined, pressing with the force of her whole body. Aggressive and bold, yeah, but in rising and ebbing waves. Giving him space to claim her in return as the currents carried them together.

While their tongues tumbled against each other and she clutched his back, he stroked her neck. He followed her smooth, graceful curves out toward her shoulders, again and again. From the pointed tips of her pixie cut past the open vee on her dress. Christ Jesus, she'd worn a dress for him.

And not only the dress. Sweet little heels and cock-hardening black stockings his hands had been begging to touch for the last two hours.

Withholding sex from her now would make him the coward. In the language she understood, he'd be telling her he lacked faith in her. Didn't trust her to keep trying, to give their fragile relationship a chance to grow once the clothes had come off.

Her being here tonight represented a victory—an overture of peace. Compromise. And if what she needed in return was to feel desired? Well fuck. He'd held that piece in reserve from their first meeting.

He slipped free of her hungry mouth. "Katherine."

Kiss-swollen and pink-cheeked, she gazed at him with pupils dark and irises sparkling. "Are we stopping now?"

Her shoulders sagged beneath his clasping hands. From her falling lips to her shifting feet, her body confirmed she expected him to say yes. To reject her need for physical proof and bid her goodnight, as if their relationship lived or died by his rules.

"I have dessert in the fridge. Some cake thing." Damned if the name would pop in his head now. He poured the last of his confidence into his voice. God only knew whether the move would be the right one. "But what I really want to taste is you."

She gasped. "I don't—" Shaking her head, she tugged her lower lip behind her teeth.

Icy, heart-stopping plunge. He fumbled for a quip, a take-back, anything to reverse course and unwiden her eyes. Before he got the breath, she covered his mouth with her palm. Soft skin he yearned to kiss.

Her hand shaking, she traced his lips. "Yes. Because it's you."

Warmth spread from her gentle touch.

He caressed her past the swell of her breasts and down her sides, molding her dress to her flesh. The inward tuck of her waist. The sexy fucking flare of her hips. "Because it's me?"

Nuzzling alongside his nose, she brushed their mouths together. "Were you thinking of my thighs when you shaved? Because I don't think your fuzzy wanna-be beard would've been nearly enough to scratch me."

In his curled fingers, he shortened her dress an inch at a time. If she intended to distract him, she'd have to find a stronger diversion than a half-hearted jest about his facial hair. The edge of her dress folded into his palms and left him grazing bare skin. "I'm always thinking of you. Tell me what you meant."

She stiffened. He could've softened the demand with a please, but she deserved to know he'd seen the evasion. Understood how her mind worked and would chase her anyway. That he'd risk losing the surface Kit to have the real Katherine.

"I don't let them." She drew back, and the fire in her eyes flashed. "I've never wanted that from them."

The men she took to her bed. No—the men she fucked. Katherine slept alone. Maybe she would leave him, tonight, without nestling in the sheets he'd bought for them to share. And that would have to be all right. He'd damn well better reconcile himself to her skittishness before he soured them with regret. Because someday she would stay. Neither of them had caught this wave before. They'd have to learn it together.

"But you want that with me?" He ached to savor her on his tongue. To flood his senses with her from the source and not rely on her sweet musk clinging to his fingers like that first night. But he had to be certain she wanted his love, his translation from words to action.

"I've always hated"—she licked her lips and blew out a hard breath—"making myself vulnerable. The sex I wanted wasn't about that. The power belonged to me, you understand?"

"I know." He'd felt her power when she'd led him into the back room and set the rules. Whatever kernel he'd claimed for himself existed because she hadn't objected. "And that was fine. For them."

She nodded. "For them. Intimacy was never currency in that exchange. But with us…"

He waited. With her bare thighs swaying against his fingertips, a sign her stockings stopped before her panties started. He'd know if he glanced down, but watching her face mattered more, despite the opinion of his stiff cock.

"Intimacy is the language we have to practice." She smiled, finally, a cheeky grin. "I guess you'll get to take the first lesson. Better aim for high marks."

Hell yes. He edged his fingers higher. "So, your dress?"

Her face turned feral, her bared teeth a teasing threat and her eyes a blazing command. "Lose it."

He sluiced the whole thing over her head and dropped it to the carpet. With her trembling fingers clasped in his hands, he stepped back to the edge of their reach and let himself look.

He'd meant to worship her slowly. Every inch of her kissed and cradled, a lesson in the sexiness of gentleness, so when she came on his tongue she'd have no doubts about how deep his love ran.

"Fucking—fuck." His cock jerked. "Katherine, you—"

Staring at his beautiful lover, Christ himself would revise his game plan. She wrapped femininity around strength. The slim muscles he'd felt beneath her skin at the shop transformed her into a goddess here, bare and defiant, challenging him to be worthy. Black fabric, modest half-cups, lifted her breasts for his mouth. Freckles dotted her creamy stomach, falling in an arc toward the black panties with their iridescent sheen and picking up again beneath, in the space before matching stockings snuggled her thighs.

"Fuck, I don't have the words." Their arms bridged the gap between them. He could keep staring, forever, as he crushed her fingers because he couldn't stop needing to hold her tighter and remind her he'd never let go, or he could map the landscape she offered him. His Katherine, whole and complete under his tongue.

She giggled, the light trill delicate and unexpected. "It's okay, Brian. We agreed the words won't show me as much as actions." Wriggling her fingers free, she stroked his wrists and tugged. "Not half as much as your face shows me. No man's ever looked at me with so much—awe." Her skin flushed across the tops of her breasts. "So much love."

Thank God. Thank God she saw the truth he'd tried to shove deep down for weeks so as not to scare her away. Thank God she pulled him closer now, as he backed her toward the couch and left her standing as he dropped to his knees.

The curve of her belly called to him. He pressed his cheek against her. Rubbing her soft skin beneath his nose, his lips, he marked her for his own. He grasped her hips, fingers falling across bare skin and panties alike and stroking both, curling the fabric and teasing.

The rhythm of her breathing quickened with each kiss he laid on her freckled skin. Shivering, she rocked her thighs toward him.

The panties slipped lower. Deep auburn curls swept over the top edge, and he nuzzled those, too. Damp, they carried the intoxication of sweet-salt and the promise of heady flavor in her depths.

As he peeled the panties to the tops of her stockings, she laid her hands on his head. She held him firm, her fingers eight points of pressure against his skull and her thumbs ruffling the combed-down fringe of hair brushing his forehead.

Mouth closed, he kissed the rose-pink swell peeking from the center of her curls. "My language skills must not be up to par, or my memory's failing, because I could've sworn I imagined a million ways to tell you how beautiful you are, how much you squeeze my heart, and now I can't grab a single one from my databanks."

That giggle. Rippling her stomach, swaying her thighs, flashing more rose and pink for his tongue to explore. She scratched his scalp in a tugging invitation. "You're telling me." Her voice hardly rose above a whisper, but her steadiness washed him free of doubt. "Not with words, but you're telling me."

She stepped out of her shoes. Flexing her toes, she woke his desire for another nibbling feast. One for a later time, because as he guided her panties down her legs, he silently promised to leave the stockings in place. She'd put on finery for him. And though she was finer still, her gesture deserved sincere appreciation.

So he kissed his way back up. Slowly. Bent over himself like her humble servant, he mouthed the tops of her feet and the knobs of her ankles. The rounded fullness of her calves twitched in his hands as she widened her stance. He laid kisses against the soft inner creases of her knees.

As he rolled his tongue in waves, mimicking the plans he held for the bare skin tantalizingly close, she let out a low moan and sank to the couch.

Perfect. Stunning. Katherine, hazy-eyed and vulnerable, trusting him. Allowing him to set the pace and claim the intimacy they needed to move forward.

Gripping behind her knees, he slid her to the front of the cushion. An unhurried push spread her thighs, left her open as he knelt before her. His Katherine, rich with pineapple and salt and a deeper musk. Her lips shining and unfolding in a sea of curling breakers. She created her own tide with her panting breaths and her pulse, the blood rushing beneath his hands where he held her thighs.

"Paradise." With sweeping thumbs, he surfed closer to her center.

Shuddering, arching toward him, she flexed into his grip. "Please. Show me, Brian."

Now.

He buried his face in her secret hollows. With her heat cresting over him, he breathed deep and drowned himself in her. Wet and trembling, all of her. Filling his nose and mouth with her thick scent, her slippery rush. The sweet tang of the tropics, of wishes granted.

Her panting breaths turned to a siren song luring him deeper. With her groaning chorus and her biting nails in his hair, she urged him on. She broke beneath his hands, battering him in her storm.

He feasted until her hands fell slack and her toes no longer curled and danced along his ribs. Lifting his head, he gazed once more at perfection.

She lay sprawled against the cushions, her arms outflung and her head back. Heavy-lidded eyes and upturned lips greeted him.

He couldn't help but beg for more. One more intimacy, to hold her close before she regained her senses and hid herself away. "Come to bed, Katherine. Stay with me awhile."

* * * *

Brian. He'd asked her something, his lips shining as they moved. His cheeks, too. He still clasped her thighs, working his hands in a deep massage while she shivered. He'd performed miracles with his tongue. All of him might destroy her ability to remember her own name, not just to hear and understand his words.

Tumbling thoughts backward, she rewound the moment. Something about bed. Another new joy to discover. Shrugging her clothes back into place rarely took more than three minutes, and leaving took less than that. She laid her hands over his. "Time to move the party?"

But Brian, kneeling in front of her, bowed his head and glanced away. His hands clenched once more before he let go.

Fuck. She'd said the wrong thing, focused on the wrong words. Falling asleep in any bed but her own might prove impossible, but she could lie beside him. Already she ached for the feel of him, for his shoulders under her hands as he moved above her. Maybe she'd allow herself another kiss, the real and intimate kind, while they fucked.

She pushed herself forward. Without the cushion at her back, her head floated, too light to be real. She clamped her knees around Brian for balance. Gripped his face in her hands and forced him to meet her gaze. "Take me to bed, please? I want to lie down with you, and your tiny couch can't handle both of us."

Staring up at her, he let out a single laugh. "Did you hear any of what I asked you?"

"Not really, no." An honest answer for an honest man.

He lunged forward. Hands tangled in her hair, his mouth wet with her strong, salty musk, he kissed her breathless. When he drew back, their harsh gasps punctuated the silence. He slipped his hands down her arms and stood. "I love you, Katherine. Even when you can't hear how much

I'm telling you." He squeezed her forearms, his hold tight below her elbows. "Now let's get you to bed."

Her legs wobbled. As he raised her from the couch with his steady support, weak in the knees finally made sense. "So that's what they mean."

"Who mean?" He draped her arms over his shoulders and cradled her to his chest. His racing heartbeat passed beneath her lips on his neck. "About what?"

"The people who say love makes you weak in the knees. And all of those other silly things." She wrapped her arms around him and clung with all the ferocity her satisfied muscles could muster. "Because your love sweeps me off my feet."

"You think so?" The twangy amusement in his voice warned her in the second before he dipped his arm and scooped her up. "It does now."

She nestled closer without half-trying. Lazy contentment overrode her usual controlled rush. This gentleness, fuzzy and warm, with her head on his shoulder, granted more peace and joy than successfully reviving a malfunctioning gizmo. Fucking was about shutting down her worries and taking—taking control, taking the pleasure she wanted—in those few minutes. She walked away with a heady rush and zero emotion. This, though. This might be better.

Carrying her into the next room, he clutched tight behind her back and knees. He breathed into her hair, tickling her scalp, and set her down on the bed before flicking on the bedside light.

The soft cotton sheets matched the rich plum of his tie. Tucking her legs beneath her, she beckoned him forward. "You can't wear your tie to bed. Too much camouflage. How will I find you?"

"Can't have that." He whispered, low and tender, as he stepped to the edge of the bed. "I always want you to know where I stand."

She crushed his collar in both hands to stop the tremble in her fingers. The things he meant seemed bigger than the things he said. Intimacy added another level to the words. A reason to look deeper. Learning this complex language would take longer than a single night.

Flipping his collar up, she tossed lightness into her tone. "I was thinking more you'd be lying down."

The tie slipped loose, and his shirt buttons fell to her fast fingerwork. As he shrugged free, she toyed with the drawstring on his shorts. When he met her gaze, she pulled in a slow tease. No rules said she had to surrender all control. Just share with him. Trade off a bit.

As the shorts dropped, his cock sprang up in a hurry. Catching her peeking, he smirked. "Some parts take lying down less well than others."

The tip gleamed under the light. He'd been ready awhile. With both of them wanting, no sense delaying the fun. She matched his smile.

The bulk of her clothes lay on the living room floor. The bra remained to go. He'd seemed to enjoy the stockings. Kissing her through them, Jesus. Those would stay. She reached for the demi-cup's back hooks.

"Wait." Gathering her fingers, he stopped her and squeezed. His eyes glowed as green as a copper flame. "Let me."

With a nod, she handed him the power. He'd dialed up the intensity tonight, and he didn't seem inclined to downshift. The promise of seeing what he would do tweaked her pulse.

As he lowered her hands to her sides, he rubbed his thumbs across her wrists. He stroked all the way up her arms and smoothed her bra straps. Head bent, he pressed a single kiss to the upper curve of each breast. "I haven't shown you near enough appreciation here yet."

He caressed down her sloping breasts—so much more impressive in this bra than they were on a normal day—and slipped a single finger into each cup. With gentle nudging, he lifted.

Her speedy breaths raised her breasts higher, and his stare quickened her breaths, a circle promising to leave her breathless again soon. God, would he never take—

Groaning, he swept one breast into his hot mouth. His fever sank into her, achy and greedy, as he sucked as much of her breast as he could hold. In a rippling wave, he worked his tongue over her. He scraped his teeth downward, an agonizing march of anticipation. And yes, fuck, God yes, he took her nipple between his teeth and tugged.

When he let go, she cried out from the loss.

"Christ, Katherine. My new favorite color." He placed a gentle kiss on her tingling nipple and pushed her unkissed breast higher. The hooks fell to his fingers, the bra to the bedspread. "You turn a beautiful shade of deep rose for me. I'll have to make this one match."

Her breast heated before he laid his mouth to her.

In his hunger, he toppled her onto her back and climbed over her.

She unfolded her legs and welcomed him between. The weight of him, fuck, a soaring joy along every nerve but especially the knotted bundle in her clit thumping merrily with her heart. Rocking and squirming, she wrapped her arms and legs around him and tried to pull him down. She could take more of his weight. She could take him all.

He pushed up hard, his hands planted in the mattress to either side of her. Gulped in oxygen while her wet nipples throbbed in the cooling air.

"What did I tell you the first time, Katherine?" His voice rough and commanding, he dragged her arms up the bed and pinned them above her head. "These hands stay where I can see 'em." A twist transformed his smile into a wicked promise. "Don't you move, now."

She convulsed. Her back left the bed, her hips and shoulders taking the strain. Valves fully open, her engine ran hot and demanding. Brian would keep up. Her bad boy. Her good man.

He loosed her wrists. "Fuck, are you—you can move, Katherine, I didn't mean—I would never—"

"I like you bossy." Hell, she'd almost come from his take-charge attitude. But soothing him would come first, before they came for each other. "You can be a little bossy. I wore a dress for you, didn't I?" Reassurance would help him bring his bad boy out to play more often. Then she'd have the best of both worlds, the considerate man and the insistent lover. "Just you, though. I don't know another man I'd trust to boss me."

Hunched over her on his arms, he seized her neck in his teeth. Nipping, biting, he claimed every inch from her ears to her collarbone. "Because I'm your man."

He was. God, he was, entirely hers and not for a few stolen minutes. If arousal hadn't overridden her, she might've cried for the joy of his love. "I wouldn't date anyone else."

"No one else." His words landed with the weight of a bank vault, sealing out any other option. Once the lock tumbled, he flashed her a mischievous smile. "So you want another date fantasy, do you?"

"Worked the first time." And then some. This time, she burned with so much need she'd set herself ablaze in a minute. "Better hurry, though."

He turned away and dragged open the nightstand drawer. "I have—"

"Do we need them?" Condoms, obviously. If he hauled out handcuffs, she'd be shocked as hell.

He fell and caught himself on his elbow. "I thought—unbroken condoms. We both said—"

"Right, and I've always used them." Without fail, an automatic get-the-fuck-out for any man who put up a fuss. Except now a stronger urge spurred her to step out of the old pattern. To show Brian tonight meant more to her than all of those nights ever would. "But I'm also on the pill. And I'm clean. No diseases, I mean."

Wide-eyed and still, he balanced over her without breathing. Finally he sucked in a quick burst of air. "Me, too."

Jesus, she'd spooked him. Made the wrong offer, one he didn't want to claim. "Oh, good. I've never dated a man on the pill before."

Chuckling, he bent and kissed her forehead. He curled his arms tighter, until his elbows brushed her shoulders. "You've never dated any man before."

"No. I haven't." Brian, though—he'd tasted her tonight. She lay in his bed, another first. Her vulnerability no longer bled through the cracked case of a broken machine. Something stronger took shape in its place. She'd never see what made the toast jump if she stopped now. "But this is new and different, right? For both of us. So maybe it should be"—amazing, perfect, terrifying—"new and different."

He lowered his forehead to hers. "I'm ready for that. I want new and different with you." He pressed his hips into the cradle of hers. As his cock branded her with heat, he rocked against her clit. "This much, in the language you can feel. But only if you're sure, Katherine."

"I'm sure I want to take intimacy for a test drive." She raised her knees, sliding her feet along his soft cotton sheets. Matching his rocking, she connected them like live wires. "And I'm sure—" Her back arched. Fuck, he'd caught a gasp-worthy angle. She hauled in a deeper breath. "Sure I want to take that test drive with you. Because I'm sure of you, even when I'm not sure of me."

He kissed her. Hard and driving, he chased her tongue with his own. "Then I'll give you every reason to be sure of *us*."

He opened her with his fingers and centered himself. Teasing, prodding, he sent her spiraling into hazy anticipation.

"So, in this fantasy." He pushed into her, sliding until he filled her. "Christ." As he groaned, his low rumble shivered through them both. "Fuck, I love how wet you are for me."

"You turn me on." She pressed kisses against his jaw. "In more ways than I know how to count."

His breath whooshed past her ear. "I meet an amazing woman. Strong. Capable. Loyal."

The Katherine he saw—the woman she longed to be. The true face she'd never shown to a lover.

He welded their bodies together with slow, deep thrusts. "So beautiful she knocks me flat. And somehow, somehow, she takes a chance on me."

As their bodies gathered speed, so did he, pouring out words in a dizzying stream.

"She lets me show her everything I see in her, all the things she doesn't see in herself."

His fingers tightened around her wrists. As she arched, he pressed her flat with the weight of his chest.

"And this amazing woman comes home with me. Sees the man I am and shows me the woman she is."

She dug her heels into the backs of his legs, adding leverage, driving him deeper. Gathering him up to give him no escape, no chance to take back the words.

"And when we make love, when nothing lies between us and I see so deep in her eyes it's like following a ray of sunlight down to the lakebed?"

His stare, his copper-green flames, burned away the old. He illuminated his depths and her own reflected in him. Dark mysteries at the center shone brilliantly with his inner light.

"That's my fantasy, Katherine. To know you intimately, from the storm-tossed surface layer to the swells and valleys so deep you've forgotten how they've shaped the woman you are."

Fuck. He pried her mind loose, sent her swimming in unfamiliar waters. She lost her grip. Lost, lost—and he grabbed her hands.

"All of you, mine. All of me, yours." He laced their fingers together as he drove her harder. "The two of us one body, one current. One."

Gasping, they jumped together. She raged as violently as his surging sea, her shuddering body impossible to control. The fire washed through her and the sea followed. Cleansing. Unstoppable.

As the storm passed, he called her to safe harbor with his eyes. Intent on her, his gaze unwavering, he rolled sideways and wrapped her in his arms. He brushed his lips to hers.

She stole a gentle kiss in return.

His eyelids sank. Or maybe hers did. Opaque barriers blocking her beautiful view of his smile and the flush in his cheeks.

She'd wait a while, until they'd both recovered, and then she'd ask him to show her again. A cozy nap, here, together. In Brian's bed. In his arms. In his life.

Exactly where she belonged.

* * * *

The thickness of Brian's blackout blinds held back the morning sun to the best of their meager ability. Glimmers filtered in around the edges. Their sharpness struck the metal of the bedside lamp and pierced his eyelids.

Katherine no longer filled his arms. He lay on his side, with an empty embrace, and the moment he opened his eyes, reality would take hold. Drifting eyes-closed in the sun's orange haze, he imagined she'd gotten up to use the bathroom. Sauntered out to the kitchen and started the coffee.

At least her scent clung to the sheets. And the sweet rhythm of her breath—

Holy fuck.

With furious blinks, he threw off the sunny filter blinding him to the truth. Not a trick of his ears. She'd migrated out of his arms, yeah, but she'd stayed. Peaceful, asleep, the sheet leaving her shoulders bare, she lay on her back with her face turned away and her hair a pointy-clustered nest.

Beautiful.

Half-expecting her to slip away before sunrise, he'd resigned himself to the idea that he was destined to be in love with a woman who wasn't ready to commit. Who might never be. Payback for all the times he'd been a player.

Yawning, he stretched and flexed every protesting muscle. No need for a workout today when he'd exercised so well last night. He'd managed a second tour for her, a feat his dick hadn't accomplished in more years than he'd care to admit. Christ, don't let their first night together be the last.

He eased closer, gaining ground by millimeters. When she woke, she might struggle with unaccustomed morning-after awkwardness. She might flee and avoid him, take the time apart to build up regrets and doubts. This moment might remain a rare one.

Her hair flowed under his hand like tall summer grasses, as soft as the fuzzy seed-tops on the clumps that crept to the edge of the sandy beaches. The last brush of gentleness before exhilaration took hold. He hadn't surfed in so long he'd almost forgotten. Hard work paddling out. Thrilling rush riding in.

The rush had to be earned. Every time. A wise man wouldn't paddle out once and expect to ride back for the rest of his life. The happiest riders didn't blame the waves for staying true to their nature. Patient, watchful, they read the signs and merged with the beauty when the moment arrived.

Starting at the back, he finger-combed her hair into behaving. A few strands refused to take orders. Others he tucked behind her ear as he traced the outer shell. His fingers grew a will of their own and spread his touch to her cheekbone, to the tip of her nose and back.

She rolled toward him. All of the beauty in her freckled face on display for him alone, she batted her eyelids as she woke.

Ten seconds, and she hadn't leapt out of bed.

Twenty. She regarded him in silence.

Thirty.

Fuck patience.

He dared kisses along her forehead and down to her ear, the quiet flutters of morning, the barely held in check mourning for the disappearing act she'd be sure to pull any second. "Good morning, Katherine."

She fumbled an arm free of the sheets and touched his mouth. The banked embers in her eyes ignited. “Say that again.”

“Good morning.” He shaped his lips with exaggeration, the better to kiss her fingers.

She shook her head. “No, my name.”

“Katherine.” His voice dropped into the low tones he felt rumbling from his belly to his balls. Hell, he’d say her name a thousand times if she asked. “Good morning, Katherine.”

A smile erased her blank mask. Her fingers left his mouth. Closing her eyes, she let out a humming purr.

Adorable. The way she ought to look every morning, because every morning she ought to be well-loved and waking in his bed. He tickled her neck. “I had no idea you were so vain.”

Her easy giggle sent blood to his cock.

She levered herself onto her side and folded her arm into a triangular prop for her head. “I like the way you say my name, even though you aren’t making me come right now.”

Not a far-off goal, the way the slipping sheet uncovered the tops of her breasts and exposed a hint of rose-pink nipple. The first time he’d called her by name, he’d had his hand between her legs and rough-soft denim scratching his palm while she squirmed. She’d remembered his demand. Fondly. Aggressively fondly, if her shifting hips beneath the sheet suggested interest in a morning replay of last night.

“Revised parameters.” Stroking the creamy swell of her breast, he teased the fabric into falling further. Her nipple, tightening into a tempting peak, rose from concealment. “When I’m loving you, you’re Katherine.”

She arched her back, and her breast filled his wandering hand. “You haven’t called me anything but Katherine since I knocked on your door last night.”

No. He might never call her Kit again. Kit belonged to the world. To her family. Her friends. Her customers at the shop. Kit formed a piece of Katherine, but she wouldn’t have come to his bed and stayed. Only his Katherine would be so brave and vulnerable.

He shifted his hand and covered her heart. The strong beat grew faster. “Because I’m always loving you.”

She flushed pink from her cheeks down and across her chest. With her free hand, she gripped the back of his neck and dragged him forward.

Nobody but a fool would resist that claim. He might be a clown sometimes. He sure as fuck wasn’t a fool.

She kissed him. Fast, gentle brushes of lips on lips. Then deeper. She explored him with her tongue, the two of them rolling and diving in a slower rhythm. An unhurried promise.

But as he wrapped his arm around her back, torn between pushing her down and pulling her over him, she wrenched free of his mouth.

"God, what time is it?" Craning her neck, she tipped her head toward the nightstand where the alarm clock stood as a silent sentry. She swore under her breath. "C'mon. If we hurry, we can fuck in the shower and still make breakfast with my family."

Fuck, yes. And—

A fuse blew in his brain. Short circuit, monitors dark, system rebooting.

Beneath the sheet, she stroked his dick. Teasing grip. Dancing fingers. "See, we're already boarding the same thought-train."

"You—" Christ, she had him wound up on two tracks. "Food. With your family?"

"Yeah. It's a rule." She released him and kicked the covers off in a flurry. "Ever since Erin's husband walked out. Sunday brunch is family time, nonnegotiable." Naked, she rose on her knees, and fuck if she didn't smell of sex. Still. Or again. "If you aren't dead, you sit your butt at the table and talk like civilized creatures."

Breakfast at her parents' table. In their house, where she never, ever took the men she fucked. Where he hadn't been allowed to pick her up for any of their non-dates. The wave filled the horizon as he steadied his feet on the board. "I'm invited?"

She let out a snort and clapped her hands over her mouth. As she ducked, laughter pealed out anyway. "Seriously, how did I end up loving a guy who's more excited about brunch with my parents than shower sex with me?"

"You love me?" Please God, if nothing in this world ever turned in his favor again, at least let her love be true.

"Yeah." Gaze locked on his face, she whispered behind her cupped hands. "I do." She shoved his shoulder, then his chest. Hard love taps with her open palm. "You wanna make something of it?"

"Oh, I definitely do." He surged up from the mattress and bear-hugged her. He'd know by the creaking of her ribs when the time to stop arrived. "I wanna make you come so hard in the shower you walk funny all the way to brunch."

"Do it." She dotted his neck with kisses. "I dare you."

Epilogue

Moving day opened with Katherine in his arms and a crop-soaking cloudburst outside his window. The squall drifted past faster than they levered out of bed.

The last time they'd sleep together at his apartment. An end to the shuffling and commuting and the weeknights when she slept alone in her bed at her parents' house. The balance had tilted, month by month over the last year, until nights together had become more common than nights apart.

But the biggest step—buying a house together—had gone from wishing to doing when they'd signed the papers yesterday. Boxes held all but today's sheets, towels, and clothes. With a dolly and the elevator, loading the rental trailer went quick.

Lacking furniture, she'd crammed her belongings into the back of the shop's work truck yesterday. Her dad would close early and meet them at the new place after lunch. And if she'd forgotten anything, hell, her parents' place would be a ten-minute drive away.

Still, she stacked the boxes he brought to the trailer with a precise eye for dimensions. Shifting and shoving, she bent over his rough-folded cardboard junk-heaps. Her ass sat snug in a worn pair of jean shorts, and her muscled arms emerged from double-layered tank tops. Every bit as enticing as the day they'd met and then some.

He scooped her up in a behind-the-back hug. "Need a measuring tape, beautiful? Will I fit?"

Clenching his forearms, she wiggled her ass. "Gosh, I don't know. Gotta follow the old rule—measure twice. We've only measured once this morning."

She twisted in his arms and dragged him into a kiss by the back of the neck. Standing in the parking lot, in full view of his soon-to-be-ex-neighbors, she greeted him with unashamed proof of love. A year's worth of practice and promises, of kisses lasting all night and love-fucking while the sun rose.

Their lips clung as she pulled back. Pouty and fiery-eyed, she purred. "We'll have that new bed tonight."

Afternoon delivery for the mattress and frame at the new house. Their house. His apartment had come furnished. They'd decorate the house together, in their own style. A mishmash of maps and wrenches. "Mm-hmm. King size. All ours."

"Sooo…" Trailing her fingers down his chest, she pecked his mouth. "We'll have to give it a workout. Christening, right?"

"Good plan." He swayed against her. Two more loads of boxes from upstairs. Drive to the house, where Rob and Nora would meet them for unpacking, housewarming, and lunch. More unpacking when Katherine's dad arrived. Dinner. A takeout dinner on the floor would be the next alone time they'd have all day. Hours and hours away. "Let's speed up time and make it happen."

The day tromped on in a cardboard flurry. The boxes marked *GARAGE* in her precise, all-caps print outnumbered the ones labeled *BEDROOM* two to one—and the *KITCHEN* travelers three to one.

By midafternoon, the work had slowed to a crawl. He sagged on a box and rested his back on the trailer. Returning it to the rental place would be next up.

Sherwood dropped onto the next box over and passed him a beer from the cooler. "You planning to box?"

A heavy bag and a speed bag stared at them from their new perches hanging in the open garage. The three-bay monster had sold them on the house. Great home workspace for Katherine, plus room for a boxing setup for them both.

"Naw, I figured we'd unpack."

A jab caught his shoulder. "Smart-ass. Afraid you can't keep up in the gym now that you've settled into domestic bliss?"

"Katherine boxes." Correcting her form would be a hell of a fun way to spend summer evenings. With the garage door closed. "A little."

"No shit?"

"Her granddad taught her some. Army man." He tapped longnecks with Rob, and they both drank. A man who'd served, and one so dear to Katherine, deserved the moment of silence. "He died before I met her.

But he helped make her the tough, talented woman she is. I wish I'd met him. Thanked him."

Katherine passed through the living room, carrying a diaper bag. The big windows let the whole neighborhood see their business. He added curtains to his mental list of shit-to-buy-soon. Tonight, maybe. Definitely before they christened the living room floor.

"So." Rob stretched out his legs and kicked the concrete driveway. "Homeownership."

"Yessiree." Fuck yes, and hallelujah. Nudging Katherine out of her parents' house had taken months of building trust. She'd needed reassurance not just from him, but from her folks, too. So used to looking after everybody but herself. "Lifetime of adventure, right here in Podunk, Iowa."

Never had he believed Rob about the whole "knowing" thing—that two minutes of talk was enough to know, down to his marrow, he'd found the woman he wanted beside him for the rest of his life. No sense telling Sherwood he'd been right. Helping move them into their new house, he was already abrim with smug satisfaction.

Flashing his damn saw-it-coming smirk, Rob nodded. "You ready for it?"

"What's to worry about?" He spread his arms wide, swaggering comfort to mask the nerve signals tripping and resetting over the much smaller, non-cardboard box tucked away for Katherine. "My wife-to-be swears she knows how to mow a lawn, and I know the best specials at every takeout place in town. What else is there to home ownership?"

"Uh-huh." Rob snorted and swigged his beer. "Don't come crying to me when you've got leaves in your gutters and ice dams on the roof." He dangled the bottle between pinched fingers. "You tell her about the wife-to-be part yet?"

"Working on it." Marriage might take a while. He took a deep drink of his own brew. Steadying courage.

He might strike out with the whole wedding band tradition. As if Katherine's commitment nerves weren't enough, mechanics scratched up metals or got rings—or fingers—cut off in emergencies. But tonight, after she fell asleep, he'd leave the jewelry box with his message on her tinkering bench. And then the choice would be hers.

"Never thought I'd see the day." Sherwood launched into reminiscing about their first meeting at Lackland.

Eighteen years old, across-the-hall dormmates for basic training. Scared-excited for the future, full of promise and stupidity. A whole fucking raft of stupidity.

"...and not a day went by you didn't swear you'd sign up for whatever specialty got you to Hawaii fastest. Surf those ocean currents every morning." As the front door opened, Rob got to his feet. "Not a lotta waves in Iowa, Surfer Boy."

Holding the door wide, Katherine shook her head and spoke into the house. "Heck no. Better you than me."

Baby in her arms, Nora walked outside. The rug rat had stopped crying, so feeding time must've gone well.

Best stand up himself, before—

"You see these boys out here slacking off while we womenfolk are busy being domestic goddesses?" Katherine traded a glance and a giggle with Nora.

Christ, let their home be as happy as Rob and Nora's. Less fruitful and multiplying, but equally full in its own way.

Shoving himself up from the box-seat, he grabbed Rob's shoulder.

"I don't need waves." He stood steady now, after stumbling onto perfection by accident. One lucky rip of a tire. "She's my Hawaii."

* * * *

Kit slipped out of bed not long after sunrise.

Brian lay sprawled on his back, his gentle snore intermittent and squeaky-scrape familiar as a windshield wiper clearing drizzle. Their first night as live-in lovers. New bed, new house, same them.

Tiptoe-hopping around the room, she threw on shorts. She grabbed a T-shirt from an open box and dragged it over her head on her way down the hall. Sun flooded the living room. Hanging the curtains they'd picked up last night went on today's to-do list.

But first?

Workbench.

The far end of the garage had been a labor of love for the previous owner. Cabinets, drawers, a whole run of wide wood counter. Pegboard and cupboards hung clear up to lofted storage space in the peaked ceiling. They day they'd toured the place, Brian had taken one look at the garage and declared this house the one.

Because he loved her.

She skipped across the cool concrete floor in bare feet. His car straddled the centerline of the two open bays for now. The high triple window in the gable end streamed sunlight above her head. Seven o'clock. Mom and Dad would swing by around noon to give her the first pick of Dad's garage sale crop and take them out to lunch. Plenty of time to putter around in her new workshop.

First on the agenda—set up Grandpa Jake's train set. Cleaning off his bench at the shop had been a hell of a weepy-eyed weekend, for her and Dad both, but a good one. A necessary one. The engine ran now, with its six pullcars, and the whole thing would have a home here in her pristine—

Not so pristine. A tiny box sat on the otherwise empty worktable.

The box looked innocent enough. Brushed metal took on a riveted suitcase style with a luggage snap latch. But something so small, sized for her palm—might as well have been a blue velvet case with rounded corners.

She clenched her trembling hands into fists. Opening up a project and peering at its guts had fascinated her since she'd first picked up a screwdriver as a preschooler. This project, though, might be beyond her skills.

Brian would be brave. And persistent. If she pushed aside this box, left it sit for weeks, for months, he'd quietly understand. But every day, his eyes would hold a silent message for her.

I dare you, Katherine.

She snatched the box from the table and clutched it to her chest. One step at a time. Open the lid, assess the contents. She flipped on the work light. Maybe the project wasn't what she thought at all.

The clasp unsnapped and the lid raised, as smooth and silent as a fresh-greased hinge.

A navy blue band sat like a napkin ring around a rolled-up slip of paper. A gag gift?

She plucked the paper free and returned the box to the table. The note unrolled in her hands. Brian's scrawling handwriting filled the space.

> *You remember we talked about spicing up the bedroom with a few sex toys? Okay, the ring's not a toy, but it is silicone, and you can wear it if you want to.*
>
> *We don't have to set a date, and we don't have to go making an announcement. But you tried me on last summer and I've fit so far, haven't I?*
>
> *Give the ring the same chance. I promise I'll still fuck your brains out when I'm your husband.*

Tears pricked her eyes as she laughed. Trust Brian to turn a marriage proposal into a comedy.

Freeing the ring, she squished the silicone between her fingers. The soft band featured nothing sticking out to get snagged, nothing shiny to scratch, and nothing they'd need a diamond saw to get off a swollen finger.

Bouncy. She flexed the material, popping the circle between her fingers again and again.

The first time she'd fantasized about Brian, a smidge over a year ago, he'd been Prince Charming. She'd been certain she'd never want that. Never want him as anything more than a fuck on the trunk of a sun-warmed car.

But now his car sat in their garage. In their home, where they lived—together.

She slipped the band around her ring finger. For all that it claimed to be silicone, the ring sure seemed to conduct an electrical charge. Shivering, she extended her hand.

The dark blue didn't look so wrong around her finger.

"Husband and wife."

The words didn't sound so wrong, either.

"Beautiful."

As she spun around, Brian stepped through the door from the house. Barefoot and shirtless, he wore a pair of jeans hitched over his hips, the fly half-open. Slapping the back of his hand to his mouth, he covered his yawn.

Fuck, she loved a sexy, sleepy man. "Afraid you'd miss the moment, were you?"

He ambled toward her and rubbed the back of his head until his hair stuck out. "Bit of a gamble. May I kiss the bride?"

"That a ploy to get me back in bed?" Meeting him halfway, she kissed the smirk from his face.

"Might be." Lips soft and sweet, he grazed her forehead and cheeks. "The day's early." He chased his gentle brushes with harder, deeper kisses at her throat. "Is it working?"

The backs of her legs hit the bumper on the coupe. "You gonna fuck my brains out, Mr. Fix-it?"

Nuzzling her collarbone, nudging her shirt aside, he nodded. "I promise, Mrs. Fix-it." He raised her hand and kissed the flexible ring. "For the next fifty years."

"Do it." Belief came easier now, the strength of his commitment bolstered in the year of his nice-guy manners and bad-boy bedroom games. She'd accidentally gone and found a gentleman. One she couldn't resist teasing with the phrasing they both knew so well that his mouth shaped the words as she spoke.

"I dare you."

Be sure not to miss M. Q. Barber's Erotic Contemporary

HER SHIRTLESS GENTLEMAN

Her heart is in his hands…

After her marriage ends in betrayal, Eleanora Howard finds herself struggling to navigate the dating scene as a thirty-one-year-old divorcee. But feeling undesirable, and living alone in the house she once shared with her ex, is hardly the recipe for finding new love—until she meets Rob. He's just the kind of charming, old-fashioned guy she needs—but he's also eager for intimacy…

After serving in the Air Force and getting a well-paid civilian career, Rob Vanderhoff planned to settle down with the right woman and raise a family. But at thirty-six, he's still single and searching—until he meets Eleanora. She's everything he wants. All he has to do is draw her out of her shell. Soon he's taking her on high school style dates, fanning the flames of her desire—and helping Nora re-discover the sexy, adventurous woman they both know she really is…

A Lyrical Originals novel on sale now!

Learn more about M. Q. at
http://www.kensingtonbooks.com/author.aspx/29485

Chapter 1

Dead last. Again.

The four of them went out after work every Friday, and every Friday Eleanora sat and smiled while guys bought drinks for Sharilyn. Hit the dance floor with Amber. Chatted up Chelsea's breasts.

Even the sidekicks—wingmen, whatever guys called themselves—refused to give her a second glance. She couldn't blame their lack of interest on the ring. She'd taken off the meaningless metal circle before the divorce had been finalized.

But to the endless crowd of broad-smile bar-hoppers, she rated five seconds of stilted conversation between texting or checking sports scores or playing Angry Birds. The highlight of four hours of boredom. Single life almost matched the worst tedium of married life.

That's what she got for saddling herself with David and galloping through her twenties with his ring on her finger. He'd been her first. Her only.

Now she performed rotating roles as babysitter, chaperone, and charity case. She didn't belong at a too-small table packed alongside tight-skinned and perky-breasted girls who flashed their IDs with the affected nonchalance of twenty-two-year-olds.

She downed the final sip of her third beer of the night. She didn't dare hop in her car and head home yet. Given her luck, she'd end up pulled over and facing a drunk-driving charge. David would love any excuse to point out her idiocy. Hiring a lawyer without him finding out would be impossible in this town. She'd never live down the humiliation.

"—and it's deep, too."

Chelsea laughed along with what's-his-name. Dog Collar Dude. Not attractive, but he had deep pockets. Probably thought he'd be getting in deep with Chelsea tonight, payment in exchange for buying round after round of drinks. God knew he hadn't taken his eyes off her breasts.

Laughter came dangerously close to making Chelsea spill out of her silky, sleeveless v-cut. Eleanora's closet didn't hold a shirt anywhere near so revealing. Boring and staid, as much an accountant in her fashion picks as in her career choices. And in her bedroom habits.

She tilted her brown bottle. All gone. No magical extra swallows remained to knock David's voice from her head.

"Whoa." An unknown quantity stumbled to a halt beside her chair. "Your friend's hot."

Fantastic. The newest Mr. Drunk-and-Horny leaned in close and drenched her nose with the scent of teen body spray. Probably the same disgusting brand he'd used in high school. Probably lived in the same bedroom, too.

"Oh? Which one?" She'd come to this lousy bar with three friends—well, acquaintances—and he didn't have a chance with any of them.

The skinny blond kid blinked as he scanned their table. Jesus. He looked barely old enough to buy the three beers he held, and she'd celebrated thirty-one six months ago.

Sooner or later she'd have to inform her coworkers she wasn't going out with them anymore. They were twenty-four, twenty-five, and poaching college boys was fine for them. For her, the whole scene smacked of desperation. Three months of this bullshit added up to quite enough.

"Uh, all of 'em?" He presented a dopey smile.

"Damn, Ellie. Picking 'em young tonight, aren't you?" Sharilyn swung her martini glass upward, sloshing vodka over the rim. "Good for you."

"Yeah, no, I'm not—"

The kid wobbled into her chair. "I don't feel—"

Vomit splattered her shoulder and rolled down her chest. Ugh. Should've dodged faster. She shoved him back.

Stumbling over his own feet, he landed on his ass, spilled his three beers all over himself, and retched. The acrid stench of puke replaced the flood of body spray in her nose. A toss-up, really.

She laughed over the chorus of oh-my-gods from the rest of the table. At least the night wasn't boring anymore.

* * * *

"Oh, fuck."

Rob swallowed the last of his beer. Lucas had better hurry up with the refills. "What now?"

They'd hit a handful of bars already. Brian had found trouble with every damned one. With Lucas staying at his place for the summer, he'd been playing mother hen for the last three weeks.

"I think my baby brother's puking his guts out."

"Take him home. Happy beer-buying birthday and all, but he's done for the night." He'd celebrated his own twenty-first on base with a pack of fellow tech geeks. Good guys, including Brian. How had fifteen years gone by so fast? "Pour him into bed."

"Yeah." Brian grimaced. "Soon as I figure out what to say to the woman with puke running down her shirt."

"Try an apology." He shoved his chair back and stood, scanning the tables for Lucas's god-awful sea-green pullover. "Where is he?"

He spotted the vomit-splattered woman about the same time Brian answered, "Your four o'clock."

Shit. Lucas had spewed at a full table, and he couldn't get eyes on him. Man down. Threat?

No punches thrown, so far as he could tell. A circle of horrified and disgusted faces clustered to one side, their owners staring at the floor. One guy held his phone up. On the far side of the table sat a laughing woman with a beautiful smile and a stained shirt. Damn. He hadn't taken a woman home in almost four months, and Lucas had party-fouled the first to catch his eye. "C'mon, let's go rescue Lucas and get out of here."

Looked like tonight wouldn't be the night to break his sexless streak.

* * * *

"Oh my God, Ellie, seriously, how can you laugh about this?" Light glinted off glitter-speckled fingernails. Amber pushed back from the table. "Yuck. Danny, take me dancing." She dragged her boy of the night away with a theatrical flounce.

"You do kinda reek, Ellie." Sharilyn wrinkled her nose. "Not your fault, but eww."

Waving in front of her face, Chelsea nodded.

Dog Collar Dude flipped through his phone. "Fuck, I missed the kid's first splash. You think he could upchuck again? The visual'd make the video so much better."

Eleanora glanced down with care. The regurgitated beer soaking into her shirt quickly lost its amusement value. The kid had added a puddle beside her chair. He barked out coughs like a hoarse dog.

“No, I don’t think he’s got anything else in his stomach.” She poked his knee with her foot. “Kid? You all right? You got somebody we can call for you?”

No answer, unless she counted more retching. Between the sound and the smell, her stomach started to turn.

A second man with the same pale hair as the first dropped to the floor beside the kid and laid a hand on his back. “Shit, Lucas, I thought you might’ve passed out.”

“Are you all right, miss?”

Sex on a stick. Thick thighs encased in denim inches from her eyes. She launched her head back and her chin skyward. Eyes up. Ohhh, bad idea. The stranger loomed over her with his strong jaw and his short, dark hair and his no-nonsense eyes.

“No, of course you aren’t.” His aborted hand movement stopped short of her shoulder. “Ugh, he did a number on your shirt. Let me give you a hand.”

He slipped around the other side of her seat. Cupping her elbow in one hand and pressing against her back with the other, he coaxed her to her feet. Large hands. Warm hands.

Her body jangled like a change jar spilling on tile.

“Look, he’s really sorry, or he will be when he’s sober.” The stranger glanced down, shaking his head. “He’s twenty-one today.”

She nodded. The blond guy picked the younger one off the floor. First legal drinking day. Okay. She filed the data under *don’t care* and waited for details about Mr. Tall, Dark and Handsome.

“You can’t wear that home.”

Her chest had snared more attention in the last five minutes than in three months of flaunting herself at bars. She’d found the secret of dating. When introversion and modest assets failed, distress attracted the good guys. Not how she’d hoped to find someone.

The man with large hands squeezed and let her go. Peeling off his shirt, he revealed a to-die-for body. Solid, toned muscles from top to bottom. Too bad his jeans came almost to his waist. Denim blocked the enticing slope heading into his pants. God, David had never reached such nonchalant bare-chested perfection.

Her rescuer held out his shirt and gestured her toward the back of the bar. “Here, let me give you mine for tonight.”

No fucking way. This guy couldn’t be for real. She stumbled over her chair.

He steadied her with a quick hand on her clean shoulder.

“Thanks.” Oh, hallelujah. She’d started thinking she’d never find her voice. “That’s, umm, I appreciate it.”

“Least I can do, miss.” He guided her in front of him past the line for the ladies’ room and stopped at the door.

“Yo, man, you gotta put your shirt on.” A beefy guy in a black shirt with the bar’s logo over his chest held out an arm. “Carrying it don’t count. You can’t be shirtless, not in here.”

She disagreed with strenuous, silent objections. Her gentleman deserved to go shirtless wherever he liked.

“You wanna run around half-naked, you gotta head down the street to the Lazy Eight.”

Making that man put his shirt back on would be a crime. Her skin heated at the slow slide of excitement between her legs. Thirty minutes of fantasizing and foreplay with David left her dry as a desert compared to three minutes of standing next to Shirtless Gentleman. The longer she lingered in his orbit, the harder her lungs worked to serve up oxygen.

Lust walloped her with embarrassing swiftness. She lacked the looks and flirty attitude to pull a guy without adding a vomit-soaked shell to the mix. Riding off into the sunset with Shirtless Gentleman glinted so far out of the picture the location didn’t exist on her map.

“Yeah, I get that.” Shirtless Gentleman raised a hand. “You can toss me out in a minute. Right now, this pretty girl’s got someone else’s puke on her clothes, and I’m going to make sure she’s safe while she’s changing.”

Gripping his shirt, she ducked into the ladies’ room past the line of pissed-off, well-beyond-buzzed women. Shirtless Gentleman’s presence seemed to deflect any cursing about cutting the line.

“No, ma’am,” he rumbled over the din of music and chatter. “I don’t wax and you may not touch.”

Ma’am. Polite. Mannered.

She stuffed her shirt in the trash and grabbed a handful of paper towels.

Fit. Chivalrous.

The damp paper towels scraped her neck under her hardy scrubbing. At least the kid hadn’t destroyed her bra. The practical white soft-cup would serve.

Was Shirtless Gentleman military?

Tucking in the shirt didn’t give her the fitted look it had given him, but she managed to minimize her resemblance to a child swimming in her father’s clothes. Squinting hard almost made the outfit look intentional. A style choice to wear a black wide-neck tee with exposed white bra straps.

Yeah, almost.

She slipped into the hall, her skin electric. His bare chest greeted her from two feet away, his arms crossed and his feet planted in a wide, easy stance. A few hoots and drunken catcalls rose from the women waiting in line.

Shoving aside her embarrassment, she tipped her head back and met his eyes. "Thank you."

His attention stayed centered on her. The unsmiling bulk of a man sported solid pecs and a penetrating stare.

"Again." She fumbled for a classy conversation starter. "Your shirt's really soft."

Your shirt's really soft. What the fuck. Her brains had gone soft. Complete mush. Mashed potatoes held the edge in outthinking her.

His mouth twitched. "Must match your skin."

"Sorry?" She'd heard him wrong. No way had he complimented her skin. Men didn't say those things to her. "I didn't catch that."

He shook his head and dropped his arms. "Shirt looks better on you than it ever did on me, miss. Let me walk you back."

Turning, he swept his hand behind her and landed with a light touch. Five points of pressure, a half circle of fingertips keeping in contact as they returned to the table. More than a few whistles followed them.

"It doesn't bother you? Being"—she waved at the crowded tables—"stared at? Graded? Like you're on display?"

Stupid question. Of course, the attention wouldn't bother him. He had cool, calm confidence perfected. Anyone with his godlike body would want to show off.

"I got over any fear of public grading in basic training."

Military. Nailed it.

Not yet, you haven't.

Her face flamed.

"A'course, the opinions of a bunch of yappy drunks aren't worth all that much, positive or not." Shrugging, he tapped her back. "Being on display for the one woman who matters, well now, that's a whole other thing. That'll make a man nervous, sure enough, however cool he plays it."

Great. He had a woman who mattered. Smooth, too, about sliding the revelation into the conversation. No ring, but an empty finger didn't mean much these days.

"I think you've got cool down." Months of going out with the girls from work had taught her how to categorize the bar crowd. The unholy chaos broke into three groups, all ring-free, with the singular difference whether they were ring-free but committed, ring-free and open or cheating, or ring-free and actually unattached. Limiting herself to the third group hadn't done her any favors. "I hope your woman who matters sees through the facade and tells you what a great catch she's made."

He paused his tapping. "Oh, I don't—"

"Woo, I didn't know you were that kind of girl." Sharilyn slapped her hand on the table. "Swapping clothes in a stall?" Her nosy, flamboyant attitude owed nothing to the drinks she'd downed. She came by her perky personality naturally. "What else did he get on you, Ellie?"

Ugh. She smiled through her irritation. Eleanora was bad enough, thanks to her mother's obsession with family history. Every girl wanted to be named for the great-grandmother she'd never met.

Shortening her name to Ellie might as well transform her into a cow. Get along now, Bessie, Daisy, Ellie.

Sharilyn made her sound like a cow giving the milk away for free with a man she'd met ten minutes ago.

"I'm—we weren't—"

* * * *

Christ. Her little friend produced as much bile as Lucas had, and the bitter sting seemed to hit her harder. The woman who'd laughed over a ruined shirt faced her sniping girlfriend with hunched shoulders, stammering a response somewhere roundabout her shoes.

"I'll overlook that because you're young and drunk, but you might wanna think on what you're saying about your friend." He'd dropped into his gruff tone, a favorite for his square-your-shit speech. A touch of gravel worked great for rattling the nerves.

The bile-producer dropped her mouth open, amazingly without the rim of a drink glass attached. The modest beauty wearing his shirt lifted her head.

"I'm not the sort of man to take a beautiful woman in a bar bathroom for an audience." Not on the first date, at least, and not unless he'd be fulfilling a fantasy for her. "And she seems like a fine lady who deserves a better class of friends."

"Did he just—who the hell are you to say what—"

Lordy, Miss Martini could screech. The woman beside him stood silent, watching him with narrowed eyes. Not angry, so far as he could tell. Assessing, like she'd spotted something new. Good. She might spare more than a thought for something new, if he got the chance to correct her misunderstanding about his relationship status.

"Shar, be chill." The curvy blonde beside the screecher leaned forward.

He averted his eyes from her gaping shirt. His daddy'd taught him to be polite. Daddy'd also taught his sisters to have more respect for themselves than these girls possessed.

"Hey, rescue dude, your buddy took the spew monkey outside for some air or whatever. Said they'd wait for you out there."

Fuck. He'd offered to drive tonight so Brian could get smashed with his brother.

"Right. Thanks for the message." He turned to the woman in his shirt, torn between handing her down to her chair the way a gentleman ought to and asking if she'd care to go for a drive.

He should've bought the extended cab. Nothing romantic about sitting four across in the pickup with a boy sick as a dog hanging his head out the window.

Of course, he'd have the lovely lady beside him, her thigh pressed alongside his. Maybe the tickle of her honey brown hair on his shoulder. His cock twitched, eager as a teenager's for a shot at action.

"I'll walk you out," she blurted. "In case the staff gives you any more trouble. About the shirt, I mean."

Holy hell. He might have a better-than-nothing chance of getting her number yet. "My heroine. That's right kind of you, miss."

She linked her arm around his, sweet as you please, and tugged him away from the table.

"Yeah!" Stemware drained, martini girl slung the empty glass with loud, obnoxious, sloppy encouragement. "You're halfway there, girl."

At sixteen, he'd begged every night in his dreams for that type of rowdy girl. At thirty-six, he had other ideas.

"Take him out and ride him home, Ellie." The girl's shout followed them. "You deserve it!"

The one who mattered tightened her hand around his arm, and her steps quickened. She'd already been taking the better part of two to his one. Five-five, he estimated.

The top of her head came to his lips. The perfect height for tucking under his chin or dropping a kiss on. Or picking up and pressing to a wall to deliver a real kiss. Get those curvy legs wrapped around his hips.

He cleared his throat in a vain bid to distract his cock. "So your name's Ellie?"

She scrunched her nose. Cute, but not a happy scrunch. "It's Eleanora, actually."

Hell, he had experience with disliking his name. Points in common melted ice faster than taking a chisel to the deep freeze.

“Eleanora.” Nodding, he held open the door. A classy name. Old-fashioned. No wonder she didn’t appreciate her friends’ butchery.

The July heat slapped his face. Same as the inside of the bar, with all its sweaty bodies, but with added humidity.

Eleanora released his arm.

Loathe to let her slip away so soon, he extended his hand.

“I’m Rob.” Leaning close, he kept her hand clasped in his. “My mama named me Robin, but don’t be letting that get around, all right? It’s another one of those things that’ll make a man nervous.”

Had as a boy, more like. Calling him Robin constituted grounds for schoolyard fights. Though he damn well wouldn’t share how the guys in basic had settled on Sherwood, or that Brian had joked later his nickname ought to be “Sure Wood” for the string of ladies he’d taken to bed.

“You don’t have anything to be nervous about.” Her smile held a trembling hint of shyness at the corners. “I know how to keep my lips sealed.”

He hoped not. It’d be a crying shame not to taste her sweetness. “Good to know.” He spotted Brian over her shoulder, leaning against the truck with a shit-eating grin. “Lucas will pay for the damage when he sobers up. You can text me the cost.”

“Oh—that’s—he doesn’t have to.”

He resisted the urge to drop his head and kiss away her frown.

“But, I should probably get your number anyway.” Blinking like she’d startled herself, she pulled her hand free and dug in her pocket. “So I can return your shirt.”

He didn’t give a damn about the lost shirt, but he rattled off his number when she produced her phone. A smidge skittish, a mite shy, and hanging with a crowd unsuited to her reserve. His Eleanora must’ve ended a long-term relationship not so long ago. She didn’t seem keen to hop on a rebound train.

Good. Neither was he. Take things slow, help her build up her dating confidence, and with any luck she’d see the potential in him he saw in her.

He walked her to her car, said a polite goodnight, and closed the door for her. Crossing the lot back to his truck, he waved off Brian’s laugh.

“Lost your shirt to the newest Maid Marian, eh, Sherwood?” Brian opened the passenger door and swung into the middle seat, leaving the window for a green-around-the-gills Lucas. “Hope you got a little something in return.”

Lucas groaned as he hoisted himself up. “Man, tell me I didn’t puke all over that MILF.”

Rob turned over the engine. Christ. Drunk or not, twenty-one-year-olds were blind stupid about women. Anyone past twenty-five probably registered ancient-to-prehistoric on the Lucas scale.

"Sorry, man, you did, and I didn't." The chance for something more, maybe, if she—

His phone sounded with a text alert. Yanking the digital leash from his back pocket, he jammed his arm against the seat.

The message originated from a caller unknown to his address book.

Just checking. I hear people give out fake numbers sometimes, and I'd hate to leave my shirtless gentleman without his shirt for long.

Well now. That was promising. Bolder in text than in person, was she?

He typed a quick response.

Brian craned his neck. "Still got nothing?"

Lousy snoop. He threw an elbow at Brian's ribs and tucked his phone away. "Maybe a little something."

Meet the Author

USA Today Bestselling Author **M.Q. Barber** likes to get lost in thought. She writes things down so she can find herself again. Often found staring off into space or frantically scratching words on sticky notes, M.Q. lives with one very tolerant, easily amused husband and one very tolerant, easily amused puppy. She has a soft spot for romances that explore the inner workings of the heart and mind alongside all that steamy physical exertion. She loves memorable characters, witty banter, and heartfelt emotion in any genre. The former Midwestern gal is the author of the Neighborly Affection and Gentleman series as well as several other standalone romance novels. Pick a safeword, grab a partner or two, and jump in. Visit her on the web at mqbarber.com.

CPSIA information can be obtained
at www.ICGtesting.com
Printed in the USA
LVOW12s1503070916
503614LV00001B/162/P